SWEET THING

CHICAGO PLAYERS

KATE MEADER

Cover design: Qamber Designs

Editing: Kristi Yanta

Proofreading: Julia Griffis

ISBN: 978-1-954107-68-7

To all my Chicago Rebels fans, thanks for loving this team so much. I hope you're glad that the saga continues ...

PROLOGUE

Lars

THE COMBINATION OF GRILLED MEATS, perfect August blue skies, and Dua Lipa's "Levitating" blasting from the sound system could mean only one thing: A summer cookout at the Kershaws was in full flow.

These kinds of get-togethers tested the limits of my sociability, so I usually stayed away. When you had addictive personality traits in your bloodline, it was best not to tempt them to make an appearance. As this thinking coincided with my general desire to not get too close to my Chicago Rebels teammates, it worked out for everyone.

But today, my excuses had fallen on deaf ears, and those ears belonged to my captain and partner on the defensive line. Theo Kershaw, the man, the legend, and the player who showed no signs of stopping, had insisted I attend.

Be there or suffer the wrath of my better half!

That would be his wife Elle, one of the nicest people on

the planet. Even a curmudgeon like me had a hard time playing killjoy to her kindness.

"NyQuil!" Kershaw was known for his nickname game, so Nyquist became NyQuil without too much effort. His grill apron said, *Your Opinion isn't in the Recipe.* "You made it."

"Course I did." Said as if it was a foregone conclusion. I held up a six-pack of Pulaski Pils from Maplewood Brewery. "Where should I put this?"

"There's a cooler over here." Kershaw took the cans and guided me into his world, as he so often did. "Ellie? Look who showed!"

Plenty of heads turned at this announcement, Rebels old and new, a couple of them with readymade smirks. The guys on my team were great, but even after a few years a certain coolness remained between us. The stink of my dad's misdeeds still stuck to me like a particularly noxious glue.

"Lars!" A tall, dark-haired woman approached, her blue-gray eyes warming as she neared. Elle Kershaw always struck me as the family's heart, the person who kept their boisterous brood grounded. More reserved than her husband, she had an understated sense of humor I reluctantly enjoyed.

She kissed my cheek. "How's your summer been? We've hardly seen you."

"No complaints."

Her smile was sly. "Heard you were working with Reid's hockey camp for a few weeks. That must have been fun."

"Oui, c'est bon." That was the extent of my French, but hockey was its own language, thankfully. Against all odds, I'd enjoyed volunteering with Reid Durand's youth hockey group in Quebec. Some players liked to use their summers to chill, regroup, and tighten the bonds with family. Others liked to keep so busy their brains became too crowded to hold space for anything else. Guess which category I fell into.

"Well, I hope you'll spend some time with current Rebels members this season, Lars." She squeezed my arm to temper any perceived criticism, I supposed. "There's always room at our table."

"I appreciate that, though I imagine it's been pretty full this summer." During the season, Theo's grandmother Aurora and his daughters Adeline and Tilly kept the female energy high before things evened out during the summer with the return of their boys. Their eldest son Hatch played pro hockey for Denver, and their twins, Conor and Landon, were rising seniors at the University of Michigan. Golden Retriever, Eggsbee—short for Eggs Benedict because Kershaw had a tradition of naming the family's pets after breakfast items—completed the picture-perfect postcard.

"Yeah, it's been great," Kershaw said. "But once the boys are gone, I'll be the only guy in the house."

I scoffed. "Which you love, you attention-whore."

"Sure, but it gets old after a while. I've had that adoration my entire life, man. Help me out and bring your manly burps to dinner."

Before I could comment in a way that neither promised nor refused, something wet and sticky grasped my hand. Looking down, I found the youngest Kershaw, three-year-old Tilly. The spit of her dad with a dark, wavy mass of curls framing her face, she peered up at me with a mischievous calculation in her shamrock-green eyes.

"Hey, you." At the grand old age of thirty-five, you'd think I'd have kids figured out. Tilly was your typical little girl, so naturally I worried about swearing in front of her or not paying her enough attention or making her cry with my resting prick face.

On establishing eye contact, the kid used the back of my hand to wipe her nose.

"Tilly!" Elle pulled her away. "Sorry about that. She's not figured out the social niceties yet."

Kershaw was laughing his head off. "Making her mark on Uncle Lars."

Elle produced a tissue and wiped her daughter's nose, then picked her up. Tilly went for another sticky swipe—my cheek this time—and missed.

"I want Duckman!"

Elle chuckled. "That's right, Uncle Lars is Duckman. She loves that thing, her favorite gift of all time."

Last Christmas, I gave Tilly a fluffy duck toy I'd picked up in the drug store around the corner before I answered another summons for a Kershaw holiday gathering. I'd forgotten until Elle connected the dots for me.

"Hey, Mom, I can take her."

"Addy!" Kershaw pulled the new arrival, his eldest daughter, into a hug. "Don't leave me."

Standing on tip-toes, Adeline kissed her dad on the cheek. "I'll be back before you have time to miss me."

Kershaw turned to me. "My beautiful girl is finally fleeing the nest."

"After a couple of false starts," she murmured, her cheeks filling with color.

I didn't know Adeline all that well. While she had her dad's green eyes and dark hair, she favored her mom with that stubborn chin and a reserve that bordered on shyness. With the birth of Tilly, a surprise for Elle who had thought her childbearing days were long behind her, Adeline left college in Vermont and stayed home to help out. She had returned to a local community college in the last couple of years and finished up an associate's degree, and now she and her best friend, Rosie, were all set to embark on a bout of overseas travel.

Out of politeness, I asked, "Where's your first stop?"

"Lisbon. Rosie's already been, and she thinks it's a good place to get our feet wet."

"You're going to have a great time."

"Don't say that!" Kershaw hugged his daughter tighter. "She might never come home."

"How about this, Dad? I'll come home when you announce your retirement."

"I'll announce it right now if it means you're safe with us!"

"Sure, go ahead. I'll wait." She smiled, a real heavy hitter even prettier for its rarity. But there was challenge in there. This Kershaw knew exactly what she was doing.

Her dad caved immediately. "Gonna miss you, Twinkle. We all will."

"I know," she said softly. "Okay, Tilly, let's find Ducky! And when we do, we'll sing his song."

Elle waved at Jordan, wife of former Rebel Levi Hunt, and excused herself. Kershaw watched his wife and daughters move away, his face luminous, his love for them so plain that I was embarrassed at witnessing such depth of feeling. I couldn't imagine having time for that and still retaining my edge on the ice.

"Man, I worry about her," he said after a moment, and I knew he wasn't talking about his wife or youngest daughter.

"She seems like she has a good head on her shoulders." At twenty-two, Adeline was definitely old enough to be flying the coop.

Kershaw frowned. "Yeah, she does. But she's spent hardly any time away from home. She tried with college, but it wasn't for her, and now I feel like she's just doing this to prove something."

"Isn't that a kid's job? Test the boundaries while they figure things out?"

"Doesn't mean I have to like it. It's a daughter thing, which I know makes me a complete sexist. One day you'll understand."

"A good soldier never disagrees with his captain." I neglected to add that I would never know the feeling because I would never have kids.

He grinned. "Dick. Okay, let's get you a drink and a burger. I left O'Malley on the grill, so God only knows what a mess he's made of it."

Dex O'Malley was another Rebels legend, a power forward who exuded all the maturity of a baby bunny rabbit yet had somehow managed to score an amazing wife, three gorgeous daughters, and a dream life. Equally shocking, as assistant captain, he was in the running for the full gig once Kershaw decided to hang up his skates.

I had no idea how the cap did it, especially when he had so much else to occupy him: family, charity work, mentoring, various business ventures. I admired the fuck out of him, though I wouldn't want his life.

Or maybe I thought a life like that would never want me.

I PUT in a couple of hours of mingling, ate two burgers and a "Moroccan lamb slider," courtesy of Jude, Hudson Grey's husband, and enjoyed a monosyllabic chat with Bren St.

James, another retired Rebel who hated these gatherings as much as I did. I was contemplating my exit when I was accosted by Aurora Kershaw on my way into the house to use the facilities.

Theo's grandmother was a bit of a legend herself. Having raised him single-handedly, she was his biggest influence. After beating breast cancer about ten years back, she moved from Saugatuck, Michigan to Riverbrook, Illinois, twenty miles outside Chicago and home of the Rebels hockey franchise, to live with her grandson and his growing family. She was also the leader of Theo's Tarts, the fan club for women of a certain age, which she'd formed to cheer on the captain during his home games. They even had home-made jackets.

"Lars Nyquist! Come here and let me get a look at you."

Petite, with a gray bob and sharp blue eyes, she grasped my arms. Though she barely came up to my pecs, she managed to land a lipstick-stained smooch on my neck. (I couldn't see it, but I knew it was there.)

"Oh, that beard burn must drive the ladies wild!"

Self-consciously, I rubbed my facial hair and mentally shuddered at the notion of Aurora commenting on its effects on the female population.

"I've only got eyes for you, Aurora."

"See? You can charm them when you choose. And I'm not the only woman that Scandi noir vibe of yours works on. Why, I've seen the greedy gazes following you around at this party, even from some of the WAGs."

"I don't mess with married women." That came out a bit abrupt, but her words sent me hurtling back to one night a couple of months ago in the Empty Net, the team's regular watering hole. Another woman who had enjoyed my beard and had taken me unawares.

"Of course you don't! Now, I've been meaning to talk to you about my grandson. You're younger—"

"Not by much."

"Eight years! So I need you to look out for him on that ice. He'll never admit it, but he's not as tough as he used to be. You'll protect him, won't you?"

"I'll do my best, Aurora. But to be fair, he's about as tough as they come. No one's getting by Superglutes."

She smiled at my use of Kershaw's nickname. "I can't think of anyone I'd want partnering my boy in these final years. He won big when the Rebels landed you, Lars Nyquist."

No, I was the winner. Though I resisted with all my Scandi noir vibes, the Kershaws made me feel like I belonged. I'd happily spend every minute protecting Theo on that ice and his family off it.

"Oh, there's Harper." She waved at the team's CEO, the Rebel queen herself, who had just arrived with her husband, Remy. I gave a quick salute which the vivacious and still shapely blonde acknowledged with a raised eyebrow. "I need to talk to her about what else she's doing to keep my Theo safe."

Off she went, leaving me to marvel at all us minor planets orbiting Theo Kershaw, the sun in this close-knit universe. I moved through the house, taking in every signifier of its absolute fitness for purpose: keeping the Kershaws safe and demonstrating their familial perfection. Every turn revealed another sign of a life well lived. The marks on the door showing the children as they grew from Hatch to Tilly, the kids' art on the walls, the family photos on the landing. This cathedral was a testament to the Kershaws' abiding love for each other, and I couldn't help a smile as I hit that creak on the stairs then another squeak of the floorboards on the landing as I headed to the bathroom.

Something pulled me up short. I was pretty sure I'd heard my name.

"You're not going to see him for at least a year," a female voice was saying from behind a slightly ajar door. "Maybe longer. By the time you come back, he might be hooked up with some bunny."

Someone else scoffed. "Sure, and what am I supposed to do about it? Oh, Lars, haven't you heard? I think you're the sexiest guy alive. Could I have a kiss to keep me warm on the lonely nights while I travel the world?"

I froze. That was Adeline.

"Why not?" The other voice countered. I recognized it now as belonging to Rosie, daughter of Cade Burnett, a former Rebels defenseman and ex-GM, Dante Moretti. "If he bites, you get some. If he doesn't, you move on and ..." She trailed off.

Adeline groaned. "I know, I know. I *need* to move on."

"Yeah, you do. But maybe he'll go for it?" Her reply was gentle, not wholly convinced.

He won't go for it. Do not even try it. Don't put either of us in that position.

I needed to leave. That way I wouldn't have to turn anyone down, not that Adeline would truly make a move on me. That was absurd.

About as absurd as what you just heard.

Pro hockey players were known for their lightning-fast reflexes, but today this one's were way off. To my shame, the door flew open before I could get a step off.

"Conor, aren't you a little old to be listening at—?" Adeline gasped.

Shit.

"Oh, sorry, I—" She hesitated, blinking dark, inky lashes, picture frames for those somber green eyes. "I thought you were my brother."

"Nope. Not your brother. Just ..." *The guy you think is the sexiest alive.* I thumbed over my shoulder at the bathroom by way of explanation.

"Right." Her face was flushed, which I would normally think was pretty, but right now, no. It meant she was embarrassed, and that I was the dick who caused it.

Rosie appeared behind her. "Hi, Lars."

"Rosie." She was a little older than Adeline, maybe by a couple of years. With her colorful ink and dark eyes, she had always struck me as mature beyond her years, unlike Adeline, who had a wide-eyed innocence to her. Or maybe I had labeled her that way because of who she was. Theo Kershaw's adored daughter.

Rosie moved past Adeline, sending her friend a meaningful look.

"I need to talk to Hatch about that thing."

"What thi—?" The words died on Adeline's lips as fast as Rosie took the stairs behind me.

A reluctant Adeline turned back to me. "How much did you hear?"

"Enough."

She dragged her teeth along a plump lower lip and placed a hand on the doorframe. For a moment, I worried she might faint. Behind her I got a sense of a young girl's bedroom: posters of people I didn't recognize, kooky art I wouldn't understand, a computer desk, a guitar leaning against a wall.

"It's not a big deal." The words emerged from my throat rusty and a little too fast.

"I just talked about my years-long crush on you and it's not a big deal?"

I winced. This got worse and worse.

She realized her error instantly. "Maybe you should tell me which of my shocking revelations you *did* hear."

I admired her for turning it on its head. If she was going to be embarrassed, she may as well drag me down with her.

"Something about you thinking I was, uh, sexy." I couldn't believe I had just uttered that word to Adeline Kershaw. *Forgive me, captain, for I have sinned.* "Like I said, not a big deal."

"Because you hear it all the time."

That made me chuckle, the first funny thing I'd heard since I'd stood outside a bedroom door and listened to a couple of young women discussing private things I had no right to hear.

"Nah, I don't hear it all the time. I'm not exactly a fan favorite."

"People can separate fandom from lust." She closed her eyes, and those sooty lashes fluttered against her cheeks. "I'm not making this any better, am I?"

"Can't say you are. But if it's any consolation, I'm just as embarrassed as you are."

"None whatsoever," she said glumly.

I wanted to chuckle again, but she wouldn't appreciate it. Had I suspected this crush? Perhaps. Perhaps that was part of the reason I rejected all those dinner invites.

I tried to look at the upside. In a couple of days, she would be on her way, out of the country, far from this moment. New adventures would replace old hurts, and neither of us would think on this awkwardness any longer. Just a schoolgirl crush on an older man. Harmless, really.

Time to wrap this up. "Are we good, Adeline?"

She frowned, like the question was unexpected. I wanted to leave this on good terms. Didn't she?

"Yeah, we're good, Lars."

An urge to kiss her on the cheek took hold of me, a consolation prize for the loss of, well, me. I chased away that nonsense and nodded curtly instead.

"Good luck on your travels. Stay safe."

"Thanks. And sorry."

I waved it off as I bolted for the stairs with the slowest, most methodical step of my life. "Think nothing of it."

CHAPTER ONE

Fourteen months later ...

Adeline

COMING HOME MIGHT NOT HAVE BEEN SUCH a good idea. Coming home on the night of a Chicago Rebels win and choosing to stop at the Empty Net definitely ranked as one of my less inspired ones.

Despite my misgivings, I pushed my way through the heaving bodies at the team's regular hangout, a task made easier since I'd already dropped my backpack at home, said hi to my mom and great-gran, and spent a few minutes fussing over my baby sis, Tilly, who had grown into a strapping four-year-old while I wasn't looking. I had one person I needed to see.

My dad, Theo Kershaw.

With that mop of dark, wavy hair, the veteran Rebels defenseman and captain was easy enough to spot, holding court in the middle of the bar. I held back for a few seconds, watching him joking around, commanding the room as well as he did the defensive line during a game. Someone must have made a crack at him because he turned and issued a withering retort complete with a crazy-ass nickname. The man was famous for his creative monikers. The crowd guffawed, completely on his side.

"Your pop's in good form, I see." Rosie, my bestie and world travel companion for the last year, placed a hand on my shoulder. "You sure you're okay here?"

No, I wasn't. I'd had a scare a couple of months ago and crowds didn't help, but I needed to get over myself. With an injection of titanium into my spine, I adopted a cheery pose which wouldn't fool my friend for a second but might be enough to fool me and the rest of this crowd.

"I'm fine. If I could only get *the* Theo Kershaw's attention."

At my raised voice, Dad finally figured it out. His handsome face lit up like a goal light, and he practically shoved his teammate Dash Carter out of the way to get to me.

"Twinkle!"

Knowing what was good for them, Rebels goaltender Noah Boden stepped out of his path along with Peyton Bell, one of the newer forwards. My dad threw his arms around me and lifted me off the ground.

"My girl's home!"

"Hi, Dad." I giggled into his chest and held on tight, tighter than I'd intended. He was a big guy, broad-shouldered, wide-chested, huge-hearted. The best man I knew.

"I thought you weren't coming in until tomorrow." He shook his head, either at my sketchy timekeeping or his mental confusion. "Does your mom know you're back?"

"Already been. Rosie said hi to her dads, too."

His apple-green eyes went wide as he pulled my friend into a hug. "Rosie! Sorry, I was blinded by my daughter's beauty."

"That's okay, Mr. K. Story of my life on this trip."

I barely repressed an eye roll at that blatant untruth. From Brindisi to Bucharest, Rosie was the star, which suited me just fine. Ever the wallflower, I liked the comfort of the shadows.

Except that one time the shadows bit back.

"Let's get you a drink, Twinkle."

"It's okay, Dad. I don't need anything. I just wanted to say hi. I didn't mean to pull you away from your adoring public."

"Come over here then so I can take a good look at you." Tucking a hand under my elbow, he steered me to a spot near the jukebox, which I imagined was for show because everyone used Spotify now. Rosie was already chatting with Giselle DuPre and her boyfriend, Mark, so I wasn't abandoning her.

"Why are you home two months early?"

I didn't expect he'd go so hard to start. My dad might play the goof on TV, but he was sharper than a skate blade.

"No particular reason," I lied. "We were just ready to get back."

We had planned to spend an extra month in Spain, but then I made the mistake of getting mugged outside a bar on Santorini. It spooked me, and while I refused to let Rosie tell anyone, especially our nosey families, I figured it was a good reason to wrap things up.

Another one? Hockey season had started, and as this was likely my dad's last year in the pros, I wanted to support him in every way I could.

"You look like you got a lot of sun. You're healthy, right?

No problems? I've been so worried about you." Another hug, even tighter this time. My family tended to think of me as a delicate flower. My travels were supposed to instill their confidence in me as I set out to conquer the world. Unfortunately, the world had other ideas.

"I'm fine, Dad. You don't have to worry."

"It's my job. So what's the plan? You're going to stick around for a while?" The hope in his voice warmed me through. My absence had been hard on him.

"For a spell. Can't miss the old man's final season."

"Less of the old, cheeky monkey. Okay, I'm going to get you a drink because this is a celebration. My best girl's home! What's your tipple these days? Something exotic with lemongrass or lychee, I suppose."

I chuckled. "A cider would be fine, whatever's on tap. Oh, is Hatch here?"

My brother, Hatch, had been recently acquired to play on the Rebels, a move that pretty much determined my dad's trajectory this year. One of his dreams was to play on the same team as his eldest son. If he could hold on for another year until my younger brother Conor made his debut, the Kershaws would be Gordie Howe-ing it to the max.

"Yeah, he's here somewhere. Hey, man?" My father's attention snagged on some poor unfortunate as they tried to walk by. "Keep my girl company, will ya?"

"Sure, T."

My entire body went stiff. Dad was already halfway to the bar while his spot was filled with the bulk of one of his teammates.

Lars Nyquist.

He hadn't changed. Scratch that. He had become *more* handsome, which should have been impossible. A year should have dimmed those baby blues, grimmed that sensuous mouth, trimmed all that beauty. Justice was clearly on a smoke break.

The less said about the last time I saw him, the better. Thankfully, my crush had waned to barely negligible. These days, I was a new woman, well-traveled and unhindered by teenage hormones.

But when faced with this absurdity—six-two, broad as an ox, all copper-tinged jaw scruff and blues the sparkle of Lake Michigan on a clear summer day—any girl might question her willpower.

"Good to see you," he said, rubbing his beard. Rubbing it in, more like.

"You, too!" Far too enthusiastic, so I pitched my next words lower. "Congrats on the win tonight."

"Yep. Your dad was on fire. Hard to believe he's serious about retirement."

I found it hard to fathom as well. He was the second oldest player in the league, and the oldest was currently on what seemed like permanent IR, so my dad was the oldest active player. When he became a father again four years ago, we all thought that would be the clincher. So long hockey.

Mom knew better. She understood that hockey meant the world to him, and once done, he might crash into the void left by its absence.

"Yeah. And you two make a good team."

He nodded.

And that was that.

We lapsed into uncomfortable silence. Throwing a desperate glance over my shoulder, I willed my father to return, but when I turned back, Lars was looking at me like he had something to say. Whatever it was, I didn't want to hear it. Leave it in the past.

So I glared at him, hoping that would discourage any trips down memory ditch, and prayed that he had the decency to forget all about it.

Lars

WHEN I FIRST LANDED ON the Rebels, I thought being partnered with a veteran like Kershaw would be weird. That that our post-game cellies would be muted by this ancient in our midst. That he might cramp *my* style.

Fuck, was I wrong.

Theo Kershaw was Teammate with a capital T. The guy knew every bar and bartender in every city we played, and they all loved him, even when he was responsible for shutting out their team. He was player, coach, mentor, counselor, and priest, and once he retired, there would be a huge hole to fill, not just on the Rebels but in hockey.

Over the last year, he'd been there for me in more ways than one. After the initial dread of dinners at the Kershaws, I'd come to enjoy them. To see them as the highlight of my week. When my father died, Theo had been the rock I didn't know I needed.

My growing closeness to the family was made easier by Adeline's absence. That was probably a shitty thing to think, but I couldn't have become a regular at the Kershaw table if I had to sit across from his daughter. Without her presence, I could listen dispassionately when Theo talked about her. How much he missed her. About the flea-ridden hostels she was staying in, the no-name airline she was flying, the salmonella magnets she was eating in. He would try sending her money to graduate her travel experience from one-star to three, but she would refuse because she wanted to make her own way.

I admired that. Growing up the daughter of a rich, famous pro-athlete might make a kid privileged. Not Adeline. Not any of the Kershaw kids. (Except for Tilly, who at age four, was entitled to a little privilege.)

Theo talked about Adeline so much that I had actually started looking forward to her return, if only so he would shut up about her. I'd seen the photo dumps before every practice, watched the reels he sent anyone who'd listen, and heard all about the adventures of Addy and Rosie, like it was the latest YA graphic novel.

In a way, I felt I knew her better than any of the fuckers here, save her dad. So it was disconcerting to find that she didn't like me.

One bit.

I barely knew her, yet here she was, scowling away at me like I'd done something to piss her off. When she wasn't giving wistful looks over her shoulder toward her dad, she would stare at me with his eyes, a deep mossy green that now reflected suspicion where his shone nothing but goodwill.

So she was embarrassed about our previous interaction. I resolved to be the adult here and make it easy for her.

"Good trip, then?"

Another forlorn glance over her shoulder. Her dark hair, like spilled ink, was in a messy ponytail, little wisps laying damp against her neck. She wore jeans and a long sleeve T-shirt with a setting sun on the front.

"Yeah, great."

"Your photos were amazing. You have a great eye."

Her gaze sharpened. "You saw my photos?"

"Your dad was always showing them, usually over dinner at your place." Looking at them, I'd felt like I was right there in the thick of a Turkish bazaar or a religious procession through narrow, cobblestoned Italian streets.

She weighed that observation for a moment but remained silent. Jesus, this shouldn't be so hard.

"Those songs, too. For Tilly."

Another share from Kershaw. Adeline and her little sister were very close, and one of their ways of connecting was through funny little songs about butterflies and birds. I didn't pay as much attention to those, but I recall being struck by Adeline's voice, sweet and clear.

"Just silliness."

"Good to be home, I bet. You must have missed everyone."

Her eyes took on a subtle tilt, like some movie goddess from the forties.

"I did. But it was good for me to get away."

Another awkward pause. Maybe I should let her off the hook.

"I'm guessing you have other people you want to talk to."

She shook her head, color high on her cheekbones that not even her sun-kissed skin could mask. "Sorry, Lars. As you can probably guess, travel hasn't made me any less awkward in my dealings with other humans. I'm still a weirdo."

"Sure, but the world needs weirdos."

That loosened her up, might even have reminded her of a conversation we had years ago at a Rebels holiday party about embracing her weird and carving her own path. Her shoulders relaxed and I got the sense she wasn't as uncomfortable as she was a couple of minutes ago. Her next words confirmed it:

"I was sorry to hear about your dad."

"Thanks. No love lost, though." Everyone was aware of our estrangement, but I needed her to be clear on it.

Sven Nyquist was an asshole and I'm nothing like him.

"That probably made it all the harder." She placed a soft hand on my forearm and squeezed. Shockwaves sizzled through me at that skin-to-skin contact, and I froze, barely able to reckon with how her sympathy practically undid me.

Seeming to recognize her effect, she withdrew her hand and changed the subject.

"So are we going to address the elephant in the room?"

Finally. This was good. Lay it out there and clear the air, which was now polluted by an unearthly squall in the distance that sounded like a baby.

"Are you still thinking about that?" I tried to infuse it with casual, maybe even a touch of absurdity that it would be on anyone's mind at all.

The prettiest blush suffused her cheeks and that gulp in the slender column of her throat? I shouldn't have been enjoying that at all.

"It was kind of embarrassing."

"Nah. Anyway, we've all grown and moved on, right?" Taking joint responsibility seemed like the gentlemanly thing to do.

The corner of her mouth hooked like an inverted comma.

Maybe I shouldn't have said that word. *Grown.* Because Adeline certainly had since I saw her last. Still serious, but self-effacing with it. A touch of the been there, done that about her. Not the kind of girl who carried a torch for an ancient, broken-down athlete.

"Yep. We have." That mobile mouth curved into a smile that hit me square in the solar plexus. Dazzling in its intensity. And those movie goddess eyes ... "So, we're good?"

We should have been. I should have been thrilled we'd smoothed over the awkwardness. Her dad and I had to work together, and it was likely I'd see more of Adeline in the coming months. I didn't need the hassle of his daughter crushing on me. This year was too important.

"Yeah, we're good." I tried to smile back, but I couldn't get my lips to curve. My pulse had picked up. My hands felt clammy, the back of my neck hot. Was I disappointed that absence had not made her heart grow fonder? Surely, I wasn't so desperate for female attention that Adeline's mature handling of our reunion was irritating me.

This was my captain's kid we were talking about.

Speaking of kids, the baby was on an absolute crying jag now, and people were starting to send dirty looks in the poor infant's direction. I couldn't see it, but it felt close, and what the fuck was a baby doing in the Empty Net?

I cast a quick look toward the bar because now the skate was on the other foot and I wanted out. Kershaw was talking to Rebels D-man, Rowan MacFarlane. With two glasses in his hands, he was evidently trying to escape but MacFarlane had him pinned.

I didn't like that guy. Since his trade in right before the playoffs last season, he'd had his eye on my spot in the Kershaw-Nyquist 'ship, and while he was a decent D-man, no way in hell was I giving up my position in the final year of Theo's career. As if the dickhead knew I was thinking uncharitable thoughts, he sent a scowl my way. I sent it right back with interest.

Pro-hockey dynamics. Welcome to middle school.

Baby-in-the-bar status update: still acting like a baby.

"Looks like you're gonna be thirsty for a while."

"That's my dad, friend to all."

Someone appeared at my shoulder, a little too close for comfort. Pretty standard in the Empty Net post-game, so I shifted a step closer to Adeline and turned.

The first thing I saw was a baby, likely *the* baby.

And this baby was pissed.

The appearance of this red-faced, mewling alien in my orbit was good. I was annoyed at my reaction to Adeline and could have done with the distraction of giving whoever brought a baby into a bar a piece of my mind. I raised my gaze to the responsible adult, a blonde with a great rack, and got the shock of my life.

I knew this woman.

Let me back up a bit here. I'd met her about a year and half ago in this very bar. I'd like to say we made it *out* of the bar to a bed, but the bathroom was as good as any for what we both had in mind. I rarely messed about on my own doorstep, but my father had just fucked up again in a very public way. I was in a foul mood, and this woman was there, all comfort and curves. I didn't take much persuading and when I asked for her number afterwards, more polite formality than true interest, she informed me that she was married.

Now, if I'd been possessed of this information, I would have run the other direction. My dad was notorious for messing about with otherwise-occupied women while he himself was also occupied. No way was I going down that road. So we parted amicably and I vowed to be more careful in the future. (I now had a questionnaire for all potential bedmates.)

Seeing her after all this time—and damn if I could remember her name—was jarring. Even more jarring was that Adeline was standing there, completely over me, which was more irksome than it should have been.

"Hello ...?"

"Vicki," she said with a touch of affront.

"Right. Vicki."

"Can you hold her a second?"

A quick glance around to see if I was being punked. No one was paying attention except Adeline who was regarding the situation with the same healthy suspicion as me.

"Um—"

Vicki was already bundling the kid into my arms. I truly believe she would have dropped her if I didn't play ball.

The baby was young, maybe six months. Or ten. I knew nothing about baby ages. Weirdly, the second she landed in my arms, she stopped crying and stared up at me with the bluest eyes I'd ever seen.

"Oh good, she likes you!" Vicki unshouldered a carry-all bag and dumped it at my feet. "Here's the thing, Lars. I can't do this right now."

My gaze snapped to hers as a sense of foreboding over-came me, or more than what I'd experienced the second I laid eyes on my one-night stand and wondered what the hell she was doing here.

"Do what?"

"I'm sorry I didn't reach out earlier."

Dread seeped deeper into my bones.

"What's going on here?" The words sounded muffled, like I was speaking underwater.

"She's yours, Lars. Meet your daughter."

CHAPTER TWO

Lars

I THINK she just said this kid was mine.

She said something else, about not being able to do *this*, whatever this was, but for now I had to focus on the first part of the shit equation.

This kid was ... *mine?*

Because Vicki had omitted pertinent details about her relationship status the first time we met, my reaction was slow. Should I take it at face value? Assume it was a shake-down? Laugh at the fact my teammates were yanking my nerves-taut chain?

People were starting to pay attention now. A woman had just handed a baby to a professional hockey player in a bar, dropped a bag, and was now backing away.

As in dumping and dashing.

A baby.

I finally found my voice. "You need to explain this."

"What's to explain? Sometimes condoms fail." She took another step back, a prelude to a breakaway.

I moved to follow her, like a tiger stalking prey, but a zombified one who was only learning to lurch. The baby was starting to feel heavier than the pit of dread forming in my gut.

So many questions. I tried to prioritize them into immediate need-to-knows.

"Why am I only hearing about this now?"

"I'll be in touch in a few days." She turned tail and fled.

I couldn't chase her down, not with this new weight in my arms. I turned to Adeline. "Could you hold it?"

To be honest, I could have asked anyone else nearby. A teammate, a bartender, hell, Theo Kershaw had more experience with babies than anyone else I knew. But something innate knew that Adeline would know what to do.

My confidence was rewarded when she jumped into the fray with no hesitation and accepted the bundle into her safe embrace. Instinctively, I took an extra couple of seconds to make sure the little one was settled and ignored that peculiar shift in my chest at the sight of Adeline holding her.

If she was really mine …

"Vicki!" I quickstepped out of there and caught up with her outside the bar, which was probably better. Less teammate interference and more chance to scream my head off without some looky-loo filming it.

"I need an explanation here."

She turned, teary-eyed, and my heart melted a fraction.

I placed a hand on her shoulder. "Don't run. Let's talk about this."

"I-I can't. My husband just found out that she's not his. He said I had to give her up and you know, Lars, I'm not ready to be a mom! She's already ruined my figure, and Brad says he wants the woman he married back."

Okay, that was a lot.

"Your husband is making you give up your child?"

"He's not the bad guy here! But I have to choose, and he comes first." She glared at me. "Don't look at me like that."

"Like what? Like you've blown up my world? Like you went months without telling me I'm a dad? Like you've just dropped off a baby like an Uber Eats delivery? Like that?"

More tears. "Don't shout at me! I've had too many people shouting at me lately!"

"Okay, okay, I'm sorry." That I was the one apologizing pissed me off, but I could tell she was walking a razor's edge. "Can we go back inside and talk about it? Or go get coffee somewhere?"

"Maybe in a couple of days." She turned to a waiting cab.

Not only had this woman dumped a kid on me and already had her getaway planned, she hadn't shown a drop of interest about where her child was this very moment. My sympathy dried on the spot.

"Vicki, you can't do this." Because I was having a hard time picking the primary reason from the million reasons why she couldn't do this, I added weakly, "I don't even have your number."

"I left it with the bag. A few days, okay?" She opened the cab's door and clambered inside.

Before she could shut it, I yelled, "At least tell me the kid's name."

"Mabel."

And then she was gone.

I'm not sure how long I stood outside, but long enough to feel a chill that couldn't be credited to the October weather. Had I ever considered fatherhood? Sure, every guy thinks on it occasionally, maybe more than that if you're in a serious relationship with commitment and a future on the cards. But that wasn't me. That was never likely to be me. With my genetics *and* upbringing, I wouldn't have dreamed of inflicting that on a kid.

A hand landed on my shoulder, and my first instinct was: *Adeline.* When I turned, Kershaw was standing there, his eyebrow raised in semi-permanent shock.

"What the fuck just happened, dude?"

Here was the thing about Theo Kershaw. He was almost a decade older than me, a family man, the definition of responsibility, and he still sounded like a bro. It didn't make him an idiot, but he was one of the guys and I loved him for it.

"She said that kid is mine."

Theo blew out a breath. "That's mighty fucked up."

"Yep." I had no words beyond that terse reply. What came next? I prayed my teammate and good friend would have some ideas. The man was usually full of them.

"She just skedaddled? Are you going to see her again?"

"In a few days, she said. She's married and she's been lying to her husband about the paternity."

"Aw, hell, that's not good."

"No, it is not. How do I even know that kid is mine?"

"Well, you don't. Not yet, but that's easy enough to verify." He squeezed my shoulder. "First things first."

I eyed him expectantly. *Tell me all the things, Kershaw.*

"There's a baby in that bar that could be yours, so you have to step up and take care of her, friend. But know that you're not alone."

It sure felt like I was. But I trusted Kershaw to have my back.

Adeline

LARS WAS A FATHER.

Hard to believe, but the evidence was here before me, literally in my arms. The mother must have been in pretty dire straits to drop this on her baby daddy like that. He had looked so shocked, and who could blame him? The woman hadn't breathed a word.

Rosie moved in, her dark eyes wide with wonder.

"If someone had told me it happened I wouldn't have believed it."

"I know. It's kind of nuts."

"Absolutely. And how are you on the hook for holding the kid?"

"I was on the spot. What was I supposed to do—drop her?"

The baby gurgled a little and gave what looked like a smile, though maybe that was gas. Here in the middle of all this craziness, she was the calmest one in the place.

"You need to sit down." Rosie pointed at Dash Carter, the Rebels left winger, who was seated at one of the corner tables near the darts board. "Carter, make room for the woman with the child!"

Dash jumped up just as his fiancée Summer Landry appeared, her face agog. "Whose baby is this?"

"Nyquist's." Dash smirked at Summer. "Don't be getting any ideas, babe. Let's get the wedding done first."

Summer blushed. "Did I say anything? Here, let's sit you down."

I didn't know the pretty blonde all that well, but I'd always liked her. She was assistant to Ryder Calloway, the Rebels' general manager, and was getting married to Dash when this season ended. She budged up beside me while Rosie stood, shielding us from the rest of the bar. Everyone was eying us with interest and who could blame them? I was holding Lars Nyquist's baby.

"Hey, Ro, grab that bag, would you?"

The mom had left what looked like a diaper bag at Lars's feet. Rosie picked it up and placed it on the table.

Summer looked at us both. "Should we open it—okay, then."

Rosie was already unzipping and rifling through the contents. Diapers, a couple of baby bottles, formula, a few onesies.

"Anything identifying?"

"Like a baby passport?" Rosie smirked. "Or the kid's driver's license?"

"We don't even know her name."

Summer stroked under the baby's chin. "She's so dang cute."

The little one wore a yellow onesie with a picture of a baby bottle and the slogan, "It's 5 a.m. somewhere." Summer tickled the baby and earned another grin. "Baby Larina? Or maybe Baby Nyquista?"

"Here we go. A birth certificate." Rosie held up a piece of paper. "Mabel—aw! Born on ..." She did the calculations in her head. "Just turned seven months. And the mother is Vicki Stevenson with the dad's name listed as Michael Stevenson. I bet *that* guy isn't too happy. He thought he was a dad and now, uh oh."

Speaking of fathers ... "Any sign of *my* dad?"

Rosie scanned the bar. "Pretty sure I saw him follow

Lars out. He's probably giving him the fatherhood spiel now. Or the kiss of life after the poor guy passed out from shock."

I didn't doubt it. My dad had a lot of experience, and he was both the captain and the oldest guy on the team, so that accorded him elder statesman status. Everyone looked to him for advice, comfort, and leadership.

A tall, dark, and instantly recognizable figure appeared at Rosie's side. I hadn't seen my brother in person in over a year and usually I'd be up to give him a hug, but the baby.

"What the fuck, Addy?"

"Language, Dino Boy. Baby ears."

"Did you just come home from traveling the world with a ... kid?"

Rosie nudged Hatch. "Not hers, dickhead. And hello? Great to see you, too."

"Damn, sorry. I just saw the baby and—" He pulled Rosie into his arms. "Hey, Ro, it's so good to see you."

I pretended not to notice how Rosie closed her eyes and inhaled in Hatch's embrace.

I called out, "You can hug me later, H."

Rosie pulled away first, which was good for her mental health, though who knew if it made a difference. Crushes were a blight, for sure.

Summer laughed, a musical tinkle. "Did you really think your sister hid a baby from you all year?"

Hatch's smiling expression shifted to stormy at Summer's words. For some reason, he didn't like her, and he was terrible at hiding it.

Ignoring Summer, he addressed me. "You want to fill me in?"

"NyQuil's in *big* trouble." Dash had returned, a beer in his hand, ready for the gossip. "Some chick waltzed in, handed over the kid, and waltzed out again. He chased after her and now, no sign of him. Real soap opera stuff."

My brother whistled. "That's wild."

"Right?" Dash jerked his chin toward the bar's entrance. "Looks like he decided not to do a runner after all."

The crowd parted as Lars returned, resolute focus on his face, grim determination in his tread. My father walked behind him, the mental and emotional support this surprise dad needed. Rosie stepped aside to let Lars get closer.

He looked down.

I looked up.

Our eyes locked and the intensity in his gaze shivered through me. Not that it was for me. It was for the baby. The situation. Maybe even the woman who had just left.

"Is she okay?" he asked.

My heart went out to him, forced to be so vulnerable in front of all these people. I wanted to protect him and the best way to do that was to take this somewhere private.

I stood, still holding the child, who seemed to be getting heavier with each passing second. "She's fine. Let's find somewhere to talk, okay?"

Look at me taking charge! Rosie narrowed her eyes at me. I fixed on a smile. "Ro, could you pack that bag up for Lars?"

"Oh, yeah, sure!" She restuffed the baby paraphenalia haphazardly and handed the diaper bag to a stunned Lars.

I caught my dad's eye, who was watching me with a curious amusement. "Dad, do you think we could use the back office?"

No slouch, he grabbed the bag from Lars, curled a hand around his arm, and said, "Let's go."

A minute later we were in the back office of the Empty

Net. My dad took the baby from me and started cooing away while Lars watched. He hadn't said a word since asking if she was okay and now, he was standing at the door, hands crossed defensively against that superhero chest, probably wondering how his world could have blown up in such spectacular style.

"Did you catch up with her?"

He turned to me, as if surprised I'd spoken. "Vicki? Yeah. She's out."

"Oh. Wow."

My dad looked up from making raspberry sounds. "She told her husband the kid was his. He found out she was not. And now we're here."

"That's messed up."

"Fuck yeah, it is." Lars rubbed his mouth. Now probably wasn't the time to get puritanical about the swearing. "What's my play here?"

"I suppose you could call social services or ..." I trailed off at the look of horror on my dad's face. "You have to come up with a plan."

Dad took a seat at the desk, still with the baby in his arms. "We have tons of stuff left over from Tilly. A crib. Stroller. Everything you need for a baby. We never got around to donating it."

Lars glared at him. "I can buy stuff for the kid. That's not the problem here. The problem, in case you haven't noticed, is that I have a full-time fucking job that involves time on the road, so I'm not seeing how I can take care of her *and* play hockey."

My dad grinned, like these were nonsense obstacles. "Don't worry about that. We can help and there are a million people in this org who'll have your back. For tonight, we're going to take her home to our place and get her fed and changed. She doesn't stink yet but give it time." He nuzzled the baby's forehead. "Right, future poopy pants?"

He sounded so calm, exactly what Lars needed to hear. The panic hadn't quite left his expression, but his shoulders softened a degree.

"I can't ask you for that." But it emerged half-heartedly because he really needed someone to take the reins.

"You're not. Ellie will help." He winked. "If my baby mama could have another kid this week, she would totally do it."

I pointed at him. "I'll tell her you said that."

"Best not, Twinkle." His gaze dipped to the baby and damn, he looked cute holding her. Even Lars appeared transfixed, though that could be a residual stunning effect.

"Listen, I should give Elle a heads up," Dad said. "Addy, would you hold her for a second?" My dad had evidently decided Lars wasn't ready for prime time.

"No problem." I took over while he headed outside to call Mom.

Which left me alone with Lars and his daughter. The silence was deafening; not even a baby gurgle to break the tension. Back in the bar—pre-baby bombshell—we had made great progress, with both of us acknowledging my crush and its beautiful demise. I'd never felt so adult. Now we were mired in another, albeit different, quagmire.

Nervously, I filled the void with some babbling of my own. "She's so good!"

Lars brooded away in the corner.

I tried again. "Did you want to hold her?"

"Might not be a good idea."

"No?"

His expression turned even more stern. "I won't be keeping her."

CHAPTER THREE

Lars

I WAS STILL IN SHOCK.

I hadn't touched the baby since I chased Vicki out of the bar. When I came back Adeline was holding her and my first thought was: *she's got this.*

The second? *I'm fucked.*

Typically, I wasn't the kind of guy who let things happen to him. I made the plays and tackled the problems head on, but this situation had me frozen, barely able to think of the next move. That's why I said what I did.

I won't be keeping her.

It sounded harsh, but common sense dictated I figure out what was best for the baby, which in this instance happened to coincide with what was best for me. We were all selfish fuckers at heart, right? There was no way I could look after a kid. I was not father material.

But you'd swear that with that declarative statement, I had ripped Adeline's heart out and skated through it on a rusty blade. She refused to look at me when Theo came back into the office with the happy-happy news that Elle was getting the crib out of storage and that everything would work out. As soon as Adeline saw him, she stood and headed to the door without a glance in my direction.

Not only was I fucked but I had fucked up.

I would have offered to take the baby, but Adeline was already gone, so I picked up the bag and nudged Theo with my shoulder.

"You sure Elle's okay with this?" Still not sure what *this* was.

"She's fine. You can make some calls tomorrow and we can figure out a plan. It's wild but hey, wild is our brand!"

His brand, maybe, with his boisterous brood around the table. Right now, I didn't need wild. I needed assurance.

Out in the corridor, Adeline had turned left toward the back exit, so we let her lead the way. We arrived at Theo's car first because his seniority meant he got dibs on one of the two precious parking spots behind the bar.

"We don't have a car seat, so I'll drive slowly while Addy holds her," Theo said. "I'll strap you in, Twinkle. Lars, you can follow us."

"Sure."

Ten minutes later, I parked outside the Kershaws' house in Winnetka, one suburb over from Riverbrook, home of the Rebels and about twenty miles north of downtown Chicago. Most of the older players lived on Chicago's North Shore, prioritizing closeness to work over the need to be within walking distance of the hottest clubs and Michelin-starred restaurants. Elle was already out the door, moving toward her husband and daughter and ... my child.

I have a child.

If this was real, I needed it to make sense. That meant not issuing knee-jerk statements about this little girl's future without sorting through the facts. The panic was still there, a low-level hum through my body, but the shrieking of my heart had subsided.

Elle took the baby from Adeline just as I met her at the door.

"Oh, she is gorgeous! And those eyes? Lars, she looks just like you."

"Don't say that, Mom." Adeline avoided looking at me. "He's hoping the exact opposite."

"No, I'm not." *Yes, I was.*

Adeline snorted. "Whatever, Nyquist."

Whatever, Nyquist? Before I had a chance to respond, she was inside the house.

Elle's eyes went wide. "What's going on there?"

"Apparently, I'm not living up to her lofty expectations for surprise fatherhood."

"Well, this is a shock, and everyone should be giving you grace while you adjust. Let's get her fed and settled." She smiled, all sympathy. "You're not alone, Lars."

ELLE HAD WORKED miracles in the ten minutes it took us to drive from the Empty Net to the Kershaws' house. In the warm and homey kitchen, where I'd attended once-weekly meals for the last year, she had laid out a shit-ton of baby supplies from bottles to clothes to one of those baby beds that probably had a fancy name I'd be forced to learn.

I was in for a real education, no doubt.

"You had all this stuff close to hand?"

"Just a few things. And we have plenty more in the basement to get you started."

Someone came in behind me. I turned hoping for Adeline—I needed to apologize—but it was Theo. Eggsbee followed and settled into the dog bed in the corner. *Someone give that pup a bucket of popcorn.*

"Sit down, NyQuil. Looks like you need off your feet."

Suddenly tired as hell, I sank into a seat at the kitchen table. All I could see was baby detritus and long years of never getting laid again.

Elle cocked her head, a hopefulness in her expression that made me itchy. "I need to get her something to eat. Would you like to hold her?"

No, but I needed to be a team player.

"Sure, hand her over." Did I sound terrified? A grown-ass man worried about a tiny little doll that supposedly had his eyes?

"Here you go. Just like that, support her head ... perfect!" Quick glance of—was that amusement?—at her husband.

"I suppose you think this is hilarious."

"Abso-fucking-lutely," Theo chirped. "I mean, that chick sure showed you in the middle of the Empty Net."

She sure did. But right now, I wasn't thinking of Vicki. My mind rewound to the disappointment in Adeline's gaze when I told her I'd be bailing on this baby biz ASAP.

I refocused on the primary problem. "There should be a number for the mother in that bag."

Theo laid all the bag's contents on the table with the rest. Diapers, boxes that looked like formula, a couple of those one-piece jumpsuits with built-in socks, and a birth certificate. I noted my name was listed nowhere, and that the date of birth roughly corresponded to nine months after I'd met Vicki the first time.

I flipped the birth certificate over while Theo searched the side pockets of the bag.

"No number." He shrugged. "Should be easy enough to find, though. No one can ever truly disappear."

Too right. The sooner I found her the sooner I could fix this mess.

For the first time since the bar, I looked down into the supposedly Nyquist eyes. This kid had been crying havoc as Vicki sought me out in the bar but since finding me, she hadn't made much of a fuss. Was it possible she had my stoicism baked into her genes or did she recognize me in some way that only evolutionary biology could explain?

She looked up at me, those big blues snagging all my attention and pulling hard at my ice-compacted heart. *Don't even think of relying on me, kid. Go work your blue-eyed mojo on some other sucker.*

"Aw, look at that! She likes you." Exactly what Vicki had said before she unloaded her bombshell news. I read that, and Elle's observation now, as reassurance for my fragile male ego.

Thank God for the Kershaws.

But I wondered about one Kershaw in particular, and if she still thought I was an asshole.

Adeline

LARS NYQUIST IS A DICK.

Sure, the man had just been blindsided with staggering news but did his first instinct have to be how to get rid of the problem? That was an actual baby in that kitchen, and the man wanted nothing to do with her.

It was late, close to midnight, but I knew the one person I could talk to was probably still up. Rather than walk through the kitchen, I headed out the front door and circled around back to the coach house. The light was on, a beacon to weary old me, and the door opened as soon as I toed the threshold.

"So Lars Nyquist is a daddy!"

My great grandmother—Aurora to everyone—stood at the coach house entrance, hip cocked, a martini glass in hand. (Filled with water as she never imbibed alcohol after 10 p.m. She just liked the silhouette of the glass.)

"News travels fast."

"Your brother texted, though I would've thought I'd hear it first from my favorite great-granddaughter."

"Your favorite? Poor Tilly."

Aurora waved that off. "She's too young to understand such nuances. Come in and tell me everything!"

Armed with a cup of cinnamon-apple tea, I sat and filled her in. This kitchen was my favorite room in the Kershaw Compound. Warm cherry wood cabinets formed a semi-circle, like an amphitheater where the French country style table was the stage.

When I finished, she tilted her head and asked, "And why are you here?"

"Sharing the gossip. Why else?"

Aurora hoisted a well-shaped eyebrow and pushed her stylish gray bob behind one ear. She might be eighty-three, but she looked not a day past seventy.

"No, you're not. You came to express your disapproval—or maybe, disappointment? Though why you'd care whether Lars Nyquist accepts his fate with grace and maturity, I have no idea."

My shrug was stiff with effort. "I just don't like seeing men get away with things or not stepping up to accept responsibility. His first instinct is to think of how to bail. That kid needs him."

"Of course she does. And knowing what I do of Lars, he needs her."

I startled. "What does that mean?"

"Oh, he's become quite the fixture at our dinner table over the last year. Almost one of the family at this point, and I get the impression he needs someone to love. Other than us Kershaws. Sure there's plenty of love to go around here, but a man like Lars needs something dramatic to make him see it. Give him focus other than hockey, especially after how his father left God's green earth."

A once-great Finnish hockey player, Lars's dad, Sven Nyquist, had trashed his NHL career with a gambling ban, then decided he could probably one-up that on the road to ruin his reputation. After several years of substance abuse, drunk-driving arrests, and bar brawling, he'd died instantly when his car wrapped around a tree six months ago.

In the past year, my family had brought Lars into the fold, it seemed. I balked at the idea that Aurora, and possibly my whole family, had the inside scoop on Lars Nyquist and his "needs." The man was supposed to be *my* secret crush, not everyone else's!

"Well, if he has his way, the baby will be returned to her mother or the state, he'll be absolved of all responsibility, and his life will go on without a care."

Aurora studied me. "Still taking things so seriously."

"This is serious business. We're talking about a baby."

"I know, I know." She patted my hand. "But neither Lars nor the baby are your responsibility. The man has the resources of a billion-dollar franchise at his disposal. The baby will be fine."

Would she? Was that the only concern, that she was fed and sheltered? I hated to think of her most basic needs being efficiently met yet no one was worried about the impact this change would have on her emotional growth and development. But Aurora was right: not my monkeys, not my circus. That should have left me relieved instead of irritable.

"I'll let you sleep." I rinsed out my cup and put it in the dish rack. "I'll keep you updated."

"Or I can just drop in for breakfast tomorrow and hear it myself. I assume the baby's staying the night here?"

"Where else?" Lars had my parents wrapped around his little finger.

Aurora stood and gave me a hug. "I'm so glad you're home, honey. I've missed you. Talking on video call wasn't the same."

"No, it wasn't. I missed you so much." Seeing her in person reminded me that she wasn't getting any younger. I wanted to hear her stories, learn all about her daughter, the grandmother I never met who had died when my dad was a teen. "Could I come see you tomorrow? I'd love to chat about *you*, not all this Rebels drama."

I also needed some homespun wisdom to get me through the next few weeks and months. Aurora always knew the right thing to say, plus she was a hoot.

"I have Tai Chi in the morning, so stop by in the afternoon."

With one last kiss to her forehead—she was a tiny thing

—I returned to the house, back through the front door. Standing at the entrance to the kitchen, I remained half-hidden so I could assess the situation. Mom was at the stove heating up some of the formula Vicki had included in the diaper bag. Dad was inventorying the baby supplies on the table. Eggsbee snored softly in his doggie daybed. As for Lars? The man of the hour was holding the baby, probably under sufferance. Yet my heart contracted at the sight.

He still looked scared, but there was something else.

Curiosity. Like the baby was a puzzle.

I found this amusing, and because I found it amusing, I was no longer angry with him. Aurora was right, I needed to be kinder about this. Maybe he wasn't going to bail as soon as someone said he could do so legally. Or maybe he would. But you know what? It was none of my business. Lars Nyquist was none of my business.

That torch I'd carried was well and surely doused. A man who could barely look at his own flesh and blood was not romance material. I could move on, not even be embarrassed about what happened last year because Lars had shown me a side of himself I didn't enjoy.

Then he caught my eye and arched an eyebrow as if to say, *can you believe it?* And there went my heart again, skittering like an oversexed bunny.

Yeah, I could believe it. I could believe that this man could assess a situation, recalibrate as needed, and figure out a new game plan. Hockey players were professionals at adapting. That initial panic appeared to have subsided, and in its place was a man who saw a challenge. Who might even be up to it.

Was that sexy? It shouldn't have been, but maybe I saw sexiness in everything Lars Nyquist.

"Addy." My dad smiled at me. "Could you do me a

favor and get the second bassinet out of the basement? And anything else you see down there that might be useful?"

Lars looked up with a frown. "Kershaw, you don't need to give me all this stuff."

"Why not? Unless you're planning on sending your non-existent PA out to shop for you, you may as well take it. And our help."

Lars gave a brusque nod, followed with a quick glance my way. "Thanks, Adeline."

It didn't take long to find what we needed. My mom had packed everything away, labeling all the plastic totes clearly. Clothes, toys, equipment. Through one of the transparent boxes, something familiar caught my eye.

Bear! My soft teddy, given to me by Erik Jorgenson, the legendary former Rebels goaltender. I'd been obsessed with it as a kid, and the way my life had been going lately, I probably wouldn't mind holding onto it to see me through the night.

Something else in the box snagged my attention—blue copybooks. I opened one and flipped through the pages of stats in my girlish script. I wasn't sporty like the boys, but this was my way to contribute to the Kershaw family business. After each game, I would show my dad how he'd done, as if he didn't have a team of experts at Rebels HQ to give him the goods.

Your TOI isn't as good these last three games, Dad. That's one of the stats GMs care most about! And points are becoming really important to defense. I'd obviously read that somewhere. I lived in constant fear of my dad being traded, taking me away from my best friend Rosie and upending my life as I knew it.

"I can take that."

I jumped so high, I almost hit the low ceiling. I turned

to find Lars at the bottom of the stairs. "Hey, don't sneak up on me like that!"

"Sorry, thought you heard me." He stepped forward, out of the shadows, and took a long, hard look at me. "What's wrong?"

"N-nothing."

Closer again. "You're shaking."

I inhaled a couple of short, sharp breaths. "Just got a fright, that's all."

His look of concern almost undid me. I turned away, grabbed Bear, and placed it in the tote box along with the supplies.

"That's your guitar, I'm guessing," he said.

I looked at the instrument's hard case in the corner, covered in Hello Kitty stickers and other labels that screamed "little girl." "That's my old one. My newer one, a Martin, is upstairs. But it needs to be restrung after I was away for so long. Old strings become brittle and prone to breaking."

Quit your babbling. You're worse than Mabel.

"I bet Tilly will love hearing whatever new songs you come up with."

Nonsense songs for babies were about the limits of my intellect right now.

Lars reached for the bassinet and our hands brushed. I pulled back quickly, not liking how I felt around him, all fluttery and floaty. I should have been over it, and now this new situation was dragging me into his orbit again. This crush needed to die.

He frowned. "Adeline, are you still pissed at me?"

Yes, but not because of what you think. "No. I'm sorry I got all judgy back there."

"I get it. I didn't respond as graciously as I could have. It was a knee-jerk reaction to very surprising news. I'm not even sure she's mine."

"Mom says she has your eyes." I agreed. I'd spent enough time gazing into them at the Empty Net. That kid was Lars's through and through.

"Not sure that's definitive. People say I don't look like my dad but there's no doubt I'm his son."

He sounded somewhat bitter, though whether it was because of the lack of likeness or the certainty that he was Sven Nyquist's son, I couldn't discern. I didn't know the entire story, but I gathered the gambling issues had driven a wedge between them. I couldn't imagine never speaking to my father, or him leaving this earth knowing I didn't want to see him.

I searched for something to say to smooth over the awkwardness.

"Not sure I look like my dad all that much. The boys all do."

"You favor your mom more. But your eyes—those are the Kershaw green. And beautiful."

My body flushed, but then I remembered that he was likely trying to pacify me because he needed my family's help.

"Spend a lot of time gazing into Theo Kershaw's eyes, do you?"

"Gotta practice our telepathy for the games, y'know."

I laughed. It wasn't so much funny as it was a welcome release of tension.

Another tilt of his head. "Are we friends again?"

"We weren't before."

"But everything's changed. And I need all the friends I can get right now, Adeline."

Adeline. It sounded sensual on his tongue.

Above our heads, the faint cry of the baby could be heard. Lars winced at the reminder that his life had changed irrevocably.

"I'd better see what the little madam wants." He took a step back with the bassinet and one of the larger totes. "Thanks for your help. I won't forget it."

CHAPTER FOUR

Lars Nyquist Baby Mama Drama!

In a scene straight out of a telenovela, Lars Nyquist found out he was a father when last night, an unnamed woman dropped off his child at the Empty Net, a known Chicago Rebels player hangout. Inside sources tell us that Lars was blindsided by the news that he has a daughter and was seen arguing with his baby mama outside the bar before she made a quick getaway in a taxi. Lars, son of hellraising hockey player Sven Nyquist, was clearly upset with the situation as it was unveiled in front of teammates and fans. Uh oh!

Regular readers of this column will remember that Nyquist Senior died several months ago in a single car collision after years in forced retirement from the NHL owing to his part in an illegal gambling ring. Toxicology results indicated that he was under the influence of alcohol and cocaine at the time of his death. While Nyquist Junior has never shown signs of following in his father's footsteps, it's clear he has more in common with the old man than everyone thought!

- Hot Goss

Adeline

"NOT IN A MILLION YEARS!"

The morning after The Baby Bombshell, I was seated at the kitchen table, which was still covered with baby stuff. The baby in question was in one of the borrowed bassinets, sleeping like an angel, while the sperm donor was in the other room on the phone with his agent looking for an exit strategy.

Evidently, I was part of it.

Seated in my lap, my heavier-by-the-second baby sister munched on a piece of naan—the kid was obsessed with all things bread. Dad was standing at the kitchen island making one of his kale-o-riffic smoothies. (His words, not mine.)

He held up the sludge-filled jug and started pouring. "Twinkle, it would be for a few weeks, maximum. Just while he gets things sorted with the baby's mom."

"But I'm not qualified to look after a baby."

My father scoffed. "You were practically Tilly's mom her first year of life. She hardly knew her incubator."

"Hey." Mom grinned and shook her head. "It takes a village and that's what we are around here." She leaned over and rubbed Mabel's chest, earning a sleepy snuffle in return. "But he's not completely wrong. Tilly did say 'Addy' before she said 'Mom' or 'Dad'."

"Addy, this is for you!" Tilly held out a piece of naan, then put it in her mouth with a giggle as soon as I showed any interest. Out came the massive, toothy grin that made my heart melt. I'd missed her so much. I'd missed them all.

But if I'd known I'd be on the hook as nanny for Lars Nyquist's surprise love child, I would have stayed far, far away.

"Why am I being asked? Is it because I'm at a loose end or is it because I've got tits?"

"Addy!" My dad frowned, like plain-speaking wasn't this family's lingua franca. "The first one."

I might have needed something to occupy my time, but a baby was a full-time job. Not exactly the kind of gig I had in mind while I pondered the great questions of who I was and what I should be doing.

"Tits!" Tilly giggled and sucked juice from her Captain America sippy cup.

"My good influence continues."

Mom reached over and squeezed my hand. "It was just an idea. You do not have to do this at all. Besides, the Rebels org is on the case, working with an au pair agency."

Au pair. Defined as "sexy nanny," usually British or Spanish or worst of all, Swedish. Likely to fall in love with the hunky single dad at the drop of her French knickers. I didn't enjoy how my lungs hitched at the idea of Lars getting his (childcare) needs attended to by this hot little number of my imagination.

My father was having none of it. "We can't have some strange woman looking after baby Mabel!"

"There you go again, assuming that the nanny will be female." I pointed at him. "Sexist."

"Completely," a deep voice cut in. Lars entered the kitchen, pocketing his phone in his jeans. "And stop hounding Adeline to take a job she doesn't need or want. She's barely been home for five minutes." He turned to me and mouthed, "Sorry" and just that intimate communication sent my pulse rocketing.

If that wasn't the assurance I needed that staying out of Lars's orbit was a top-shelf idea, then I didn't know what was.

Dad was still on his soap box. "So you're fine with some stranger feeding your kid?"

"People hire strangers to look after their children all the time." Lars inhaled deeply and arced a tired and troubled gaze over the kitchen and its inhabitants, skimming Mabel with barely a glance. "I'll get out of your way."

You would think he'd announced the coming of the end times. My parents shot up. Well, Dad was already standing but he seemed to grow five inches.

"You're heading ... home?" My confused mother not-so-subtly placed her body between Lars and the bassinet.

"Alone?" Dad's shocked utterance contained a healthy infusion of *fuck, no.*

Sensing the drama, Eggsbee jumped to his feet, barked once, and wagged his tail.

Even Tilly got in on the act. "Duckman, have some bread!"

Lars frowned at Tilly, caught my eye—more of the *us v. them* communication—then returned his attention to the guardians of Mabel's galaxy.

"Gotta do it sometime. For now, the wheels are in motion. The paternity test, the lawyer, the nanny hunt, trying to get ahold of Vicki." He sounded especially irritated by that last to-do. "I can't stay with you guys forever."

I doubted he got a wink of sleep. My parents had set him up in the guest room, with the crib beside the bed. Mom told me Lars had been awake the entire night and even fed his daughter once, under her knowing direction.

When Tilly was seven months old, she was already sleeping through, but each baby was different.

My heart keened in sympathy. I was on my parents' side here. He should stay longer because once he left, he was truly on his own.

"Yeah, but do you have to leave right this minute? We only just got Mabel down."

This ploy by master strategist Theo Kershaw was enough to throw Lars off his game. Uncertainty crossed his brow.

"I don't want to take advantage." Less sure now.

"You are not taking advantage." Pushing for home, my mom squeezed his arm. "You didn't get any sleep, Lars, so we're ordering you to lie down and take a nap. Just an hour or so, because you'll be no good to that kid if you don't get some rest."

"You've already helped out so much—"

"And we can do it for a few more hours. Theo, talk to him."

My dad placed a comforting hand on his shoulder. "Go ahead, get some shuteye."

Lars exhaled. "Okay. I'll set my alarm for an hour and then ..." He trailed off, his gaze drifting to his daughter. Stories were written in that look, ones with unknowable endings.

Once he left, my mom and dad shared one of those familiar knowing glances I'd been privy to my entire life. My parents were #relationshipgoals, the Great Love Story I envied and craved for myself. After a one-night stand resulted in a surprise pregnancy, my father had pursued my mom relentlessly and charmed her prickly Black Cat with his pure Golden Retriever energy. Five kids later, they were still madly in love.

Eager to escape what I suspected came next—my parents making out like teenagers—I headed upstairs and ran into Lars coming out of the bathroom.

"Could I have a word?" he asked.

"Sure."

"I overheard some of the conversation you were having with your parents about taking on nanny duty."

I tried to recall if I'd said anything negative. "I'm sorry if it sounds like I'm not being a team player—"

He held up a hand. "Stop right there. I just want you to know I would never expect that. Your parents are out of order to even ask it of you. So please don't think I'd want you to step up like that."

"You wouldn't?"

He rubbed his mouth, something he did when he was thinking about how to phrase his next words. I wished I didn't know that.

"Well, no. You're a young girl, with your whole life ahead of you. Cleaning up after my mistakes is not your responsibility."

Not sure I liked being described as a "young girl," as if I wasn't mature enough to be in the running for this nanny gig. Or anything else.

Setting that aside, I asked, "Is that what you think? That Mabel is a mistake?"

He blew out a breath. "I mean, in the sense of me fucking up with a married woman. The kid can't help being born. What I'm trying to say is that this is *my* problem, and I don't want other people feeling they need to fix it. No one else can fix it but me."

My natural empathy rose to the fore.

"Yet good things can still come out of it. I know it's hard

to see that right now when your life has been tossed on its head like this. People want to help."

"Yeah, I see that. And I'm grateful. Truly." He shook his head. "I'm not used to accepting it, I suppose."

"How come?"

He scoffed. "How long have you got?"

Forever.

He didn't wait for my answer. "I'd best let you get on. Just don't let your parents boss you around, okay?"

"Says the man who was ordered to take a nap by the Kershaw Sleep Police."

He laughed, and wow, that sound wrapped me up in a Lars hug. The guy was dead on his feet yet that laugh gave me life.

With one last smile, he headed into the guest room and closed the door.

Lars

HOW HARD COULD THIS BE?

I could tell Theo and Elle were terrified at the thought of me taking on solo father duties. Hell, I was right there with them, but I couldn't show it. I had to project calm, so I watched like a daddy hawk while my co-defenseman strapped the kid into the car seat. It didn't look too difficult as long as you made sure the belt looped through the right holes. If only the rest were that easy.

I thrust my hand toward Theo, who looked at it like it was a foreign object.

"Jesus, NyQuil, you're gonna need more than a handshake to get you through this." He wrapped me in a hug and patted my back while I regarded Elle over his shoulder. Her brittle smile barely covered the cracks. She didn't have much confidence in me, either.

"Thanks, Elle, for staying up to feed her and giving me the crash course in parenting. And for all the stuff." The trunk was stuffed to the gills.

"Are you sure you don't want us to come home with you?"

I waved it off, so blasé, like I learned I was a new dad every day. "I've got this. The agency will be sending over nanny prospects tomorrow, and hopefully one of them can start immediately."

I was supposed to leave for an away game the day after, so I sure as hell needed childcare to be squared away by then. Which meant I would probably end up choosing the first nanny who didn't radiate serial killer vibes.

My next moves felt weirdly robotic, the same as how I felt when Sven would watch every one of my motions on the ice in that first year of living with him. As a professional athlete I should've been used to multiple peepers on me. Coaches, players, fans, media. But this new pressure took me back to those early days learning how to play hockey under the critical eye of my father.

Pick up your toe.

Quit dragging your heel.

Not like that, you fucking idiot.

Are you sure you're my kid?

Yeah, Sven had any number of "critiques" at the ready to spur me on to greatness. He labored under the weird misapprehension that a six-year-old would pick it up naturally purely because of genetics. I thought I'd moved on from that feeling, but here I was again, a bug under a glass, with everyone waiting for me to fail.

Open the door.

One more glance in the back at the kid to make sure she was locked in tight.

Maybe I should tug on the strap to check its tautness? But that would look like I didn't trust Kershaw when he and Elle were the only reason I wasn't completely falling apart.

Now or never. But before I could climb in, a strong voice called out, "Hold up! Wait!"

Adeline.

She bounded toward us, her dark ponytail bobbing behind her, determination in her expression. She wore jeans and a tight, fluffy lilac sweater that molded to her in ways I should not be noticing.

"I'll head back with him and get his place set up."

"Perfect!" Theo grinned and gave his daughter a hug.

"I'm not staying longer than an hour or two," Adeline insisted, though no one had asked.

"Just long enough to dot the i's and cross the t's," Elle said, obvious relief in her voice, expression, in her whole demeanor. "You'll be in and out."

Adeline turned those movie goddess eyes on me. "You okay with this?"

Her tone was, *you're taking my help whether you want it or not*, which I assumed was related to that brief convo we had a couple of hours ago. I hoped she didn't think I'd been planting the seeds of weaponized incompetence. While my cluelessness around babies was a real and verifiable thing, I sure as hell wasn't using it to get Adeline to take on this gig.

"Wouldn't dare say no with the daggers you're shooting me right now."

She opened her mouth, shut it quickly, then murmured, "Just want to be sure we're on the same page."

Strangely, I thought we were. Even more strange, I kind of liked it. And I liked this bossy version of Adeline.

To hell with it. I gave one last pull of the strap across the baby car seat, then took a proper look at the baby for what felt like the first time. Of course I'd looked at her before, noted that cupid mouth, her apple-blossomed cheeks, those blue eyes that people insisted were copies of my own. But this time I held her gaze and made a promise: *I'll take care of you, whether your DNA is mine or not.*

That was the crux of the conversation this morning with my agent, Quinn Huxley, and the lawyer he hired to get me out of this mess. Determine paternity, then determine next steps. When I'd mentioned that even if she wasn't biologically mine, I wanted to help her financially, my consiglieres had exploded in indignation.

Quinn had led the chorus. "Let's not make any rash decisions. You don't owe this kid or her mom a thing until the courts say so."

"I have to agree," the lawyer chimed in. "Information gathering first, decisions later."

I let them think I was on board with that plan, but I'd had plenty of time to think during my sleepless night. Lying on my side, my eyes glued to the crib where a tiny human got more sleep than I did, I'd wondered why that was? Why was I awake and terrified while she was asleep and content?

Because she felt safe—and I was the reason for it.

Okay, not me specifically, but the adults taking care of her. I hadn't felt that when I was a kid, first being used as a pawn while my parents hammered out custody. Then the revolving door of stepmoms and "aunts," none of whom stayed for long enough to give me a real sense of security. Sven and his temper would inevitably drive them away.

The whole situation made me think about Vicki and the home she'd given Mabel so far. One where the child wasn't wanted or could be thrown out at the drop of a hat. Where the only father she'd ever known made his wife choose "the kid or me." Where her mom would think that was a viable choice, just give her up to some stranger in a bar.

Stranger or not, I would still be looking after her. A scholarship or a trust fund or something along those lines, even if she weren't mine.

Mabel babbled, like she knew all these crazy thoughts inside my head. Like she understood just how much she had upended my life: *yeah, man, you are in so much trouble— and it's all on me!*

The little she-devil was hella cute, though.

I lifted my head to catch Adeline giving me what could best be termed a "soft look." Better than the disdain-dripping darts she'd been shooting my way since I received the joyful tidings. At the same time, I didn't want her getting the wrong idea, thinking I might be cut out for this nonsense.

I nodded my thanks to Elle and Theo, climbed into the driver's seat, and pulled out very, very slowly.

CHAPTER FIVE

Adeline

I HAD no idea what possessed me to come rushing out and offer my services. Maybe it was my dad's pleading or my mom's insistence I didn't have to do a thing. Maybe it was the helplessness of that kid who was being shoved from pillar to post and needed stability more than anything else.

Spoiler: none of the above.

It was because Lars had been honest about his inability to ask for help, which I took as his way of putting himself out there and well, asking for help in a typically male way. I couldn't refuse a man in need, especially when a child's welfare was on the line.

"So, do you live in a house?"

"No, I live in a shack under the bridge."

I chuckled because that did sound stupid. "I meant, versus a condo. Just thinking about your square footage."

He raised an eyebrow. "My square footage?"

My cheeks heated. I couldn't win here.

I caught his reflection in the mirror. That was exactly how he interpreted it, and look at us, joking around. Ah, progress.

"My square footage is more than adequate."

I rolled my eyes, which earned me another Lars laugh, warm as whiskey and twice as potent.

"How come you're doing this, Adeline? Did you fall for my hard luck story back there?"

"Maybe I'm curious to see where you live. And if you can turn your bachelor pad into a suitable home for a kid."

He sighed. "This is madness, isn't it?"

"A little. But guys find out they've knocked someone up all the time. Witness the Great Love Story, Trademark, of Theo and Elle Kershaw."

"The Great Love Story, Trademark?"

"Just a family joke. Like this epic love they have is so unique it has to be trademarked." I paused a second, so my curiosity didn't come off as too rabid. "What happened with you and Mabel's mom?"

"Boy meets girl, girl neglects to mention she's married, boy and girl have a whale of a time, boy's left thinking he's in the clear but then his world implodes over a year later. Definitely not a great love story, trademark or otherwise."

"And her solution is to drop the baby off at the Empty Net after a game?" I gave a low whistle. "That's one way of handling it."

"She's not in a good place. The mom, that is. I have people looking for her. Given her marital situation and the desperate measures, I'd like some assurance that she's safe."

I would never have thought of that. This woman had lied her ass off, landed him in hot water, and upended his life, yet he was concerned for her well-being. Point to Nyquist.

"You don't think she's going to do something stupid, do you?"

"No, nothing like that. If anything I got the impression that she was doing this to save her marriage. But if this guy told her it was the baby or him, then that makes me concerned for her safety. He might be violent or abusive. Also, I'd like to talk to her. Tell her that we can figure out a plan. I have resources."

"That's probably why she dropped her off—because you are the ultimate resource. Financially, anyway." That came out harsher than intended.

"True, I can throw money at the situation but I'm not sure I can do much else."

I didn't have a chance to respond because we'd turned into the driveway of a townhouse. It was faux Tudor style, and I could tell the square footage would be just fine.

As for the man beside me, I wasn't so sure about that.

This was a huge change for him. Luckily Mabel seemed like a good-natured kid, but still, she was barely seven months old. She needed twenty-four-seven care.

Not your problem, Adeline. You're here to get him set up and go on your way.

Leaving Lars to figure out unstrapping the car seat, I gathered as many supplies as I could and started stacking them at the door. By the time I was beginning the third trip from the car, Lars had freed Mabel and was carrying her up the steps.

"Leave the rest of the stuff. You're not a porter."

"You're going to have your hands full for a while, so I'd take all the help I could get if I were you."

He shook his head. "Sorry, I didn't mean to sound like an ingrate. Thanks for being here."

He sounded so sincere, and my heart fluttered a little. *Enough of that, silly girl.*

I busied myself with taking in all the baby equipment, a task that worked semi-decently to calm my racing pulse. It wasn't as if I was starved for affection or kindness—my family were the kindest and most embarrassingly affectionate people on the planet. Yet here I was, simpering at Lars Nyquist's gratitude. Or maybe it was that softness that came over him when he realized he was coming off as too gruff.

I was a sucker for it, so I needed to shore up those defenses as quickly as possible.

WHAT A DIFFERENCE TWENTY-FOUR HOURS MADE.

One day later the Empty Net was no longer the rowdy, spectacle-drenched bar where one-night stands dumped babies into the arms of shocked professional hockey players. Though I wasn't convinced the drama-free atmosphere would last long.

"You did what?" Punctuating the screeching in my face, Rosie added a good shoulder shake.

Let me tell you more about my friend. Rosie was what could be best described as an experimenter and a truth-teller, except when it came to herself. I could always count on her in good times and bad, and though she was a couple of years older than me, she never treated me like a kid. She did, on occasion, treat me as an innocent in the ways of the world, particularly as she had no problem attracting men while I was generally man-repellent. I was the stick-in-the-mud to her free spirit, and we balanced each other beautifully.

"I just helped carry some stuff into his house. That's all."

Then I left. After two hours and ten minutes.

I couldn't just drop and dash. We set up the crib in Lars's bedroom—his idea, so he could keep an eye on her—and I organized the supplies while trying not to nose about his space, which was expectedly masculine, shockingly neat, and boringly impersonal. I showed him how to heat up the formula using the bottle warmer and watched while he fed the baby.

It was a lot of information for the guy to take in. It bothered me to go but if I hadn't left then, I don't think I would have left at all. Before I did, I made an emergency appointment with Pepper, who was married to former Rebels player, Bast Durand. An early childhood education specialist with a childproofing business, she would come in tomorrow and make sure Lars's home was safe for Mabel.

"So, you're like his personal assistant," Summer said, completely straight-faced. She'd always struck me as a gentle soul and not given to heavy dollops of sarcasm.

"More like a family friend."

Rosie snorted.

Summer stared at her. "What's that about?"

Rosie shot a quick look of semi-apology at me. My historical hankering for Lars Nyquist was not common knowledge. As I was 99% certain that I was long over it, discussion was *probably* harmless, plus giving it air would prove I was on the right side of this thing.

"I may have once harbored a minor crush on Lars." Summer's eyes went wide while I pointed at Rosie. "I'm over him."

"Didn't say a word."

"You didn't have to. And even if I wasn't, then it wouldn't matter. I won't be working for him as his nanny."

Summer's mouth dropped open. "He asked you to do that?"

"No, my parents did. He's in a bind but he'll be interviewing candidates tomorrow. An agency is sending them over."

Rosie took a sip of her Dovetail Hefeweizen (the Empty Net had really stepped up its local brewery game). "Does anyone really think he can get someone hired and installed in a day, though? That's majorly wishful. He needs to be on a plane the day after tomorrow for the New York game."

Summer's mouth twitched. "Zara Jacobs took three months to hire the right nanny. Then she fired her, and took another two for her second round." Zara was married to Cody, one of the players. "It takes time to do that process correctly. Never mind that, though! I want to know more about this crush of yours."

I thought I'd gotten away with it. "Like I said, a school-girl thing. When he arrived on the team, oh, five-ish years ago, I was gaga for him. Mrs. Adeline Nyquist in my note-books, social media stalking, the usual. And then—" I paused and sent a glance toward Rosie, who looked sympa-thetic. "About a year ago, he overheard me talking about how I thought he was the sexiest guy alive."

Summer clamped a hand over her mouth. "No!"

"Oh, but yes."

"How did he respond?"

"He was cool about it, and we were re-clearing the air last night when he was bamboozled by a baby."

"That's wild!" Summer touched a finger to her chin. "He's probably forgotten all about it, now that he has other things on his mind."

"Not sure he even remembered it at all until I ran into him last night." That was how low on Lars Nyquist's radar I fell. The worst—or second worst—thing that had ever happened to me was barely a blip for him. "But you're right, he definitely has his hands full."

"And you don't have a crush on him anymore?" Summer's sharp look gave the question an uncomfortable weight.

"Not at all! I've done a lot of growing up this last year." I exchanged a quick glance with Rosie, who gave me a smile of support. She was the only person who knew about the assault in Greece, and while I was sharing light-hearted crushes with Summer, I wouldn't be talking about that.

"So he overheard you saying something nice about him." Summer waved it off. "No big deal!"

"Exactly. It was just a crazy lapse in judgment, but no harm, no foul." Rosie was being remarkably quiet about it all, so I gave her a chance to weigh in. "Right?"

"Sure. You know your limits."

"What does that mean?"

"If you're going to take this nanny job, you have to understand the boundaries."

I bristled. "Who said anything about taking this nanny job? I specifically said I would *not* be taking it."

"Yeah, but that was before you helped him with his equipment."

"Hilarious."

Rosie grinned. "His baby equipment."

I shivered, not unpleasantly. "I'm not taking that job."

"You heard Summer. How likely is it he'll have a nanny by—" Rosie checked an imaginary time piece on her wrist. "Tomorrow? And when that doesn't happen, who'll be on the hook to watch this baby?"

My heart sank as the obvious conclusion dawned on me. "My mom."

"Your mom. The same mom who just got through raising a toddler and already has her hands full now that said toddler is in the fearsome fours."

"That's not a thing," I interjected. "It's terrible twos. And Tilly's in preschool."

"My point still stands. Your parents are the nearest Lars has to family in this town. Your dad's practically his best friend and your mom is always cooking him meals. Aurora even named a martini after him."

"She did?"

"Yeah, Hatch said. Scandi Noir, she called it. Finlandia vodka with grapefruit."

"Oh, that sounds awesome," Summer cut in.

"Doesn't it?" Rosie went on. "So in the absence of an actual nanny, your mom will take it upon herself to look after the kid and it'll be weeks before official childcare comes through. And she has her job, right? Your brother was saying she just contracted a new project."

My mom ran an information consultancy firm where she helped companies manage and leverage their knowledge assets. It was deep, in the weeds work. One of the reasons why I'd stayed home to look after Tilly was so she could continue to run her business without interruption.

As well as being remarkably well-informed, Rosie was right. Elle Kershaw was a freakin' saint and who else would volunteer to help? Sure, there were other hockey WAGs, but which of them would jump in at the deep end like my mom had done already?

It didn't mean that I should be volunteering my services, though. "He'll find someone."

Rosie nodded wisely. "Sure, he will."

CHAPTER SIX

Lars

A WAIL that could wake the dead—or at the very least Dex O'Malley, my Rebels teammate who could sleep through anything—sent shockwaves throughout the house.

So much for a good-natured baby.

The moment Adeline left the house, it was as if Mabel knew that she was on her own. That the one person now responsible for her welfare was the definition of disaster. Over three hours since our trusty threesome became a desolate twosome, and Mabel's lungs would not let up.

The only time she was quiet was with a bottle in her mouth, but I couldn't feed her twenty-four seven, could I? That would be a negative. And yes, I checked online. Now I was learning from the World's Teacher, aka YouTube. One woman with Mary Poppins vibes, including the accent, seemed to know what she was talking about, so I bookmarked her channel and played a couple of relevant videos. I'd burped the baby—shirt ruined—and now I was holding her to my shoulder and pacing around the house because apparently movement was supposed to calm her.

It sure as hell wasn't calming *me*. Mabel's impression of a banshee continued to assault my eardrums.

"It's okay, sweetheart." *No it's not ...*

"We're going to be alright." *Liar, liar.*

"I've got you ..." *But who's got me?*

I considered my options while the baby's wail dialed up several octaves. Call Elle and Theo was top of the list. I knew they'd be over here in 0.4 seconds if I put out the Rebel signal, but they'd already helped so much. They had their own family to take care of and didn't need to add me to their very full plate.

There were probably other teammates who could offer an assist, or their wives, which was likely sexist of me. But in this game, the wives took on most of the child-rearing duties. What did I expect? The WAGs to set up some sort of rotation-for-sad-sacks to make sure this poor kid and her doofus hockey player dad survived the night? Not exactly realistic. Nor did I have that kind of relationship with any of them.

The only person I could imagine giving me the help I needed was Adeline. She had set up the baby's crib and showed me around the supplies—not that a single word went in beyond "formula"—and had given me a look of such pity when she left. She didn't fake it and tell me I'd get through this ... because she knew I was up shit creek without a nanny.

As I did laps of my house with a distressed baby, I took in how much my environment had already changed. I was used to neatness, order, everything in its place. Organizing my existence with a military precision had helped me manage the chaos of my upbringing, and those tenets had stayed with me. Tidy life, tidy mind.

Now everything around me was fraying at the edges. Bits and bobs and baby stuff strewn haphazardly. Onesies and bibs in piles on the sofa, the foyer stuffed with a stroller, bassinet, and equipment my brain had yet to label. The kitchen, previously neat as a pin and my haven in times of stress, was now a bombsite filled with baby rubble.

"Shush, sweetheart. Let's stop with all this fuss."

The wails continued, and I was thankful my neighbors lived several hundred feet away, so they weren't likely to contact social services to report my terrible parenting.

At least, that's what I thought until I heard the doorbell ring. Someone must have called about the noise, and to be honest, I was at the point where I needed to surrender to the authorities and accept that I was not cut out for this line of work.

"Let's see who that is. Maybe it's the police to arrest you for disturbing the peace."

I opened the door to find a vision on my threshold: Adeline.

"Hey!"

"Hi, how are things?"

"Absolutely fantastic." Mabel's shrieks branded me a liar, but I was foolishly electing to brazen it out. "Did you forget something?"

"Uh, no, it's just—is she okay?"

"No idea. I've fed her and walked around with her and tried talking like some supposed guru on YouTube suggested. I thought she'd have cried herself out by now."

"Babies can pretty much cry forever if they have a mind to do so." She held out her hands. "Could I?"

Please. "Sure." I had no idea why she'd returned except that she probably heard Mabel from miles away.

Adeline took the baby into her arms with a deftness I envied. "I think I know what's up. This little mite needs to be changed."

"Into a baby that doesn't scream?"

"Into a new diaper."

Jesus, I was a complete idiot. I'd fed her and that food had to go somewhere. How did babies survive at all? Now that I thought of it, she did stink a bit, but I'd assumed that was just how my house was supposed to smell from this day forward.

"You told me that before. About the diapers and I watched Elle do it—it kind of went out of my head."

Adeline smiled, and I suddenly felt hope bloom in my chest. Not that I expected her to stick around but when this woman was here, things were simply better. Seeing her hold Mabel with such care and consideration left a lump in my throat ... well, I was probably just feeling overwhelmed with the emotion of it all.

"Let's get her taken care of and hopefully, she'll be less cranky."

I nodded in awe, silently thanking the universe for sending this *enkelini* back to me. *My angel.* I watched closely as Adeline lay out the mat (canvas, really, that could be seriously Jackson Pollocked if we weren't careful). But she *was* careful, absolutely assured in her movements. She unwrapped the baby from the diaper—and yeah, sorry, kid, for leaving you like that—and moved through the steps quickly and efficiently. Dirty diaper popped in the pail, baby cleaned up and repackaged like a little gift, then back in a clean onesie which I passed off like the nurse assisting a surgeon. As soon as she was clean and dry, a beatific peace came over her.

That's all she wanted: food, comfort, and a dry booty.

While Adeline worked her magic, I couldn't help watching her, not just for her sure way with Mabel, but because she had changed outfits since I saw her last. Now she wore a cute dress, one of those wrap-around deals that bisected her breasts and cinched at the waist. The skirt was full but as she leaned forward during the diaper-changing, the fabric draped over her hips and ass, giving her curves a sensual silhouette. Her hair was no longer in a ponytail, but fell in soft, blue-black waves over her shoulders. She looked ... sexy.

Snap out of it, man.

As a baby's literal shit made the best distraction, I did my best to clean up the mess, noting that I was going to need a boatload of supplies and/or have my cleaning lady up her schedule to daily. Washing my hands, I surreptitiously studied Adeline who sat at my kitchen table holding Mabel. The image was like something out of an Americana tribute, one of those fifties' era paintings about perfect suburban life.

It should have made me shudder. I'd grown up with that perfect American life, at least on the outside. No one would have thought differently. I was the son of Sven Nyquist, who was drafted from Finland at nineteen, married a puck bunny he knocked up, then took sole guardianship of me when my mom died. I'd had nannies as a kid, interspersed with girlfriends and stepmoms who liked the idea of life with a famous hockey player until the reality set in. Sven's temper and my neediness did not make for a happiness equation.

With my father's relationships with women a mess, he

turned to me to salvage his personal life. If he could coach me to be a professional hockey player, then he'd feel like he hadn't failed in other aspects of his life. I might not have been wanted, but I could be of service and restore his pride.

Now here I was, faced with having to look after a child I didn't want—maybe not the same situation as dear old dad, but certainly not the ideal way to go about bringing a baby into this world. I was pissed at myself, if I was being honest. Pissed at getting myself into this fix and at how my life was about to become so much smaller.

"She's happier now." Adeline looked up with a smile that vanished at the utter panic she saw on my face. "It's going to be okay, Lars."

"You sure about that? Because right now, if you hadn't shown up, I'm not sure I would have figured this out without damaging her."

"She would have had a little booty rash, and you would have had no sleep. Not the end of the world. You would have figured it out."

It was kind of her to say so. "Is there a reason why you came back?"

"Just on my way home and thought I'd do a quick check-in. I know you must be feeling overwhelmed."

With her empathy making my chest tighten in a way I did not appreciate, I moved on to practicalities. "I'll be interviewing the nannies they send over tomorrow. But I don't even know how to pick one, other than 'can you start today?' Probably not a good criterion."

"Not the best." She bit her lip, and I looked away because ... I didn't know.

More like, I didn't *want* to know. I was so tired that my mind was straying to inconceivable things.

I heaved a breath. "This is probably out there but—"

"I'll help with the interviews."

I blinked. "You will?"

"I know you have to travel for a game the day after."

"I already told the brass I need personal leave."

"You did?"

She didn't have to sound so shocked.

"I might know zero about looking after a kid, but I do know that I won't be finding childcare in less than twenty-four hours. This is my problem, and I need to be here for this kid until I've hired someone. I can't be in two places at once, so something had to give." I crossed my arms. "But if you can help me vet the candidates, that would be amazing."

"I can do that. What did your Rebels bosses say about you missing the game?"

"Ryder said they'd get a temp nanny in, and I shouldn't worry about it." Ryder Calloway, the general manager, had been full of ideas after he spent the first three minutes of the conversation laughing his head off. "But I told him I can't leave my kid with just *anyone*. I had plenty of that as a kid and as shitty a dad as I'll probably be, it would be even shittier to leave her with someone I've never met. I need a few days to get all my ducks in a row."

Mabel yawned and seemed to settle, oblivious to my agitation. Evidently this little girl felt safe in Adeline's arms. I felt two ways about that; the part of me that needed to see Mabel comforted evicted the envy—mostly—at knowing I couldn't make this child as happy.

But I could pay for decent help.

"The fact that you don't want to palm her off on just anyone tells me you're not going to be a shitty dad. Did you get any sleep last night?"

My bleary-eyed expression must have said it all. "Not much, but your mom got even less."

"It's not a contest."

It was always a contest. I was a winner on the ice and there was no way in hell I was going to be a loser when it came to fatherhood. I would be better than *him*.

"Here, I can take her." Mabel had fallen asleep in Adeline's arms, so I was loath to wake her. But neither could I keep this vibrant woman in my kitchen doing her Madonna and Child impression all night.

We made the transfer without waking the baby. "Worn ragged by my stellar parenting skills."

She gave a low chuckle. "You'll get there."

Maybe I would—with her help.

CHAPTER SEVEN

Lars

WHERE DID people find the time to have children?

I understood the sex part. Hell, I always had time for the sex part, but the rest. The feeding and changing and cleaning and interviewing.

Several hours into the nanny hunt and I was having a hard time keeping my eyes open. To force my mind to attention, I thought back to Theo's call this morning, the one he'd made as soon as word of my request for a leave of absence had filtered back to him.

"Are you fucking kidding me with this, NyQuil?"

At a good thirty-six hours in, I was inordinately sleep-deprived. I had managed a couple of fitful hours last night, unable to fall deeper because (a) Mabel might need me and (b) I was still furious with myself for this mess of my own making. All my life, I'd been careful not to behave in any way that drew comparisons with my father. He was the rabblerouser, the partier, the guy who wasted all his gifts. That wasn't me.

Yet it looked like the apple didn't fall far.

I didn't need Kershaw to tell me I was handling this all wrong. My inner voice was more than up to the job.

"This is the only way forward I can see, T. I don't want to compromise on the nanny and it's not fair to expect Elle, Adeline, or anyone else to fix this."

Theo had uttered a long string of epithets that would have made a nun blush.

"How important is this year, Lars?"

"I know how—"

"How important?" He sounded as serious as I'd ever heard him. It was likely his last year in the pros. This was it for him.

"Very."

"There's only so far you can take this lone wolf act. You're part of a team. The Rebels, sure, but more importantly, mine. Team Fucking Kershaw. Never mind Mabel, I'm the person you need to be pleasing!" That made me smile. I knew his game, but his argument was mighty entertaining, so I let him run with it. "And you think that taking time off and upsetting the greatest defensive partnership in the league is your best move?"

"Selfish of me, I know."

"Damn right it's selfish! And if Mabel knew anything about hockey or could even talk, she'd tell you I'm right. Also, you seem to have forgotten that you've never won the Cup." As if that data point had escaped me. "I've already won it four times, so another one is just gravy, but I'm going all out this year to solidify *your* legacy. I'll talk to Addy again about taking on the gig."

"She's already helping with interviews. That's the extent of her involvement, so leave it be."

I had hung up on a grumbling Kershaw and tried not to get hung up on the fact that Adeline as Mabel's nanny would solve most of my problems, while creating several more.

All because of what I'd overheard a year ago.

I think you're the sexiest guy alive.

I wasn't fool enough to think Adeline still felt that way. She'd traveled the world, gained a wealth of experience, probably met some scruffy backpacker closer to her age, and had forgotten all about me. In the bar the other night, she'd been cool about it, mature and even-handed. Since then, she'd given no indication that her crush might be still operational.

In my line of work, I had women throwing themselves at me a lot—witness my current predicament—but rarely did I have women *un*throwing themselves. Denying their intent after an initial showing of cards. I had a feeling that if Adeline stuck around to help in a more hands-on capacity, I might start wondering more about this woman and how sexy she looked in that dress last night.

I couldn't think about that, not if I valued my career, my sanity, and frankly, my balls.

"Lars?"

I blinked my way back into the conversation. Adeline was trying to get my attention.

"What's that?"

"Did you have any additional questions for Janet?"

Janet. Candidate number four. Or was it five? I took a quick glance down at the clipboard Adeline had dropped in my lap several hours ago, observed wryly that I'd made zero notations, and decided to end this farce before I said anything that made me look more foolish than I felt.

"No, nothing." Standing, I extended my hand, the same move that ended all the other interviews.

"Thanks for coming in." Adeline smiled and led Janet toward the door. "We'll be in touch with the agency when we've reviewed all the applications."

The door closed and Adeline pivoted to face me. "She's probably the best one of the bunch. Though the girl with the childhood education degree was nice as well."

"Book learning," I muttered. "What good is that without experience?" I could read a book. Would it make me a good father? Negative.

"She has experience as well with a family in Wisconsin. Good references."

"If they're to be believed."

She squinted at me. "What's wrong?"

"What's wrong? We just spent ten hours—"

"Three."

Was that all? "Talking to these strangers about looking after this little stranger, who sees *me* as a stranger. Don't you think that's weird?"

"No weirder than a woman doing a drive-by after a hockey game and dropping your kid off in a bar. This is uncharted territory, Lars."

She sounded so calm about it, but this wasn't her life. She would go home and get on with her day, her week, her year. If Mabel was really my kid, and I suspected she was, then I needed to sack up.

I rubbed my mouth, wishing I could rub on a smile.

The baby monitor burst into life. During the interviews, I'd listened to it while Adeline asked the questions. Every now and then, there'd be a breathy murmur, and my feet would itch to investigate. But nothing much would follow, so I supposed Mabel was okay. Sleeping while everyone else worked their asses off to take care of her.

Babies, what a life.

"I'd better go check on her."

I headed toward the kitchen where Adeline had stashed Mabel during the interviews, reasoning that we wanted her close in case we needed to spring into action. The baby was awake, her wide blue eyes gazing up at the ceiling. Did she have any idea what was going on?

Note to self: buy a book on baby brain development.

Her little cry had sounded more urgent on the monitor. Now, she was just gurgling away happily, clearly an attention-seeker like her mom. As a strategy, I couldn't fault it. I stood over her, checking her out and making sure my instinct—that she was doing fine—was the correct one.

"She needs to be fed," Adeline prompted behind me.

So much for instinct. Of course Mabel wanted something. I would need to learn this babble lingo of hers quickly.

Heating formula and using the bottle warmer was now officially in my daddy skillset yet I was still conscious of Adeline's eyes on me as I went through the steps. Once I'd pressed the button on the warmer, I turned to her.

"How'd I do?"

"With what?" She had averted her gaze to the clipboard.

"Did I get the formula warming right?" I worried that the baby didn't have breast milk. What was Vicki doing? Was she pumping and dumping, a phrase I'd always assumed was sexual, but now I understood in a different context? Because that sounded wasteful, and now I was mad at her all over again.

"You seem to be doing just fine."

"Well, it's hard to fuck up." I winced at swearing in front of the kid. In front of Adeline, who was my teammate's daughter. Not that it made her a child, but she occupied a weird place in my psyche.

"You're going to get through this, Lars. And speaking of getting through it ..." She consulted the clipboard on which she'd made a shit-ton of notes because she was diligent like that. "If I had to pick, I'd say Janet was the best candidate."

That was the last one. While I hadn't paid complete attention to the questioning, I'd picked up on a vibe from her. She'd spent much of the interview trying to meet my gaze, and when it happened a couple of times, she'd push out her chest. Like I needed to know she had tits or something.

"She seemed ... forward."

"You want someone who's sure and certain around the baby. This isn't a job for wilting violets."

"Yeah, but I don't want to be fighting off the nanny either."

She looked like I'd slapped her. "What does that mean?"

"Didn't you see how she was kind of making eyes at me?"

Her lips parted. "Well, yes. But they all were, even the grandmotherly one. Shona."

"The one who asked about 'extra duties'—"

"And winked. Yeah." Adeline laughed softly. "That got your attention."

I shook my head. "Sorry if it looked like I wasn't

completely present. I was listening out for Her Majesty. Worried she might choke or something."

"So you're going to have some admirers. As long as they're professional."

Sure, but if they couldn't stay professional throughout the interview, I didn't hold out much hope for ongoing boundaries.

The warmer beeped and I extracted the bottle like I was dismantling a nuclear bomb. Out it came, without touching the sides. I wiped my brow.

"Need a napkin there, Doctor?"

That made me chuckle. Adeline had a dry sense of humor, much more deadpan than her dad. More like Elle.

I placed the bottle on the counter. "Every little thing seems fraught with peril. I get one thing wrong, and it'll all come crashing down."

"Catastrophizing is your go-to, it seems."

Maybe. As a kid, I lived in fear of doing the wrong thing, upsetting the great Sven. Mistakes led to verbal put-downs, slaps, and worse.

Now I'd made a huge unforced error, fathering the child of a married woman, and I could hear Sven's voice, my constant critic. *Loser screws up again. Why am I surprised?*

"Let's get this princess fed, then." I picked her up, and once satisfied she was comfortable, I nudged her tiny pink lips with the teat of the bottle. She latched on like a barnacle, which made me laugh.

"She knows who's got the goods." Adeline's voice was soft and empathetic.

"What do you think I should do, Adeline?"

"About?"

Everything. But one thing at a time. "The nanny. Which one would work the best?"

"Probably Janet. You're going to be too tired to sleep with her, so I wouldn't worry about her making advances. Unless you come home and find her in your bed, then I guess all bets are off."

I couldn't help my surprise at such direct teasing and when I looked up from Mabel's fierce suckling, I found a blushing Adeline.

"That's kind of specific."

"I don't know why I—forget I even went there."

Okay. "Thing is, I'm not sure any of these candidates are right. Maybe we should interview more."

She bit her lip. "This is your call, Lars. Of course you want the right person for Mabel. But in the meantime, you have a dilemma. The team needs you, so taking time away from your job isn't really the answer. This is likely my dad's final season, so you know he wants to go out with a bang. In fact, your time on ice could be better and if you're distracted with your home life, then how is that going to improve?"

"My TOI? How'd you make that out?"

She waved that off. "Oh, I just watch the stats. It's kind of a hobby of mine. Listen, maybe I could help with the childcare aspect for longer. Only I don't want to shoehorn my way in if that's not what—"

I held up a hand. "Yes! Of course I need your help. I'm not going to look that gift horse in the mouth."

At which point my gaze dipped to her mouth in anticipation of the gift it would truly be. I dragged my eyes away to find her staring at me. Busted. This was so not the complication I needed, yet rush-importing a stranger into my house to look after my daughter sounded worse. I didn't want to look back on these days and regret that I handled her childcare in a half-assed manner, even if Mabel turned out not to be mine.

She's yours. Just accept it.

"I could stay for a few days to tide you over for the next couple of games and more nanny interviews? How does that sound?"

Absolutely perfect. The weird sexual awareness I felt around her was something I could control. I had no choice. Still, I needed to be sure I wasn't pressuring her.

"Adeline, are you sure you want to do this?"

CHAPTER EIGHT

Adeline

SURELY THIS WAS A MISTAKE. But I wondered if it might help me, too. Helping someone while helping myself to heal.

I couldn't avoid my future forever. At the same time, I wasn't quite ready for the navel-gazing therapizing necessary to truly get over what had happened to me in Greece. A couple of weeks looking after someone weaker than myself would be a good way to ease back into the routine of life.

"Adeline?"

The way he said my name sent a shiver through me, which was absurd because I had thoroughly convinced myself that he did nothing for me.

"Hmm?"

"Are you sure?"

"Yes, it's just—"

He cut me off. "No, you're right, it's a terrible idea. You've already helped so much and here I am, asking for more. That's just greedy."

Never mind that I was the one who had offered. "No, it's not. Not at all. Only ..." Rosie was worried about me accepting this gig for a few days—how the hell would she react when I said I might be stepping in for a longer period?

She would think I had it bad for Lars Nyquist.

I didn't. If anything, I felt sympathy for him, maybe even pity, and pity generally crushed lady boners to dust. A clueless Lars wasn't all that sexy, which was great for me, and allowed me to see this assignment for what it was: a chance to be a good Rebel citizen.

But first things first.

"There's the crush thing."

The words slipped out, crashing off the walls like discombobulated bats looking for an escape.

"Okay," he said slowly.

"I just wanted to be clear that it's in the past. I'm not here so I can get closer to you or go all stalker on your ass."

I closed my mouth, waiting for him to respond, hopefully in a way that would minimize the flush of my skin and patter of my heart.

His brows drew together. "Never thought you were."

He was closer to me now, still holding Mabel, who was surgically attached to the bottle, suckling away. When he wasn't thinking too hard about it, he was quite the natural.

He continued. "I wouldn't for a second believe that a lovely young woman like you would actually think that after all this time." Before I could weigh in with "why not?" or "you think I'm lovely?" he moved on. "As far as I'm concerned that's water under the bridge. It's as if it never happened."

Easy for him to say, but I appreciated his effort to put me at ease.

"Just schoolgirl stuff," I reiterated.

"Think no more of it." He was swaying a little now, with Mabel in his arms. The sight made me melt. "But I understand how this might make working for me awkward. If it makes things easier, you wouldn't see me much. You'd only be here when I wasn't, and when I am, your time would be your own. I know you probably have plans or are thinking about next steps in your life. Maybe this would give you a little breathing room while you figure that out?"

I would never have expected that level of insight from a jock like Lars Nyquist. The shock of fatherhood must have opened new neural pathways in his brain.

"You're not ... wrong. I *am* starting to think about what comes next. I also need a job because I can't leech off my parents forever. This might help us both."

Something shifted between us, a burgeoning recognition of the other's needs, and the moment was only broken when Mabel gurgled, now that she'd finished the bottle.

"I can take her," I said, holding out my arms.

"Is that a yes?"

I nodded. "While we set up more interviews and get someone qualified in permanently." A few weeks, maximum.

"Thanks, Adeline." He placed her carefully in my embrace, and for a moment we were close enough to kiss. Instead he inhaled, his nostrils flared, and he looked away. "I need to pack right now for the away game. You got her?"

"I do."

Lars

TO SAY that hockey players were a superstitious lot was an understatement, and the Rebels were no different. The crazy rituals, the eccentric prep, the don't-fuck-with-what-works routines. That meant I had an assigned seat on the team bus to the airport because everyone sat in the same spot going out and coming back. No one would risk a change-up.

And because everyone knew where I sat, I guessed that blow-up baby with a mask that looked uncannily like me was not accidental.

I picked up my doppelganger, dropped it in the place beside me, and took my usual seat by the window.

"Welcome to fatherhood, dude!" Cody Jacobs, one of the centers and a father himself, called out.

"Uh, thanks."

I hadn't seen the boys in a couple of days as I was given personal time yesterday, allowing me to skip practice while I interviewed women who would take care of my child.

As the bus filled, people either commented on my new life status, dropped off "gifts," or both. Rattles, baby toys, a dildo with indecipherable Sharpie markings (from Peyton Bell, the most inappropriate guy on a team of reprobates). The baby-themed gifts were no better than dollar store junk, nothing I'd give to Mabel, which pretty much said it all. No one was taking this seriously. By the time Theo arrived, his seat was piled high with baby junk.

He smirked, which reminded me of Adeline. *Do not need that.* "Need to be alone with your haul, NyQuil?"

"Nope."

With his help, I did my best to offload my stash into the overhead storage. It reminded me of how cluttered my life had become in the last couple of days. I didn't like it.

The captain finally sat in the vacated spot and turned to me. "This might be the best thing to happen to you."

"How'd you make that out?"

"Well, you're kind of distant with the guys, even after a few years with the team."

"Can't help my sparkling personality." My Scandi noir vibes as Aurora labeled it. More useful with women, apparently.

"It's okay. You make up for it by your association with me."

This was true. In the last year I'd accepted more invitations to the Kershaws, and while I'd never admit it, I loved how they'd thrown their arms wide and invited me in. Growing up the way I did, I wasn't used to that level of intimacy. But since this baby surprise I felt a need to both stay close and pull away. I hated that I was taking advantage of them.

My least favorite D-man, MacFarlane, walked by. I eyed him as he passed, daring him to fuck with me.

"Anyone taking bets yet?" he called out. "Is Nyquist the daddy or not?"

It might sound like harmless joshing, but everyone knew why he'd phrased it like that. Taking bets, indeed. Like my father.

"Sit your ass down, MacFarlane," Theo said with a glare.

I waited until the asshole had found a seat at the back of the bus. "You don't need to fight my battles."

My captain raised an eyebrow. "Uh, that's my job, kid."

I laughed at that. "Listen, can I ask you something?"

"Sure."

I did a quick review of our space, making sure no one was listening. "Are you sure you're okay with Adeline helping out with Mabel?"

He squinted. "Is there a problem? Look, I suggested it, but she didn't have to do it. In fact, she changed her mind all by herself."

Sure, after she saw what a disaster I was. After I told her none of the nannies were good enough. Now I was having second thoughts, especially given her insistence she did not have a crush on me.

"Yeah, I get that. But maybe she's feeling pressured."

"She needs a job, she wants to feel independent with her own money—you are paying her, right?"

"Of course."

"And she won't feel like she's under our feet all the time. Though I hope she doesn't think I'm trying to shove her out of the house the minute she's back in the country." He looked thoughtful, then whipped out his phone and started typing.

I leaned in.

> Twinkle, I'm so pumped you're home but don't take that nanny gig for NyQuil if you don't want it. I just want you to be happy.

Not more than ten seconds later, a text appeared.

> I know, Dad. Lars needs the help so I don't mind. He's kind of pathetic.

Theo held his phone up. "See? She's fine with it."

I remained unconvinced but she was right about one thing: I was kind of pathetic.

"Why do you call her Twinkle?"

"You ever heard the expression 'twinkle in my eye'?"

I nodded.

"After we had Hatch, it took a while for Ellie to get pregnant again. Who knew, after my swimmers hit the jackpot immediately the first time? We were kind of worried, so I started imagining this new baby. I'd talk to her in my head, the twinkle in my eye, this beautiful life we hadn't yet conceived. I guess it gave me hope that it would happen. And then it did. My twinkle came to life, and here she was."

"You're crazy about her."

He chuckled. "Yep. It'll happen to you, too. Daughters are different. Nothing I wouldn't do for my kids, but when it comes to Adeline, I've always worried about her. It's been hard for her to grow up in an environment where hockey rules everything."

I imagined that would be tough, but Adeline didn't seem bitter about the hockey mania. She'd even found time to comment on my room-for-improvement TOI.

"I'm just glad she's home," Theo went on. "And if she's not living with us, then you're the next best thing. Uncle Lars!"

The trust in his expression almost broke me. All these people expecting me to be the good guy.

Theo was also the only person who truly understood how difficult my relationship was with my father. Sure, anyone could see from the outside that I'd stopped talking to him over fifteen years ago. The reasons were plain enough, on the record for all to see. But that didn't stop me from getting so drunk I couldn't play the day I found out he was dead. Theo covered for me. My captain always had my back.

Meanwhile, I was looking at Adeline Kershaw's mouth like it was a tasty treat.

I inhaled a breath. "Listen, thanks for ... everything."

"Who else is going to put up with your moods?"

My phone pinged with a text, and I looked at it quickly, maybe with a touch of hope. Adeline might need to contact me about something.

But it wasn't Adeline. It was my lawyer, the one my agent had hired the minute I vomited out my sad sack story.

Call me.

We were twenty minutes out from the airport. Yesterday, before the nanny interviews, I'd stopped by his office to give blood. I needed to know, so I hit dial.

"It's Lars Nyquist."

"Mr. Nyquist, I have the results of the paternity test." His tone was even, not giving a clue about what was coming next. "The baby is biologically yours."

I snatched a quick breath. No more doubts, at least not about my genetic contribution to Mabel. As for the rest, I was a doubt-ridden lump of Jello.

"Now what?"

"I would recommend that you work out a custody arrangement with the mother as well as child support arrangements."

"She's not interested in being a mother. At least not to my kid."

My kid. I could feel Theo's eyes on me, drawing conclusions from my side of the conversation.

"If that's the case, then you'll still want to figure out where you stand legally. The child is yours, but we need to make sure the documentation is in order."

My name was not on Mabel's birth certificate. Could that be changed? Did it need to be?

"Could you figure out my options and get back to me? I'm about to head out of town for a game."

"Understood. Send me any documents you already have and check back in with me when you return."

I clicked off and stared at my screen for all the good it would do me.

Theo coughed. "You okay?"

"As you probably heard, it's official. I'm a dad."

Tender Noah Boden turned around and leaned his elbows on the seat. "Daddy Defenseman? Woo hoo!" He called out to the rest of the bus. "You hear that, boys? Nyquist just passed the paternity test. His swimmers did the job after all."

People started throwing stuff at me from a spare stash of toys and dildos that needed a target.

My dumbass head was as good as any.

CHAPTER NINE

Adeline

ROSIE WALKED INTO MY PARENTS' kitchen, took one look at me with Baby Mabel in my arms, and shook her head.

"You're a goner."

"Oh, shut it," I said affectionately. Rosie was always talking about my "mom energy" because I was usually the one trying to reel in the good times. My friend had a tendency toward reckless and needed someone to read a situation and tell her it might be dangerous. She got that from her mom, Violet, who had been a notorious wild child in her youth.

"Looks like you'll be pumping out more of Nyquist's spawn soon. Knocked up and so in lurve."

"Like I said, just doing the guy a favor." I prayed my blush wouldn't be obvious.

I didn't need such intrusive thoughts entering my head.

I couldn't afford to think of Lars that way, not when everything was so complicated. The last thing he needed was for me to fawn all over him. He'd barely reacted when we discussed my crush. Probably heard it all the time.

Rosie helped herself to a Revolution IPA from the fridge. "Is the gang all here?"

We were playing host to the WAGs and fams for tonight's game in New York. The Kershaw house was the unofficial seat of team fandom for away game viewings, and while I wouldn't have minded a quiet night in, it was nice to see everyone.

"Yeah, Violet arrived a few minutes ago. She said you haven't gone around to see her yet."

Rosie rolled her eyes. "What a liar! I ran into her at the coffee shop with Devon yesterday. He's obsessed with my new ink."

Devon was Rosie's fourteen-year-old half-brother and absolutely adored his sister. The feeling was mutual.

My mom put her head around the door. "Rosie, finally! Your mom's been asking where you were." She called back. "She's here!"

Violet Vasquez-St. James came thundering into the kitchen. "My beautiful girl, where have you been?"

Rosie laughed as her mother hugged her. Though Violet didn't raise her daughter, they still had an incredibly close relationship. As surrogate for Cade and Dante, Rosie's dads, she had remained an integral part of her daughter's life. Both dark-eyed and curvy, with glorious ink adorning their skin, they could easily pass as sisters.

"Mom, why are you telling everyone I haven't been to see you?"

"Well, not officially. Bren thought you'd come over and see us yesterday, and if I hadn't run into you at the coffee shop, I'm wondering if you would have bothered! Also, Harper can't wait to see you tomorrow."

Rosie caught my eye. Her aunt Harper, the Rebels CEO, had offered her an internship with the team, but my friend had confided in me that she didn't really see herself in that corporate structure.

"Can't wait to see her," Rosie said diplomatically.

Violet waved a hand at me. "And what do you think of all this? Nyquist's love child?"

My mom kissed my cheek. "I think my daughter is very kind to step up."

"She's a saint." Violet smiled at me, though the way she said it, *saint* rhymed with *sucker*. "And is he sure she's his?"

"Theo just texted. Lars heard from his lawyer and it's a yes."

Oh. It felt odd to hear this information from anyone other than Lars. I wondered how he was doing, though knowing my dad, he was in good hands. The media were already all over it, especially given Lars's family history; now that it was official, they would be like sharks to blood.

Everyone was chattering about the situation, who the mom was, why she'd done what she did, what came next.

"What's the PR plan?" I asked.

"I'm sure the Rebels have it under control," my mom said.

"I haven't seen anything on the Rebels website or socials. No statement, no mention of it. I'd think they'd want to get ahead of it."

Rosie shrugged. "What can they say? '"Don't worry, Lars Nyquist is *not* like his dad. He's one of the good ones.'"

I must have scowled at her because she raised her eyebrows and mouthed, "What?" They couldn't help being gossipy old hens, but I didn't have to like it. These were real people, not tawdry tabloid fodder.

"Mom, could you ..." I held the baby out to her. "I need to pee."

"Of course. I've been dying for some snuggle time with this little one."

I went to the upstairs bathroom for privacy. Maybe I should leave it alone. Lars would be prepping for the game and didn't need to hear from me. But I could send a message, and he'd see it afterward?

> Hey. Just heard the tidings of great joy. 😉

He could interpret that how he wished.

I checked my reflection in the mirror, noting the dark circles under my eyes. I hadn't slept well last night at Lars's place, lying awake, worried that the doors were locked. More than once, I got up to check all the windows at one point and reset the alarm. The house was safe. I was safe.

But I didn't *feel* safe.

Perhaps returning home and immediately jumping into this nanny gig was too much change in too short a time. Was this truly a good way for me to get over what happened in Greece *and* my crush?

My phone buzzed with a text from Lars.

> Yeah, poor kid, lumbered with me for an isa.

ME

> What's isa?

LARS

> Finnish for dad.

My phone rang. *Lars.* I answered it quickly, not because I wanted to hear his voice but because time was of the essence.

"Don't you have a game to prep for?"

"Yeah, but I have a few minutes. How's the gossip mill grinding back in Chicago?"

I laughed softly. "Don't worry, you're still the talk of the town."

"That's something, at least. Would hate to give up that crown."

There was a pause while I tried to think of what to say.

"It's just—"

"How are you—"

We both laughed, mine nervous, his ... maybe nervous, too? After all, he had just found out officially he was on the hook for eighteen years of child-rearing.

"What were you going to say?" he asked gently.

"I was going to ask how you were doing with the news. Even though you knew it was a possibility, maybe even likely, it still must be weird."

"Sure, it was more likely than not given the circumstances. But I wasn't quite prepared for how it would make me feel."

"Which is?"

"Even *more* terrified of fucking up. Given how I grew up, I know what *not* to do, but I worry about the execution. How to switch up the patterns. How do I ensure I don't screw up a kid's life?" He made a sound deep in his throat. "Sorry, not what you signed on for."

My heart hitched for him. "Big changes can bring up all sorts of emotions. Make you think about what's gone before, what needs to happen. Get you all up in your feels."

"Yeah, that's what's happening. I'm all up in my feels."

But he didn't sound annoyed, more amused at my take on it. "Is Mabel with you?"

"She's downstairs with Mom. I came up to the bathroom to get a quiet moment."

"Ah." He sounded disappointed. "Is she okay?"

"She's fine. Everyone here is completely doting on her. The new Rebels princess."

"Adeline, I—" He cut off as someone spoke in the background. When he came back, his voice was lower, so muted I could barely hear him. The intimacy of it made my skin tingle. "They're calling us to line up."

"We'll talk more when you get back." *Right*. The poor guy didn't want to be discussing this with me. I was just the help.

"Yeah, we will. And Adeline?"

"Hmm?"

"Thank you."

My heart went into a pitter patter. Foolish, so foolish. "I'm happy to help. Go get 'em, tiger."

The line went dead. I closed my eyes, cringing at my absolute absurdity. *Go get 'em, tiger*. How was I still upright after that?

MABEL WAS TUCKERED OUT, so I was able to put her down in Mom and Dad's room just as the game was starting. I kept the baby monitor on the end table as I settled in with the women I'd watched games with for the last twenty years. All my life, I'd known this crew—my mom, my great-gran, Vi, Rosie, Ashley, who was married to Dex O'Malley, and their daughters, Willa, Jenny, and Bea. The Kershaw women wore pink Theo's Tarts jackets, a tradition started by Aurora who used to gather her granny brigade and bring them along to home games. We were a noisy lot, with the constant trash talk masking the worry that our guys might fall victim to injury at any minute.

Seeing Dad gliding onto the ice always got our blood pumping, but it was extra fun to see Hatch on the bench as well. Dad's dream was to play with his eldest son—*now I can retire happy*, he'd say, but I knew he wanted more. Like playoffs-more. Finals-more. He had played with the Rebels for most of his career, and that team had won the Cup four times. A fifth wasn't outside the realm of possibility, and to do it with his son? That would be legendary.

At the first break, the Rebels were up 2-0, and Tilly was yawning.

"Silly Tilly needs her Zs," I said, nuzzling her head. Her hair was starting to come in thick, leaving us in no doubt as to her Kershaw bona fides.

"No Zs!"

Before my mom could make a move, I stood and reached for my little sister. "Come on, Til."

She jutted her bottom lip and pouted. "I need a song."

I sighed heavily, my usual opening salvo in the negotiation. "Okay. But only if you brush your teeth for the whole five minutes."

"One minute."

"Two, or I won't be able to find my guitar."

Tilly bolted for the stairs, which made everyone laugh. My mom sent me a look of gratitude, and four minutes later after arguments about rinsing her mouth (*swallowing your toothpaste won't keep your stomach clean*), whether she could sleep in her Theo's Tarts jacket (*it's only for games*), and which of her jim-jams should get the royal nod (*you only need one pair of Baby Shark shorts, not two*), she was settled under the covers with Ducky, her favorite toy. Lars had given it to her two Christmases ago, and I had assumed she'd have moved on by now, but us Kershaw girls had a lot in common. It was hard to leave the fine Finn in your rearview.

"What should we sing about?"

"Duckman."

"Ducky?" I patted the soft and worn toy, tucked in beside her. I had a song for him, like I had for most of her toys and favorite things.

"No, Duckman! Uncle Lars!"

Uncle Lars, huh?

I picked up the Martin guitar, pulled the strap over my shoulder, and settled it in my lap. The weight was familiar against my body, like welcoming an old friend. After my family, I'd missed playing guitar the most. It wasn't feasible to carry it around on my travels, but I kept my hand in by playing recorded background music when I called home to sing to Tilly.

Strumming the strings, I picked out a C chord. The guitar was slightly out of tune and would need to be restrung, but it was good enough for a lullaby. To the tune of *Twinkle, Twinkle, Little Star*, I started quietly so as not to wake Mabel in the room next door.

"Duckman, Duckman, on the ice ... Skating faster than the mice."

Tilly whispered, "Mice."

"With your silly beard so thick ... How you move about so quick ..."

"Duckmaaaan ..."

I strummed and waited until Tilly joined in, "Duckmaaaan!"

"On the ice," I continued. "Skating faster than the ..."

"Mice!" Tilly screamed and broke out in a flurry of giggles.

"Shush, Til, you'll wake the baby."

I unstrapped the guitar, but Tilly was having none of it. "More!"

I'd known I wouldn't get away with a single verse. "Okay, how about the Butterfly Song?"

Ten minutes and three songs later, including a reprise of *Duckman, Duckman, On the Ice*, I finally escaped. A quick check-in with Mabel assured me she'd slept through the entertainment, so I headed downstairs and was working on replenishing snacks in the kitchen when Rosie walked in with Eggsbee on her heels.

She leaned against the counter. "How were things at Lars's house last night?"

"Good. I'm in the guest room with Mabel in the crib." Lars had left yesterday morning, so I spent the day tidying, doing Mabel's laundry, and ordering groceries and supplies.

"Right." She ran a finger along the countertop. "And you were okay on your own?"

I looked up from my task of arranging Trader Joe Laceys on a plate, as if this careful placement would somehow stop people from inhaling them the minute I put them down.

"I was fine. He left instructions for the alarm." I pushed the plate of Laceys toward my friend, who picked one up and took a bite. "Don't worry about me. I haven't had a nightmare in ages."

Rosie had been the one to hold me tight every time I woke up terrified after another bad dream.

"You should tell them."

We'd had this conversation several times. "They don't need to know, Ro. They'll just worry and want to wrap me up in cotton wool. Plus, this year is so important. For Dad, for Hatch, for the team. No way do I want this to distract from that."

She looked both sympathetic and fierce, with a touch of guilt mingled in there. She still blamed herself for letting me walk home alone. "I wish I'd caught that guy and de-balled him," she said around her chewing.

And end up in some Greek prison? "Thankfully, there was no lasting damage!" I added another Lacey to replace the one she'd eaten. "Now, take these into the marauding hordes."

CHAPTER TEN

Adeline

A TEXT CAME in on the Kershaw Kinder chain from my brother Landon, quickly followed by one from Conor.

> Is this true about Nyquist?
>
> CONOR
>
> Which part? That he knocked up some chick or that Addy's living in a sitcom playing the guy's nanny?
>
> LANDON
>
> All of it.

Now University of Michigan seniors, the twins were two years younger than me, but the gap had always felt wider, especially where Conor was concerned.

ME

Is it so strange I'm helping? Oh, right, you guys are so self-absorbed, helping someone else isn't on your radar.

CONOR

Ooh, big sis is testy!

LANDON

Only yourself to blame, Addy. Shouldn't have let #Elleo boss you around.

ME

My choice.

CONOR

Heard it happened in the bathroom of the Empty Net. Would've thought Nyquist was old enough to know better.

Was that true? I didn't want to think of Lars with someone else and I especially didn't want to think of the sex they had in a bar bathroom that resulted in a child.

ME

And you know this how?

CONOR

Boden told H. Says he remembers the night *very well* because Nyquist was in a foul mood, something about his dad being interviewed after a DUI and the news dredging up all the old shit between them in the media. Meets this chick, bang-a-thon in the head, and nine months later we've got baby Nyquist.

ME

Shouldn't you guys be out drinking or picking up casual sex partners instead of gossiping? I hear that's what college is all about.

I wouldn't know from my own college experience, but my brothers were immensely popular. Men and women were constantly sliding into *my* DMs, looking to hook up with them.

LANDON

I'm studying. And Conor is ... not.

CONOR

I'm waiting for this girl I know to end her shift at the bar. And then the fun begins.

ME

TMI! You should be studying too. You can't rely on hockey.

He'd already been drafted and his future was set. I liked to poke fun at him all the same.

CONOR

Think I can. The genes are strong with this one. And if it doesn't work out, Landon will support me with whatever app he creates.

LANDON

In your dreams. Addy, are you living with Nyquist?

ME

Short-term, looking after the baby. She's so cute.

I sent a pic of Mabel.

CONOR

That just makes me want to double-wrap my dick from here on out.

LANDON

But with Nyquist? Is he treating you okay?

The more intuitive and sensitive of my little brothers, for sure.

ME

I barely see him. That's kind of the point— I'm here when he's not.

CONOR

Addy, don't go falling for Nyquist. He's much too old for you.

My cheeks heated. Had Rosie said something? She wouldn't have shared with Conor, I knew that much. They did *not* get along.

ME

Not interested. Hockey players are all assholes. Present company *not* excepted.

LANDON

Agreed.

Landon had dated one last year who broke his heart, the bastard.

He added:

Plus, Addy's not going to waste her time on some guy who impregnates puck bunnies against the urinal. So classy. She wants the Great Love Story like Mom and Dad.

This was true, and I certainly wasn't expecting my former crush to mature into something as epic as Theo and Elle Kershaw.

ME

Trademark!

LANDON

Trademark!

As kids, the last person to yell "trademark" after the first mention of the "Great Love Story" got a punch. These days, we were rarely in each other's physical presence enough to continue the tradition but still scored points against each other any way we could.

CONOR

My girl's here, so gotta go. Talk soon after
🍆 + 💦 = 🤤

LANDON

Bro, no one cares about your orgasms.

CONOR

I do. I care about them a lot.

HATCH

What have I missed?

Never mind, educational as always. Also, trademark! Conor, last again.

CONOR

But I'm about to get laid, so who's the loser now?

ME

Good game tonight, H. You on the plane yet?

HATCH

At the airport. And thanks. We did good.

Before the thread could launch into a blow-by-blow

account of the game, I bowed out. A minute later, Hatch called.

I answered quickly. "Hey, is everything okay?"

"It's fine. I just wanted to check in. I feel like I've barely seen you since you came home."

Hatch and I were usually close; at two years older, he felt protective of me, and I had always adored him. As a kid, I'd followed him around constantly, and he'd never once told me to get lost. Yet, since returning home, I'd placed distance between us, mostly because I hated lying to him. Not sharing what happened in Greece felt dishonest.

"I know. We should make some time to get together when you're back in town."

"Yep. Or you could just tell me what's going on now."

Anxiety made my hands itch. "Going on?"

"Yeah, you've been quiet. Or quieter than usual. And this nanny thing is kind of out there."

"Like I said, Lars needed help."

He passed over that. "How come you came home early? Rosie said you guys were loving Italy and you still had Spain to do. What changed your mind?"

I squirmed, hating myself for keeping it from him. "Just homesick. I missed everyone."

"Well, I missed you, too."

"Oh, everyone but you."

"Ha ha."

I changed the subject. "You haven't said how you like working with Dad."

"Dad's gonna dad, y'know? It's cool. I always knew he was the hardest worker in the league but seeing it up close is ... well, inspiring."

I smiled, loving that he was in this enviable position. "I

think I'm going to have to put a video together. You and Dad tearing it up on the ice." When I was younger, I loved creating highlight reels of my dad's best moves. My brothers, too.

"That'd be cool. Mostly I just want to be there for him this season because it could be the last. I worry this Nyquist drama will have a negative impact on the team. We need everyone on deck."

"That's why I'm trying to help. Keep everything on an even keel. Go Rebels." Which meant my own drama needed to stay well and truly buried. We chit-chatted some more and rang off with promises to meet up when he returned.

With no more family to occupy me, I lay back in the bed in the guest room, feeling the shadows draw in. Perhaps I should have bunked with my mom and Tilly tonight or taken Rosie up on her offer to stay over, but a show of strength was almost as important as actual strength. I reopened the guest bedroom window, closed it, and made sure it was secure.

I rechecked the alarm. Again.

Not yet ready to sleep, I took out my computer and started pulling clips of the game into my editing software. My dad's tenacity and perseverance still amazed me. Sure, his stats had slipped a touch over the last couple of years, but that was understandable. Defenseman statistics weren't as flashy as the offensive ones anyway.

He had made a couple of minor mistakes tonight, but Lars was always there to cover. The two of them were a well-oiled machine, cogs in each other's engines. To the soundtrack of Mabel's baby snores, I worked on creating a video of the defense's greatest hits since the season had started.

Then I took a walk around downstairs, checking doors and windows once more.

I was overdoing it, I knew that much. Before my travels, I was devil-may-care about my safety. I thought nothing of walking home with headphones on or barely noting my surroundings after dark. Used to people and cars, I was a city-raised girl with what I thought was an innate common sense and spatial awareness. Slickers like me grew up with Spidey senses, but that night, six weeks ago on the island of Santorini, they failed me.

I should have stayed with Rosie, but of the two Australian guys we'd met at the village bar, the one "assigned" to me wasn't really digging it. Neither was I, but I was trying to be more open to new adventures. My guy Shane was already hedging his bets: yawning and talking about getting up early to hike while his gaze wandered to a couple of cute French girls at the bar.

I decided to make it easy for him. "I'm going to turn in."

Rosie lifted her head and frowned. She leaned around Galen, the surfer she'd been flirting with all evening. "Just one more drink."

I waved off the offer and stood, smoothing my shorts, which had ridden up to reveal my tan lines. Shane didn't even look, only turning back from his obvious attentions to the bar when Galen nudged him in the ribs.

"You should walk Aveline back."

"It's Adeline ... Never mind. I'm fine! It's just a few blocks up the hill."

A polite Shane made a half-hearted effort to pull himself upright all the same. "No worries, happy to."

"I'll get a cab." I didn't want to cramp anyone's fun. That was my brand. Let everyone enjoy themselves. No Debbie Downer vibes here.

I raised my hand in a wave and turned to go. My arm was caught by Rosie.

"Are you sure you don't want me to come back with you?"

"I'm fine!" I grinned. "But maybe I should stay to make sure you're okay?"

"I'm drinking water," she said. "And believe me, I can handle this one."

Rosie was the strongest person I knew. She knew how to look after herself, and I hated to interfere with her fun. Besides, she'd just seen a photo of my brother online with a girl at a club back home, so she was on some sort of revenge sex mission. Not that Hatch even knew or cared about her crush, but Rosie knew, and I cared, so I was fully on board with any plan to bone away her sadness.

"So, we're both where we need to be." Smiling, I pulled her in for a hug. "I'll text you when I get home."

The hostel was a third of a kilometer away, less than a ten-minute walk. I could cab it, but I didn't want dirty looks from some taxi driver because the fare was hardly worth his time. A brisk walk and alert posture would do the trick. I'd be in bed before I even had a chance to get worried.

A fat fingernail moon shone above, though every now and then, clouds scudded across the crescent and an eerie darkness fell over the sandy streets. Bougainvillea with hints of coconut scented the air. As I moved away from the village and up the hill, the gravel beneath my sandals gave a dry squelch. A couple of minutes in, that was the only sound I could hear as the bar's music receded. Alone at last. Don't get me wrong, I loved traveling with Rosie, but her extrovert nature sometimes wore me out. I needed some solo down time, and this walk back was the perfect respite.

Then I heard it, a soft patter behind me. I looked over my shoulder to see a dark figure following at some distance.

Probably someone heading home or another reveler on their way to the hostel. Up ahead was the entrance to a villa Rosie had pointed out earlier in the evening, its lights shining bright into the night, and for a mad moment, I thought about banging left, sprinting down the driveway, pounding on the door for sanctuary. But a few seconds later, I had passed it, leaving behind my crazy thoughts. I worried about looking foolish.

Better foolish than dead, Aurora would say.

I increased my pace, putting distance between me and the phantom. I looked behind to see him or her making the turn into the villa. A local on their way home, and I'd let my brain run a mile thinking he was on my tail.

My relief was so obvious that I didn't even notice him until I bumped into a wall of muscle. He was tall. Heavyset. I smelled alcohol—grappa, perhaps—and tobacco.

He said something in Greek. I shook my head, assuming it was a question, and stepped around him.

He pulled my arm. I jerked away. I didn't even see it coming until the blow landed like a bomb against my cheek.

Reeling from the shock, I lost my footing. This guy hit me! Only then did I feel truly scared. Our positions magnified the threat, him looming above, the moon halo-ing his head like an avenging angel. Me on the gravel, exposed with my legs splayed because of the way I'd fallen. More Greek muttering, then he pulled at the strap of my purse, a crossbody.

He only wants my money. My phone. My possessions.
Not me.

I should have pulled it over my head, handed it over, but

I was paralyzed with fear. He yanked on the strap, drawing me closer to him, close enough I could smell body odor and alcohol fumes.

"Give," he growled. Finally, a word I could understand.

Still, I did nothing. My cheek stung from where he'd struck me, but mostly I was stunned that this could happen to me.

White, privileged, American.

Stupid.

Another strike came, this time to my mouth. I felt my lip bust open, the ooze of blood. Then someone was shouting.

Not me. I was too passive. Too absurdly quiet about this assault on my person.

Those yells were from Rosie.

By the time she reached me, he was gone, sprinting back up the hill toward the hostel, taking with him any self-assurance I'd possessed, any modicum of bravery I felt about striding out into the world.

"Addy! Oh fucking hell, what did he do to you?" She cradled my head and held me close. "I'm so sorry. I shouldn't have let you go alone. I had this weird feeling and decided to call it a night."

"It's okay," I muttered into the crook of her arm. "You didn't know."

Six weeks later after a visit to Lucca, Florence, and Siena in Italy, we came home, cutting the travels short by two months and pleading homesickness as our excuse. It wasn't entirely untrue. I wanted the bosom of my family, the familiarity of home, the safety of being a Kershaw. I swore Rosie to secrecy because if my family knew, it would confirm everything they thought they knew of me: that I was weak, delicate, in need of protection.

It would confirm what I knew of myself.

I had taken on this nanny gig, not just to help Lars or to ensure Mabel was cared for, but to heal and find the one thing I needed.

A way back to myself.

CHAPTER ELEVEN

Lars

FUCK, I was tired. I expected I could sleep for a week after the trip to New York. We'd had a good game, a 4-2 win, and the flight back was in a word, raucous. I tried to join in but all I could think of were my new responsibilities.

I was someone's father and what I knew about parenting could fit on the surface of a puck. The last three days were spent in a fugue: practice, gym, run, skate, eat, sleep—barely—and start all over again. I was a wreck. I needed to get to grips with this monumental change in my life or my game was going to suffer.

Thank God for Adeline. Reaching out to me when she heard about the paternity test was not on my bingo card. I shouldn't have called her from the locker room, but I'd needed to hear her voice, a calm I took with me into the game.

Just after four in the morning, I let myself in, reset the

alarm, and tiptoed through the house. We had moved Mabel's crib to the guest room, so I knew that's where Adeline would be sleeping. She had said she wanted to be close as it made things easier when the baby woke up. All good. To be fair, I didn't need to check in on the baby. I had no doubt that she was sleeping, in good hands, doing better without me—or a combination of all of the above.

I checked the guest room anyway.

Empty.

My pulse spiked in panic. Maybe Adeline had taken Mabel to her parents' house, but surely, she would have told me. She'd texted about everything else, not that I really needed to know things like, *Mabel sucked down her bottle like a champ* or *Mabel slept for four hours!* My lack of excitement about this stuff affirmed I was a bad choice and the sooner I could get Vicki back in the mix, the better.

I whipped out my phone. No message. Stepping into my bedroom, I got the shock of my life.

Adeline, in my bed, like some sort of Goldilocks checking out the mattress situation. Beside her, on the same mattress, was the bassinet with a chubby little fist resting on the edge, playing peek-a-boo. Adeline's hand was close, as if she was God reaching out to Michelangelo's Adam to give him life.

My thundering heart calmed, relieved at finding them both safe, but that state didn't last as my senses recalibrated and recalled that a very attractive woman was in my bed. The duvet cover was pulled back to reveal a shapely leg joined to an even more shapely ass, the curve of it enough to make my mouth water. Her underwear was that boy short type, but nothing about this woman's form suggested "boy." I'd never expected to see it and because of that, I wasn't ready.

But my cock was. There it went, stirring up a storm, and it wasn't just her ass that had me in tatters. One perfectly rounded shoulder with what I imagined was silky, touchable skin, just begged for my lips.

Why was she in my bed? What was wrong with the guest room? And was Mabel okay?

On cue, the baby made a gurgling noise and gave a fist pump like she was celebrating my win—all of them: hockey, fatherhood, a hot woman in my bed. The thought made me chuckle and the sound made Adeline stir.

She turned over, blinked, and pulled at the duvet, an instinctive move to cover herself. But there was more. She jerked her body away so quickly her head thumped the headboard. I got the impression she would've drilled through the wall if she could, so eager was she to put distance between us.

The light from the corridor highlighted more than shapely curves and soft skin. It shone on the fear in her eyes.

I took a step back. "Sorry, I didn't realize you'd be here."

"I—" She shook her head and turned to the baby. Relief passed over her features, though she didn't relax. Her body remained on high alert. "I planned to be awake before you came back."

"We made good time." I leaned against the doorframe, aiming for casual. "I didn't mean to scare you."

Her smile was thin. "No problem. She almost slept the whole night through."

"Except I just woke her—and you. Go back to sleep."

She passed over that. "You won your game. Congrats."

"Yep. It was a good one. How were things here?"

The duvet cover had slipped enough to reveal the swell of her breasts hugged by a camisole. I receded further into the shadows where this inappropriate leap in sexual awareness belonged.

Adeline chuckled, completely unaware of my discomfort, but it was better than the frightened deer look. "I probably overshared about Mabel's bodily functions."

"No, it was good to hear. Normal stuff." And it put this, whatever *this* was, on a clearer footing. Baby poop, erection killer. "So, how come you're in here?"

In my bed.

"She doesn't like the crib, but she loves the bassinet. I wanted to have her at eye level or close enough, but the guest room bed is a little small for both of us and this California King is the bomb. I hope you don't mind."

"Not at all." Mabel let out a little cry and Adeline reached over to soothe her, though not before she paused a moment, perhaps waiting for me to step in. When I didn't make a move—an unfeeling monster, here—she took over with the surety I'd come to expect. "Is she okay?"

"She's fine. Just hungry."

"I'll feed her."

She looked up. "You sure?"

"I'm up and you should get back to sleep." I moved forward and leaned over my daughter. *Mine.* I still couldn't believe it.

Rather than scoop her out, I picked up the handles of the bassinet, a move that made Mabel expel a strange noise.

"Was that ..." I checked in with Adeline. "A giggle?"

"It was!" Adeline's mouth stretched wide. Damn, that was a pretty smile and—

Keep your happy for your own daughter, not someone else's.

I turned back to Mabel, anything to avoid Adeline's smile and how it made me feel. "You liked when I swayed this bucket thing, huh?" I did it again, giving it a swoosh back and forth. The motion yielded more gorgeous giggles.

From both of them.

I FED MABEL, burped her like a pro, and returned her to her crib in the empty guest room. Adeline had said she didn't like it, so I left her inside the bassinet, cradled by the crib. She'd also told me that on the baby's back was the best position, at least until she was twelve months or could roll over on her own. So much to learn, and I didn't know how I could keep all this information in my head. Mabel seemed happy right now and soon enough her translucent eyelids shuttered closed.

I felt grimy after traveling back on the plane. Usually, I'd take a shower before hitting the sack, only Adeline was asleep in my bed, so the master bath was out. That left the guest one. Luckily, I had spare underwear in my holdall, so I slipped into the shower and turned it on.

This bathroom didn't have my soap or shampoo, but what must have been Adeline's sat in the caddy. I uncapped the shampoo bottle and took a sniff.

Instant hard-on. Fuck.

That's what her hair smelled like. I'd noticed it when she handed off the baby last week, when we stood so close her scent had lodged in my brain and stayed there, waiting to be reactivated like a sleeper spy. I checked the label. Orange blossom and jasmine. I didn't think I'd smelled that before, or if I had, I had no idea what to call it. But now, all I could think was this scent was Adeline.

Adeline in my nostrils, curling into my lungs, giving my

cock a burst of life it hadn't had in months. Years. Apparently, there were hard-ons and there were Adeline hard-ons.

Christ, I needed to ignore that and wash my damn hair. I lathered up, and of course that only made my cock harder. That sleepy smile of hers snuck into my brain and made itself at home. Her shapely leg, the curve of her ass, peeking out of the duvet cover in my bed.

My bed.

Harder again. Hard enough to slam through the shower tile.

I refused to touch my dick. That was a first, unable to stroke myself because the fantasy that inspired it was so taboo. My teammate's daughter. The man's child.

No longer a child, though, but a gorgeous, curvaceous woman.

The cami strap slipping off her shoulder, the swell of her tits straining against the stretchy fabric. Those full, red lips, a little puffy from—from what? From wrapping around my rampant cock, that's what. At this rate I wouldn't need to touch myself because I was getting there on filthy thoughts alone.

I rinsed my hair, then picked up the body wash. Not mine. Hers. I didn't recall the scent which was good as it didn't send me into a raging need to stroke myself dry. I applied the wash to my body, careful to avoid my groin, at least until I came back down to earth. Until I had descended from the clouds of fantasy where Adeline was on her knees, her ponytail at hand level.

In my dream, I refused to grab it. Ignored it like I ignored my hard-on.

I rested my forehead on the tile, looking to cool down. Anything to bank the need. But it was no use. Images of a sexy, sleep-pliant woman swirled in the suds, heading to the drain. Adeline's moss-green eyes, with that movie goddess tilt, half-lidded as she hauled herself to wakefulness.

I couldn't, but ... why? Fantasies were rocket-fueled by the forbidden. This one would be harmless because I would never act on it in real life. No one would ever know.

Having given myself permission, I encouraged her lips to nudge my cock, just a kiss, but it wasn't enough. I needed more, the sweet, velvet suction of her mouth. I needed control. I grabbed hold of that ponytail—in reality, my dick. One touch was enough to set my balls alight with pleasure. Lust bolted through me. The scent of orange blossom permeated the steam as my hand gripped hard and stroked roughly from base to tip.

Make it quick. Get it over with, send the guilt down the drain. The wrong girl—no, woman—with her lips moving up and down my cock. I squeezed the tip, held tight to the base. Holding onto the perfect picture of Adeline sucking me off, her lips swollen, her cheeks hollowed out as she blew me and my mind.

My balls sizzled, heavy with spunk, and with one last tug, I came in thick spurts against the wall and with Adeline's name on my lips.

CHAPTER TWELVE

Adeline

WHAT WAS that saying about intentions and the road to a particularly hot place?

I'd had such good ones when I slipped under Lars's covers last night. Keep the baby at eye level without smothering her or having her fall off the side of the bed. I wasn't lying when I said she was fussy in the crib. Oddly, I also felt safer in his bed, like knowing it belonged to him was a tangible thing I could hold onto.

But then I realized I should probably have changed the sheets first because they smelled like hot, studly hockey player. Thankfully, I had a baby on hand to keep me honest because if Mabel hadn't been playing chaperone, I might have let that tantalizing man scent tantalize me all the way to an orgasm.

I had set an alarm for 4:30 so I could feed Mabel and

take myself back to the guest room. He wasn't supposed to know I'd even been here.

Instead he arrived home early and I was on hand to contribute to the narrative of Adeline's embarrassing crush on Lars Nyquist. My dad's teammate no less! I'd certainly walked—or slept—into that one. I'd also acted like a frightened little rabbit when I saw him silhouetted in the doorframe. Large, hulking, reminiscent of my Greek ogre.

Annoyed with myself, I stretched, and my fingers brushed Bear. He must have fallen out of Mabel's bassinet. I would return him and go back to the guest room where I belonged.

On my way downstairs, I passed the guest room with its open door. Mabel was in the crib, already asleep, which meant Lars had worked fast, feeding her and putting her down. Clearly becoming a pro at this parenting lark.

Guilt panged me at hearing the pitter-patter of the shower. What a great guest I was, evicting the poor guy from his ensuite. I dropped Bear in beside Mabel, set him near her hand so she would feel him when she awoke, and that's when I heard it.

A moan.

The door to the bathroom was ajar, and that sound could mean only one thing: Lars was having a private moment.

Another moan went up, more of a groan this time. That was how lust sounded, and it immediately found a corresponding throb between my legs.

I had to leave. I couldn't stay here while Lars did *that*.

Yet, I remained frozen, like that night on a Greek isle a couple of months ago. Only this time, it wasn't fear that molded my feet of clay.

It was desire.

Something about knowing the difference made me braver than I'd felt in a long time. Oh, it was all wrong, but it was also feeding something within me, something a little crazy. I was never the one who took chances or made moves. Rosie said I'd never met a line I wanted to cross.

This felt different. This felt like a situation I could handle.

What I truly wanted to handle was whatever Lars Nyquist was stroking in there. I wanted to touch him, taste him, feel him, and because I would never have a chance to, this might be the closest I would get. A little eavesdropping to fuel the lonely nights ahead. Harmless, because he would never know. As soon as he finished, I would exit stage left.

The moans were increasing in volume, which meant he must be close. I gripped the dresser, pushed my thighs together, and tried not to think too hard about the sheer wrongness of what I was doing.

"Oh, oh fuck, *ohhh*." Then one groan that *had* to be Lars's climax coupled with a very loud "Adeliiiiine!"

My mouth fell open. No, that couldn't be right. I must have substituted my deepest fantasy for that final cry of release, taking the desire to be in Lars's sexual crosshairs to its logical conclusion. Of course, he would think of me when he came. That was all part of *my* wicked fantasy.

I played it back in my mind, rewound to the moment before, and ... shit, that really happened.

"Adeline?"

Oh. This time, my name was not spoken as a groan or punctuating an orgasm, but in shock. Maybe even disgust at my creeper behavior.

And this creeper was pretty bad at covering her tracks.

I snapped my gaze to Lars who stood before me, his broad shoulders beaded with moisture, a towel raised to his chest and draped down the center-line. It covered most of the good stuff, but I still got an excellent view of sheer, tightly-packed muscle on either side of it. Those thick thighs I'd dreamed of. The curvature of his rock-solid ass. Hints of the V-cut. All there, for my viewing pleasure.

"What are you doing here?"

"I ..." I gestured to the sleeping baby. "Mabel must have pushed Bear out of the bassinet. I brought it back in and didn't realize you were, uh, busy."

Busy. What a word choice!

Lars continued to stare, his cheeks darkly flushed, his lips a straight line of disapproval.

"How long were you out here?"

The query was bitten out. He didn't know how much I had heard, but even if he assumed I'd heard that last part— my name on his lips when he came—then that was hardly my fault.

You stayed, Adeline. You stayed to listen, though you knew it was wrong.

"I'm sorry. I didn't mean to ..."

His eyes darkened, swallowing all the blue. "Didn't mean to what?"

I barely managed to gut the word out. "Listen."

I wasn't sure what I expected. A denial? An apology? A quick ushering me out of the room? Whatever it was, it wasn't this.

Deathly, accusing silence.

I finally broke it. "I should leave."

"Yeah, you should."

Humiliated, I took a step backwards and my heel caught on something. Before I could stumble, Lars and his battle-hewn reflexes grasped my elbow and kept me upright. The movement brought him close, too close, and all that separated us was a towel, a hairsbreadth of erotically charged space, and the flood of embarrassment that was rushing in to fill it.

"Careful," he murmured, low and husky, more warning than counsel.

His fingers burned through my skin, rivaling my shame in a flush across my body. I pulled away, sidestepped the overnight bag I'd almost tripped over, and fled the room on rubbery legs.

CHAPTER THIRTEEN

We're happy to report that the dream team of Kershaw and Nyquist managed to keep New York at bay last night. An inside source tells us that Nyquist wanted to take time off to deal with the surprise addition to his family, but this plan was met with resistance from his captain and the Rebels front office. Despite rumors of a rift between the D-men over the threat these changes impose to Theo Kershaw's likely final year in the pros, they've managed to put that aside as the Rebels org rallied around to resolve Nyquist's childcare issues.

In an interesting development, Kershaw's daughter, Adeline, has stepped up as temporary nanny to Nyquist's love child, a solution that no doubt ensures the Rebels captain maintains control over a volatile situation. Still no word on the mysterious woman who left the typically unflappable Finn in the lurch, but we have to wonder if Lars's baby drama has more plot twists in store!

- @RebelsInsider

Lars

I HAD ROYALLY FUCKED UP.

Not just the fact I'd jerked off to fantasies of my nanny—what a cliché—but how I'd reacted.

Who has two thumbs, jacks off to an out-of-bounds woman, then acts like it's her fault when she catches him in the act?

This guy!

So maybe she should have stepped out the second she realized what was happening in that shower. Was it possible she didn't know? Or was I projecting some brand of innocence on her that didn't exist? The virginal daughter of my teammate, too curious to flee when confronted with a man in the throes of an orgasm.

As if I needed any more fuel to this fire.

Yet the thought of her there, listening to my desperate moans, stayed with me for the rest of the day. I imagined her rosy nipples hardening to sweet, suckable peaks. Her thighs rubbing together, seeking delicious friction. Her pussy quivering and gushing as I came with her name on my lips.

She was forbidden for a million reasons. I had to weigh every move and decision around her, so I didn't mess up her life and mine. If she still had that crush on me, then I had the capacity to hurt her.

We had agreed before the away trip that Adeline should take days off when I was back in town and had a break from practice or games. She had taken yesterday off, spending overnight back at her parents' house, while I tried to manage

Mabel solo. The kid had slept through the night, if sleeping between midnight and five a.m. was considered a full night's sleep. Now she was sitting in the highchair the Kershaws had donated, her face covered with papaya mush, the worst of the baby foods. I was partial to pear and banana myself, but my daughter had more exotic tastes.

"You like that, huh?"

"Yabby!"

"Yabby," I agreed while I took a wet cloth to her face and wiped her down, a losing battle because she just smeared the next spoonful over her mouth, heedless of my efforts. Then, because she knew I wasn't a fan, she flicked her spoon, shooting the mush in my eye with a precision that made me proud.

I rubbed my face with the cloth. "Nice wrist move, sweetheart. I see hockey in your future."

The lawyer was working on the options, specifically custody and financial arrangements. Vicki had vanished back to Cleveland. I'd assumed she lived in Chicago but no, she'd driven over five hours to abandon her kid to a guy with no child-rearing experience whatsoever, and five hours back. Neither had she done anything illegal by dropping her kid off with her bio-dad, so we couldn't get the law involved. *Not that you want that,* Quinn had said. *This should be handled privately, for everyone's sake.*

I agreed. Torn between anger and sympathy, I knew that bandying about accusations of criminality wouldn't make this more palatable.

My phone rang with a call from Natalie, the Rebels' publicist.

"Yeah?"

"Hi, Lars! We were hoping you'd stop by the front office after practice today."

Sure, if my nanny shows after I scarred her for life. I half-expected her to text and tell me she was out. That she'd talked to Rosie or God forbid, her mom, and told them she didn't feel safe in the same house as me with my hungry gaze and dirty fantasies.

"What's up?"

"We'd like to run through some possible statements about your situation. While everyone loves a single dad, the press on this one so far has been, shall we say, negative?"

I'd read several articles, posts, and comments about my "situation," and I didn't think anyone could shine this turd up. Anytime I was mentioned, the media inevitably brought up my father or my imaginary rift with Kershaw.

"Ignore it."

"We can't. People will want a statement about your plans, if you're going to build a life with the mother, and—"

"That's easy: 'none of your business' and 'I banged the mom in a bar bathroom while she was married to someone else so that's a non-starter'."

Not even a gasp. Publicists and their nerves of steel.

"And your father?"

"What about him?" I winced at my sharp tone and sent an apologetic glance toward my daughter.

"We want to offer a clear distinction between the past and the present."

"Sure, do that. Try to steer them away from the old man's drugs, gambling, and whoring. Along with his three ex-wives and the army of former business partners he fucked over. Let's try to avoid all the comparisons."

A tingling sensation flushed across my skin.

I looked up and there was Adeline, her cheeks pink, her lips wet, and looking just as I'd imagined her during that sexy shower session. The floodgates had opened and there was no stopping this porno now.

Natalie had said something while I tried to wrangle my thoughts. Problem was that lately whenever Adeline was in my orbit, those thoughts became mushy. Scattered. Incomprehensible.

"Say 'gain."

"Let's start with the family wants privacy at this time."

"Sounds like a winner."

Natalie had the bit between the teeth. "And maybe we could send a photographer, do a photo shoot with the baby—"

"I don't want to use the kid like that."

"Think about it."

"Sure," I said to end the conversation.

I looked up and met Adeline's gaze.

"You okay?"

After what had happened yesterday, she was asking if *I* was okay?

"Fine," I clipped back.

"What was all that about your father?"

"Apparently there's concern in Rebels circles that this recent drama is a little too reminiscent of good ole Sven's rabble-rousing back in the day. The guy's dead but his hell-raiser spirit lives on in me, that kind of thing."

"That's ridiculous!" Not going to deny it, her outrage gave me a little thrill. "You're nothing like him."

"You don't know that. To be honest, given his reckless tendencies, I'm surprised I don't have more half-siblings beating down my door."

Her lips tightened. "What about your mom?"

"She died when I was a kid. Dad wasn't too happy to have to take over, so he decided the way to make it worth his while was to mold me into the best darn hockey player he could. And yeah, he was kind of a dick about it. Took a while for me to measure up to his standard for greatness."

I had obviously surprised her with my backstory vomit. Sometimes I surprised myself.

"I don't know much about him except for ..." She trailed off.

"The fact he was banned from the league for illegal betting?"

The first person since the fifties. Of all the professional leagues, hockey was the most easygoing when it came to gambling. They only asked that players and franchise staff not wager on pro hockey games. NCAA? Place your bets. Fantasy football? Have at it. Other sports were complete hard asses about it: no wagering on anything ever. All my dad had to do was obey that one simple rule and bet on any other fucking thing.

The guy had always been a self-saboteur of the highest order. He chose his own sport. Worse, his own games. Decades had passed without an acknowledged infraction by a player until Sven Nyquist called the police because a bookie wouldn't pay out on a win. The guy was as dumb as they come.

That was the first time. A ten-game ban was his punishment. Six years later, he got caught again, only that time he almost dragged me down with him.

I rubbed my beard, resolved to be more conciliatory. None of this was Adeline's problem. I needed her, which meant sharing less and keeping what we had on a professional footing.

"Well, the poor kid seems to be doing okay despite being landed with me as a dad."

"There you go again."

"What?"

"Making a self-deprecating comment about your fitness to be a father. Not even self-deprecating. More like ... self-loathing."

My hackles rose. "We didn't all grow up in the *Little House on the Prairie*."

"In the what?"

A grim smile shaped my lips. That reference was obviously way before her time, which only went to affirm a million other things. "Family perfection where everyone gets along and the sun's always shining."

"So your family wasn't perfect. Show me one that is."

Yours, sweet thing. I reached out and rubbed Mabel's tummy. As usual, she preened and bat her eyelashes like the little attention-hog she was.

"I guess what I'm trying to say is this little girl needs two parents who can be there for her. A father who has a clue what he's doing. A mom who won't run at the first sign of trouble. As far as family, she's already way behind, and I don't want to make it worse."

"Just because Sven Nyquist patterned a blueprint of bad fatherhood doesn't mean you have to follow it."

"You think I'm screwing up?"

"I think you're so *afraid of* screwing up that you won't let yourself enjoy this. Enjoy Mabel."

I stood and threw up my hands. Suddenly I was entertaining Theo Kershaw levels of drama.

"Enjoy *this*? How the hell am I supposed to enjoy this? This is a baby. A human life. A sponge waiting to absorb, hell, everything. I can't enjoy that. There's too much at stake."

My anxiety lashed the room like a thunderstorm.

She approached, like a keeper toward a cornered

animal. "You're not alone here. You have a team of people, a village for want of a better word, to make sure Mabel gets the best care in the world. She won't want for anything. But this is a two-way street. Mabel gets a dad, but you get a child. You get the joy of watching her grow, achieve milestones, be loved. That's not something to be sniffed at. That's such a privilege and I wish you could see that instead of focusing on all the ways this could go wrong." She held my gaze, clear and true. "So you're worried that people will think you're like Sven. Screw 'em."

Her words calmed me like no others could have done.

"Screw 'em?"

"Yep. People *love* seeing patterns, even where none exist. If you don't want to just ignore it, then reframe the narrative. So your baby mama dropped the result of your bang-in-a-bar-bathroom off before the world. Own it! Show everyone that you're putting in the work when it comes to fatherhood."

I frowned. "Do this photo shoot for Natalie? Sounds fake."

"It doesn't have to be. Like now. Look at how cute she is in her little Rebels onesie."

God, she was. My entire body softened, which made a change from my usual response in Adeline's presence. "It's covered in papaya junk."

"The *worst* of the baby foods."

"That's what I said. Well, to myself. Mabel seems to be a fan."

Adeline grinned. "We can clean her up. And even if she's covered in it, so what? Every parent in the world will identify with that. Let me take a few photos and we can post to your personal social media. That makes it seem less corporate and more under your control."

"I suppose ... but I get to decide which ones. Or if they go up at all."

The next twenty minutes were spent in an impromptu photo shoot. Mabel alone, clinging to her little spoon like a hockey stick. Me feeding her or holding her aloft while she giggled and yelped. Funnily enough, I enjoyed it. Or maybe I enjoyed how Adeline was able to pull joy from some deep, dark recess inside me.

Heads bent together, we looked at the photos, while I tried my best not to inhale my nanny's hair like a pervert. I let Adeline choose her favorites. She had a better eye than me.

I opened my Instagram. "What should I say?"

She thought about it, then took the phone and typed something.

I read back what she'd written. "Best Mistake Ever?"

"Own it, Lars."

She was right. I wasn't my father. I'd made mistakes but unlike him, I was going to own mine.

I hesitated for a moment, then hit post. "Natalie's gonna kill me." But what of it? I needed to fight back against the haters in my way.

"This is your daughter, and you know what's best."

Not sure how true that was, but I let it go. Somehow, through all this, I'd forgotten the tension between us. It needed to be addressed.

"Adeline, what happened yesterday—"

"I'm sorry."

"No, that was all on me."

A fiery blush crept up her cheeks. "We both made it happen. I should have left when I realized what was going on."

The ribbon of steel in her voice surprised me. She

seemed determined to take ownership over what had occurred. I was all about responsibility and I certainly appreciated seeing it demonstrated by others.

"Okay." I blew out a breath. "I worried you might not show today."

"Why?"

"I thought you might feel … unsafe around me." *Because dammit, you should.* The way she was looking at me now with all that doe-eyed innocence was doing very bad things to me. "You seemed scared when I came home yesterday morning and woke you up."

"Strange bedroom. Sudden awakening. That was all." She shifted uneasily. A lie, but about what exactly? "And to think I wouldn't show because we had a weird moment? That wouldn't be very professional. This year is big for my dad, for you, the team. It's imperative that we keep this a calm, drama-free environment for you, Mabel, and the entire Rebels ecosystem."

I appreciated that she wanted to put the needs of Mabel and the franchise ahead of all else. That was a good way to look at it.

I picked up my coffee as she went on. "I have a couple more nanny interviews set up for tomorrow. And I promise to give you your space. You won't even know I'm here."

I doubted that. Still, I could hope. "I promise to keep things professional, too."

"Oh, don't stop your … activities on my account."

I coughed up a mouthful of coffee. "My activities?"

Her blush intensified, a flush of warmth that I could feel from here. Christ, I wanted to kiss every inch of her and find out where else she pinked up.

Think of the team, Mabel, and your mental health.

"You know what I mean! Still your house, Lars. How

about I get our girl cleaned up and you can get ready for practice."

I let her take over. Now that my kid was in good hands, I'd pimped her out on social media to rehab my rep, and I had permission to jerk off to my heart's content in my own house, I was apparently golden.

CHAPTER FOURTEEN

Adeline

"OH. MY. OVARIES!" My ears almost burst at the screech. "Look at that gorgeous bundle!"

Tara Fitzpatrick, mom to my friend Esme, came bounding over on gravity-defying heels and gave me a hug.

"Hi, Tara!"

"Hey, cutie! I'm so glad to see you. Want a haircut?" As usual, she gave me the critical once-over that told me my wants were irrelevant: I *needed* a haircut, and she was right. She ran the player salon and cut the hair of everyone Rebel-adjacent. I'd dropped by her digs at Rebels HQ to say hello.

"Maybe later? I'm here to take Hatch to lunch."

"Oh, how fun. But they're still in practice, so have a seat there and tell me all about your travels while I hold this little one."

I took a seat in the big leather chair and chatted about

my favorite places—Ubud, Chiang Mai, Split, and Siena, to name a few—while Tara tickled Mabel, who loved the attention.

"And now you're on the hook as nanny? You okay with that?"

"Why does everyone think I've been hoodwinked into this gig?"

"Oh, no reason." That knowing smirk said differently.

"Has Esme said something?" I hadn't seen my friend for ages—she was at NYU—but she had been privy to my embarrassing crush back in the day.

Tara stood upright and placed a hand on her hip. The salon apron she wore dipped below her blue leather mini but did little to hide her killer legs. "Honey, I just don't want you to get hurt. Take it from me who has chased after the wrong guy far too many times."

Tara's shenanigans as a hockey husband hunter back in the day were fabled, but after a few wrong turns and a crazy fake dating scheme with Dex O'Malley (wild!), she'd eventually found her happily-ever-after with Hale Fitzpatrick, a former Rebels GM. No doubt she meant well, but I refused to be lumped in with sad and pathetic hockey bunnies like Mabel's mom. Besides, Lars and I had talked it out and we were being totally professional. Lines had been drawn!

"I didn't take this on so I could get closer to Lars. That was schoolgirl stuff, just a crush that's history. I did it because I'm a team player and I didn't want my mom to be landed with all the work. Because that's what happens, Tara. Women are expected to take on all the unpaid labor."

Tara blinked at my outburst. "Well, aren't you an absolute star?"

"Certainly sounds like it."

We both turned to the sound of a deep-voiced rumble.

Rowan MacFarlane, one of the Rebels D-men, stood at the salon's entrance. Not really on my radar, he'd been acquired by the franchise about six months ago. (Rosie said he was big on social media, which always made me suspicious.) He was good-looking, that was for sure. Blonde, square-jawed, and clean-shaven.

Had he overheard me talking about my crush on Lars? I really needed to keep my mouth zipped.

"Hi, Rowan," Tara said breezily. "Have a seat, I'll be with you in a sec." Her phone buzzed. "Oh, that's the General."

Tara moved away to talk to her husband while Rowan sidled closer and studied Mabel, his nose twitching like he'd encountered something particularly noxious. "Nyquist's kid? She doesn't look like him."

"I wouldn't say that. She has his eyes."

"My sister just had one and he already looks like her husband. Bit of a potato head." He held out a hand, weirdly formal. "I'm Rowan."

"Adeline." I stood and shook his hand, matching his formality, which made him smile. "Good to meet you."

"Yeah, about that." He was still holding my hand and used the leverage to draw me in as he bent close to my ear. "How come we haven't met yet?"

Was he flirting with me? I wish Rosie was here to tell me.

"I've been away. Traveling."

"Right, your brother said. Thailand or somewhere."

"Thailand, Malaysia, Vietnam, Laos. We did Europe, too."

He nodded. "Cool. And now you're looking after Nyquist's kid?"

"Just temporarily while he works on getting a permanent nanny." Something occurred to me. "Shouldn't you be in practice?"

"I have a wrist injury, so I was in rehab instead of on the ice. But they're finishing up any minute now."

"Oh, okay. I should probably get going then."

He was still holding my hand, using his non-injured one, I supposed. It wasn't … terrible.

"So what do you do for fun?" I must have looked surprised because he laughed. "You're not hanging with a baby and Nyquist all the time, are you?"

Lately, yes. Just listening to my crush jerking off and engaging in small talk with a seven-month-old. A real party animal.

"I haven't had much time since I got back."

"Maybe we should hang sometime."

"Okay, sorry about that!" Tara came bustling over. "Rowan, chair, please."

Finally, he released my hand. It felt clammy but then that was likely me, because clammy was my brand.

"Nice to meet you, Adeline."

Lars

I KNEW THAT CRY.

Weird that it took barely a week for me to develop the ability to recognize my daughter's voice. I looked up into the stands and there they were: *my girls.*

I couldn't help that thought nor the way it snaked inside my brain. Neither of them was mine, not really. Mabel had my genetic material, that was all. As for Adeline? I needed to nix those dangerous thoughts.

It sure was nice to see her here all the same, even if we were in this weird spot.

I skated over to the wall. "Is everything okay?"

"Of course. I'm having lunch with Hatch. Thought I'd show Mabel what Daddy does for a living."

That made me warm. *Daddy.* "I would hold her but—"

"On the ice, no. Dad dropped me once. I haven't recovered."

"What?" Theo, with that innate instinct for knowing when he was the hot topic, skated over. "Are you still holding that against me? For the fiftieth time, O'Malley bumped me and—"

"Not how it happened." O'Malley launched into a spirited defense of this decades-old incident. "You were skating backwards while carrying your kid, showing off as usual, and you crashed into me. I saved Adeline's life! Hey, Addy, you're looking well."

He kissed her cheek, and while I knew it meant nothing, I still wanted to punch his throat.

"Hi, Dex. You played great the other night. Your PPG is already stellar this season. And your Corsi score is looking good, too. Close to 58%!"

"I don't pay much attention to the stats, but if you say so."

"Addy loves her stats." Hatch leaned on the wall. "Hey, sis."

"Hey, Dino Boy."

O'Malley's face lit up. "Dino Boy! Remind me again?"

Unfortunately, I knew this origin story. "Something about the dinosaur-themed underwear Kershaw wore the night he conceived the kid."

"Shit, really?" O'Malley clearly wished he'd never asked.

Hatch shook his head. "*Not* my preferred nickname."

Theo chortled. "As we say in the biz, you don't get to choose, H-man!" He leaned over the wall and chucked Mabel under the chin. "Now, how's my goddaughter? Mabel, May-belle, Belle of the Ball, Jelly Belly? We'll work on it. Baby's gotta have a nickname."

"Oh, that'd make a good photo for the socials." Adeline snapped a few with her phone while Theo mugged it up.

He peered up at her. "Did you take those photos on NyQuil's Insta?"

I answered for her. "Yep. She really knows her stuff."

"That she does. Glad to see you coming up with some counterprogramming to the narrative."

I was pissed that I had to, but Adeline's taking charge of the situation was a blessing.

"We should probably mix it with hockey stuff, too," Adeline said. "Just a few clips. Keep it light."

"You can take complete control of it." I didn't care about that kind of thing, but I'd already had a call from Natalie congratulating me on my *social reach* and *innovative strategizing*. Owning my shit had apparently worked.

Theo was making Mabel giggle with nose boops, two shameless flirts instantly drawn to each other. A couple more players skated over.

"Aw, look at those cheeks." Jacobs leaned over and stroked Mabel's head. "As soon as Zara saw photos of Mabel, she started hinting about another kid. I wouldn't mind a boy this time." He nodded at me. "You should bring her over for a playdate. Z's got a mommy-baby group she hangs with."

"Maybe." I wasn't sure about her establishing bonds

with other kids only to have them broken when she went back to Vicki.

"She can make her debut at the party," Theo said. "Have you figured out her costume yet?"

"The party?"

"Halloween party at Chez Kershaw?" Straightening, he gripped the wall and addressed Adeline. "You haven't told him?"

"We've had other things on our minds, Dad." She caught my eye and bit her lip. We certainly had.

No one seemed to notice the awkward pause, probably because Theo plowed right through it as usual. His tactless-ness was so often a gift.

"But no one misses our Halloween party! It's legendary. Just wait until you see what I'm doing."

"Saturday night?" That was five days away and we had a game the night before. I shared a quick glance with my nanny. "Adeline needs a night off. I can't expect her to mind Mabel at a party." In other news, I was looking forward to sleeping. A Halloween party was not on my radar.

"We can probably find a costume for the little 'un," Theo said, oblivious to my objections. "Tilly's outgrown tons of stuff."

"I'll make her costume." Apparently, I *was* going to the party.

"Make it?" Jakey went wide-eyed. "Like on a sewing machine?"

Jesus, no. "I'll figure it out. I can actually buy stuff for my kid."

Theo's lips twitched. "Yeah, I know. Just trying to make it easier." He leaned over and kissed his daughter. "Sorry you have to put up with this grouch."

"It's okay. I'm an expert on grouches." She put her

tongue out at Hatch, who made a face and told her he'd see her at the exit.

The rest of them skated off, the locker room their goal.

"Looks like I'm on the hook for a Halloween costume then. Any ideas?"

"Oh, you didn't want anyone's help a minute ago."

I shook my head, feeling foolish, and not just because of how I'd snapped at my teammate. "I hate appearing helpless, like everyone needs to pitch in for sad old Lars."

"Dad's just trying to help. We all are. And on that topic, I've been thinking we probably should take her to the doctor for a check-up?" She looked like she was planning her next words carefully. "Mom will have a recommendation. That okay?"

"Of course. I don't mean to sound like a total asshole who wants to do it all his way." Especially when my way was meandering and clueless.

"You're just proud. It's not a bad thing, but Mabel comes first." She spoke with that soft strength I so admired. "I'll ask Mom and try to get a doctor's appointment for when you're available."

What would I do without this angel in my life? *Probably get a good night's sleep.*

"Also, that's not a bad idea about setting up playdates with other kids," she continued. "Socialization can't start too early, and Jane is a sweetheart."

"Jane?"

"Cody and Zara's little one. She's almost two."

Right, I'd sent a gift when she was born and thanked my lucky stars I didn't have to worry about constantly checking in with the missus and worrying about a kid. *No, not me, not ever.* How the mighty had fallen.

"You know best."

Her brow wrinkled. "So, just wanted to say hi. I should go because Hatch, lunch, and all that."

"I can take her home."

"No, you should stick to your routine. That's why I'm here. We'll see you later!"

CHAPTER FIFTEEN

Adeline

THE SUNNY SIDE UP DINER was a Riverbrook stalwart, and where our dad used to take us as kids every Sunday for brunch. (They'd named an omelet after him that was still on the menu, so he considered it his duty to give them his custom forever.) It had feta in it, which made me think of Greece, so I avoided that and went for French toast, which made me think of Paris in the spring and eating banana and Nutella crepes with Rosie while strolling the streets of Montmartre. Perfect. Hatch ordered a Theo, Belgian waffles, and a double stack of blueberry pancakes.

"So how are things? Settling in with your new team?"

"I feel like I know them already because of Dad. So that's made the transition smooth."

"Cool, cool."

He eyed me over his coffee cup. "What?"

"You tell me. You've been a touch moody of late. You should be on top of the world, but maybe you're feeling some pressure being on the same team as *the* Theo Kershaw."

"It's a lot to live up to." For a brief moment, I saw the strain in his expression. "But we don't play the same position, so there aren't the same comparisons. I can handle the old man. The press and fans are a different story, and they're going gaga with this Nyquist baby story."

His gaze sharpened, and for a moment I thought he'd heard about my crush on Lars and was worried it had the potential to make waves during this important year. But no. Looking up, I saw Dash and Summer taking seats at the counter. Summer spotted us and bounced over.

"Everyone's got brunch on their mind, I guess!" She leaned over to kiss my cheek, then nodded at Hatch. "Hey, Dino Boy."

My usually good-natured brother scowled at her. "No one calls me that."

Dash had come up behind Summer and circled her waist. "Dude, *everyone* calls you that now that O'Malley has filled us in."

Summer slipped his grip and hunkered down to rub Mabel's tummy. "Aw, aren't you adorable?"

Her fiancé rolled his eyes. "What did I say? Not even hitched yet and she's got baby fever."

Hatch hadn't let up on the glower, only now it was directed at Dash.

"How's the wedding planning coming along?" I asked to break the tension.

Summer's smile was tentative. "I actually wanted to talk to you about it."

"Me?"

"She's down a bridesmaid." Dash rolled his eyes like this was a ridiculous "bride" problem. "You're next on deck."

Summer nudged him in the ribs. "Dash! I'd like to have set the scene first."

"Uh, everyone wants to be in our wedding party, babe. Nuptials of the century, or so my mom says."

A visibly miffed Summer turned to me, mouthing an apology. "Could I call you later?"

"Of course!"

They took their leave back to the counter.

"I can't quite put my finger on those two." I shook my head. "Dash is kind of—"

"A jerk?" my brother offered without hesitation.

"I was going to say condescending. I wonder what Summer sees in him."

"His ginormous salary and even bigger trust fund."

Kind of harsh and not my impression of Summer at all. Dash was heir to a huge hotel fortune, though. We were talking billions. "You know this how?"

"He treats her like shit, and she puts up with it. Why else would she do that if she wasn't holding out for the payday?"

"Maybe she thinks she can change him." Though they'd been together for close to five years, and her sunny influence had yet to produce observable results. "Or maybe we don't know what happens behind closed doors. He could be a total sweetheart to her in private."

"You're not going to be her bridesmaid, are you?"

"If she asks, sure. Rosie's already in."

Hatch blew out an annoyed breath. "Sounds like a disaster waiting to happen. But never mind that. How about you tell me what's going on with you?"

"Just watching this little one." I checked in on Mabel

who was happily munching on a strawberry-apple-spinach rice wafer. "And thinking about next steps."

"More college?"

"God, no. I liked the business classes but I'm not sure how to apply it."

"You were a big help to Mom when Tilly was born. Is that something you'd be interested in as a career?"

"I don't think so. I'm just helping until Lars finds a nanny he clicks with."

"So Nyquist is being respectful, right?"

Sure. Says my name when he comes. Real respectful.

"Do you think Mom and Dad would be okay with me there if they didn't trust him?"

"Right, but ..." He tapped the table with his index finger. Waited. Squinted.

Awareness dawned. "Rosie said something!"

"She might have mentioned a certain crush. This information had to be shared, Addy!"

I covered my heating cheeks with my hands. "It was harmless and is now ancient history. Absolutely forgotten. We talked it out and we're fine."

Hatch looked skeptical. "You discussed this crush *with* your crush and he's fine with it?"

"There are more important things than ridiculous crushes, H. The man's world has just blown up with a baby, not that long after the father with whom he had a notoriously strained relationship passed away in painful circumstances. Believe me, he's not thinking about how I liked him once in the distant past."

"Good. 'Cause his life is a mess. He's probably feeling vulnerable right now."

And I wasn't? Still, I preferred Hatch's take on it, that poor Lars needed protection from my wiles.

"Plus, look at how it all came about. Banging a married chick in a bathroom, a one-night stand. Not so different from his dad."

"Since when are you so judgmental? Have you forgotten that *you* were the result of a one-night stand?"

"But Mom and Pop got together soon after because they were fated. The Great Love Story, Trademark. I'm the reason you're even here!" This argument was as old as the hills. "Besides, you shouldn't be dating any hockey players. They're all assholes."

"Don't I know it," I said with feeling.

Satisfied he'd done his big brother duty, he stood. "I'm heading to the john. Don't eat my bacon."

"Yes, sir." I helped myself to a strip right under his nose, then texted Rosie.

> Can't believe you blabbed about L to my brother!

ROSIE

> Sorry!!! We were bonding and I felt the need to keep the good times rolling with hot goss. Is he being a jerk?

ME

> Actually, he seems to think Lars needs protection from my claws at this difficult time.

ROSIE

> LOL. Finally, you're a maneater!

Another text came in from an unknown number.

> It was nice to meet you today.

> This is Rowan, btw.

Hmm.

How did you get this number?

UNKNOWN

I have my ways. So, would you like to hang sometime?

Straight to it. I wasn't sure I liked that. I wasn't sure I was even attracted to Rowan. My experience was that people were usually interested in me because I was a Kershaw first, a woman a distant second.

Hatch had told me to stay away from hockey player assholes. Even Rosie thought the idea of me being a maneater was hilarious. No one gave me much credit, that was for sure. But neither did I like the idea of dating someone to prove something.

ME

I'm pretty swamped these days.

UNKNOWN

I hear you. Let me know if your schedule opens up.

Lars

FOR CONSISTENCY'S SAKE, we had reworked the schedule so Adeline stayed over even on my nights off. I needed sleep and I couldn't get much if I had to attend to

Mabel's every whim. And yeah, I knew she was a baby and that whims were her brand.

Only sleep was near to impossible because this woman was in the next room with my daughter. I turned over, noting the time on my phone: 2:06 a.m. Punched the pillow. Considered a silent jerk-off, which usually did wonders to send me asleep. But now I couldn't because the woman I dreamed of was next door and I'd promised her—and myself —that I was drawing a line under it.

I stared up at the ceiling, making out shapes, turning them into plays on the ice. Defensemen didn't usually think too hard about plays, but sometimes I liked running the lines in my head, like counting sheep. It usually helped keep thoughts of Sven at bay, yet my surprise fatherhood meant he was on my mind of late. I was trying to remember good things, but I could only focus on the negative.

My father once gave a TV interview about five years after he'd been banned from the league, so a good ten years ago. His trophies filled the background, his softening body filled a leather chair. He'd aged twenty years in five and was still as bitter as the day he was kicked out of professional hockey.

"Do you regret your decision to gamble away your career?" the interviewer had asked.

"What's the point in regrets?" he'd said, his thick Finnish accent making him sound like a Bond villain. "It happened. I cannot turn back time."

"And what about your son Lars? How's your relationship with him?"

Sven's palpable disgust leeched through the screen. "Nolla."

Null. Zero. Nothing.

I couldn't forgive him. He saw nothing worth forgiving. *Nolla* was right.

My eyes fluttered closed as sleep got the better of me. But then they snapped wide open. I'd heard a noise.

Downstairs? No. Closer. I sat up, quieting my heartbeat, straining to listen.

There it was again. A whimper. Perhaps Mabel was awake.

I padded toward the door and into the corridor. The sound came again, louder, more distressed. The guest room door was ajar. I pushed it a few inches wider and poked my head in. The room wasn't completely dark. Moonlight filtered through the blinds, illuminating a sleeping Mabel in stripes.

Movement in the bed caught my eye. Adeline shifted, turned, and cried out. Mabel stirred but didn't wake.

Adeline was having a nightmare. I recalled that first night I came home early, how she'd reacted as if I was an intruder. I didn't want to scare her again, but if I let this go on, she might wake Mabel.

Cautiously, I stepped forward just as Adeline thrashed again. That decided it. I sat on the bed, figuring that would be less intimidating than being caught looming over her. Placing a hand on her shoulder, I gently shook.

"Adeline."

She was awake instantly, her body simultaneously curling in on itself and moving away.

"Adeline, it's me. Lars. You were having a nightmare."

Shallow breaths punctuated the air, her chest rising and falling quickly. She was terrified.

"It's okay. You're awake and you're safe." I leaned over to put on the nightstand lamp. It was dim enough that it shouldn't wake Mabel.

Adeline wiped at her face, drying tears.

"Hey, what's going on?"

"J-just a bad dream." Her breathing was coming more evenly now, but I didn't believe her. Sure, maybe she was embarrassed to have someone wake her up in the middle of the night—Adeline was on the shyer side when she wasn't bossing me around—but something seemed off.

"Are you that frightened of me?"

"You? No, not at all. I feel safe when you're around."

"Except you had a nightmare even though I'm in the same house, making you feel safe?"

"You can't always control your dreams."

Tell me about it. "What was it about?"

"I-I can't remember."

Another lie. "Did something happen to you, Adeline? Something that made you feel unsafe?"

She burst into tears and covered her face with her hands, her shoulders shaking. I couldn't stand it a minute longer. I pulled her into my arms and held her close to my chest.

"Tell me, sweet thing. What happened?"

"It's nothing. It's over. I-I'm fine."

I rubbed her back. "Clearly you're not. What's over?"

"Greece. It was stupid. My fault, really."

"Someone hurt you?"

"I was mugged."

Fuck. "How bad?"

"Just a couple of slaps. A busted lip. He didn't even get anything." She pulled back to look at me. "Could have been worse."

Sounded like enough, but I understood what she meant. It could have been so much worse. Anger ripped through me, and I banked it with effort. Adeline's comfort was all that mattered in this moment.

"You were alone?"

She nodded. "Walking home from a bar to my hostel. I'd left Rosie behind—it wasn't her fault. She came along a few minutes later and scared the guy off. He wanted my purse and Lars, I-I froze. I couldn't believe it was happening and when I should have been giving him what he wanted, I lay on the ground like a fool. Taking his punishment."

"This is *not* your fault. You were in the wrong place at the wrong time and if I could get my hands on this fucker, he would know exactly whose fault it was." I continued to rub close circles over her back. "Your dad never mentioned it."

Silence.

"You didn't tell him? Or anyone?"

"They'd only worry."

"Well, of course they would. But that doesn't mean you get to keep it to yourself."

She stared at me with wet eyes. "I made the call. I don't think it was wrong."

Now wasn't the time to argue with her, but God, I wanted to.

"Your parents adore you, y'know that?"

"I know. But I'm also the one they feel a bit sorry for. Silly Adeline, bumbling away with no plans. I really don't want to contribute to that narrative."

I understood wanting to counteract your family's expectations, but other than Kershaw feeling extra protective of Adeline because she was his daughter, I didn't understand her concern. She was young, not yet sure of herself. No one would critique her choices.

My hand was still on her back, where I realized now

that it was touching her skin, bare and hot, and I really should leave before I made a fool of myself.

"You okay now?"

"I will be." Then quieter, "Could you stay a while, until I fall asleep?"

Damn. "Sure."

She lay back down, then pulled the duvet back.

I stared at the spot beside her like it was a pool of lava.

"Lars, you'll freeze. I promise I won't jump you."

I gave a nervous chuckle. She wasn't the problem. On a steeling breath, I turned off the light and twisted my body to lie down beside her.

She faced me, her eyes shining in the darkness.

"You want to talk about what happened? It might help."

She paused a moment, then said, "Rosie's a bright star."

I wasn't sure how that was relevant, but I remained silent, letting her marshal her thoughts.

"When we were traveling, she attracted tons of attention. Rightly so, she's always the life of the party."

"But you felt a little dimmed by comparison?"

"Yes. I can't believe I'm saying that. When we traveled, there were always guys buzzing around and I was usually the third wheel or forced to make small talk with some guy's best friend. I got that a lot in college—people interested in me because of my father or brother—and now it was happening on my travels. I love her, but sometimes I'm envious of how easily she makes friends. Has guys crawling all over her."

I stroked her cheek. The idea of guys crawling all over Adeline did not sit well, but I also hated that she had self-esteem issues that left her thinking she wasn't worthy of having guys crawling all over her.

She went on, a slight hitch in her voice. "I don't even

want that. Casual sex, or the idea of it, doesn't appeal much. I see my mom and dad, and I want what they have. We joke about it—the Great Love Story, Trademark. But it's beautiful to see. Comforting. Only, to even get that far, I'd have to attract someone, which is hard to do when you're cowering in the corner."

I was tempted to mention that Theo and Elle had started with a one-night stand, a very casual beginning, but that probably wasn't the point.

"How does this relate to getting mugged in Greece?"

"Oh, just that not wanting to cramp Rosie's game made me a little reckless. Going off on my own. It wasn't her fault, and she feels terribly guilty about it. Also, sometimes I just want me-time, and that kind of introversion makes it hard to make an impression on someone."

"Adeline, you are no less beautiful or attractive than Rosie. You have this quiet strength that shines off you. You're amazing with my daughter." *You're amazing with me.* "Everyone brings something different to the table so comparing yourself to a friend—or teammate—is never going to make you feel better. What you should be doing is focusing on your strengths."

"Wallflower. Undecided. DUFF."

"DUFF?"

"Designated Ugly Fat Friend. Except I know I'm not ugly or fat. Maybe nondescript and ... meaty?"

I wanted to shake her. "Right, because I fantasize about nondescript and meaty all the time."

She stiffened. Huh, big mouth strikes again. Seconds ticked by painfully slowly.

I broke the strained silence. "I shouldn't have said that."

"Maybe we should talk about it."

It was the last thing I wanted to talk about, but I

couldn't deny her, not after she'd been so honest about her feelings of inadequacy.

"What I did was inappropriate, Adeline."

"But you did it all the same, Lars. You thought about me while you ... jerked off."

Adeline

THE DARKNESS MADE IT EASIER, this shield of shadows. Or at least I thought so until the silence stretched taut enough to break, and I held my breath for the moment Lars would cut this discussion off at the knees.

He answered simply. "I did."

"Why?"

He sighed, his breath a warm puff against my lips. "Do I have to spell that out? Or how wrong it is?"

"Yes, and not sure I care."

His thumb grazed my cheek. "You are so fucking beautiful."

My heart clattered like a wild thing, and I didn't know how I managed to keep my response so cool. "So that answers one question."

His lids went to half-mast. "You're the fantasy of any guy, Adeline, but you're also my teammate's daughter, my kid's nanny, and at least a decade younger than me. All those things are outside the lines but also the forbidden is ..."

"Sexy," I murmured.

"Yeah. It is. You are. The taboo adds an extra element to

the fantasy. None of this can go any further than my fevered imagination."

My entire body rebelled at that conclusion. I placed a hand on his chest, splayed my fingers to take in more. I needed him to know that this wasn't one-sided, despite those earlier claims that my crush was history.

Because it clearly was not. I had it bad for Lars Nyquist.

"So you get to use me to get off and I can only ... listen?"

I don't think I had ever been so bold in my life. If I didn't take this chance, I might never have another one.

"You weren't supposed to listen."

"And you weren't supposed to be thinking of me while you touched yourself." Point to me.

Adeline Kershaw, Debate Champion, Senior Year, come on down.

"This can't happen." His palm curled around the back of my neck, in direct contradiction to his words.

"Doesn't seem fair." I placed my hand over his and pulled his palm to my lips, where I applied a kiss to his warm, rough skin. "You get to come. And I get shown the door."

I flicked my tongue over his thumb, watching and listening with satisfaction as his breath caught. Little kitten licks. *So bold, so naughty. Could I go further? Should I?*

I didn't need to. The leash on his self-control finally snapped.

"Christ, Adeline."

Holding my face, he dropped his lips to mine, covering my mouth forcefully. Nothing gentle about it, just pure, white-hot need. His beard scratched against my chin, the sensation sending shivers through me. I gasped and that parting of lips gave him the access he needed. He licked into my mouth, and I clutched at his upper arms to stay upright, even though I was lying down.

I felt him hard against my belly, then harder still as his hand cupped my ass and cleaved me close. I moved my leg around his thigh, cradling his body, drawing him closer to my aching core. The kiss streaked through me, lighting every neural pathway, setting my blood aflame. It was thunder and lightning and a storm of desire that I couldn't have imagined in my wildest dreams.

He groaned. Pistoned his hips. Thrust his erection, barely contained in boxer briefs, against my pussy. Embarrassing dampness flooded my panties, the heat of him driving me higher. His mouth continued to devour. I couldn't help my moan.

He stopped and drew back, hand still on my ass, the other holding my head still. In the half-light, he looked stunned. Incredulous.

"This. Can't. Happen."

The words fell like blows. After a kiss like that, how could he even think them never mind give them voice? Deep down, I knew there were all sorts of reasons why this shouldn't happen, but none seemed to take precedence over the one that pounded in my brain.

You don't do it for him.

Here I was throwing myself at him. Trying to seduce him, as if I knew what the hell I was doing. The guy was wrecked after the week from hell, forced to live with a stranger, and I was taking advantage. So he said my name while he came—big deal! He clearly wasn't interested in me as anything more than a convenient stand-in for a jerk-off.

I slipped his possessive grasp—or tried to. His hand was still clamped on my ass, his hardness imprinting on me, ensuring I would be useless for any other cock.

"Y-you're right. I don't know what I was thinking."

"Adeline," he rasped. "This isn't personal."

Of course it was. He was rejecting me because of who I was. Nothing more personal than that.

"You should go."

Still, he stayed, leaning his forehead against mine for a long moment, that was both lovely and excruciating. Finally, he whispered, "I'm sorry."

He slipped out of the bed like a thief and with one last check on Mabel, left the room. I lay back against the pillow, my forearm over my eyes. At least no more bad dreams would haunt me tonight.

You would have to fall asleep for that.

CHAPTER SIXTEEN

Adeline

MY ALARM WENT OFF and I lay there for a couple of minutes, willing myself awake. I had finally fallen into a fitful sleep around 5 a.m. The crib was empty, which meant Lars had come in while I slept.

Memory of the nightmare came rushing back. I could still smell the alcohol, the tobacco, the sweat, all mixed with the bougainvillea and sea air, but it seemed more muted now. Overlaying it was the feeling of strong arms, a warm-as-whiskey chuckle, and a deep-timbred voice soothing me through my distress. How sweet he was to stay and talk me through it.

Until I embarrassed myself by throwing myself at him.

I groaned, torn between pleasure at that kiss, the feel of him against my body, the taste of him filling my senses, and the humiliation of rejection.

As much as I would have liked to bury myself beneath

the covers and never come out, I had a job to do. I needed to remember that. I slipped out of bed and threw on a Rebels jersey and Lululemon lounge shorts, then after a quick side trip to the bathroom, headed toward the kitchen.

Should have stayed longer in front of the mirror. Not because I needed to make myself presentable or hide away from the consequences of last night, but because it would have been better to miss Lars Nyquist giving his daughter a rundown of a past game. I so did not need to hear that, not when it was so adorable my ovaries did a two-step. As I lingered in the hallway, Lars said something about "the idiot left winger from Nashville."

"You'd hate this asshole, Mabel. The guy hasn't got two brain cells to rub together, so I had no problem fooling him and getting that puck off his blade."

Mabel made a sound of agreement.

Lars chuckled. "Yeah, you know exactly what kind of bozo I'm talking about."

Bozo? Who called a guy on an opposing team a bozo?

The man who just realized he'd said "asshole" in front of his daughter and was trying to cover with a dorky word, perhaps? Gah, stop being so cute!

Okay, time to get this show on the road.

I entered the kitchen just in time to witness Lars picking up Mabel and settling her against his broad shoulder. I'd seen guys holding babies before. My dad, his brothers, even Lars. This should not have been any different, but I knew something now I didn't know then.

Fatherhood wasn't easy for Lars. While it was easy to assign his difficulty to some playboy-manchild attitude, it clearly went deeper. He didn't think he was capable. A man who could thread a puck through a tiny space, who could drill for days and practice for eternity—this guy thought he wasn't good enough for this new gig.

I had thought that as well at first. But what I saw now was Lars gazing at his baby daughter with an intensity that broke my chest wide open. The man was falling hook, line, and sinker for his little girl, and I wasn't sure that he even realized it yet.

With Mabel safely ensconced in his thick, muscled arms, he moved to the bottle warmer. Skillful hands tested the temperature of the formula while keeping the baby safe. Raising the bottle to her lips, he paused a moment and said, "You want it, baby girl?"

Yes, please.

My lusty thought must have manifested in this reality because Lars's attention was diverted from Mabel for a moment. His gaze darkened as it raked over me.

And "raked" was the right word here. The way he looked at me felt positively forbidden.

"Mine?"

Mine? I pressed a hand to my chest, a move that sent his nostrils into a flare.

"What do you mean?"

"Is that my jersey?"

Oh. "No, it's mine. Well, Dad's."

Color tagged his cheeks. "Sorry, I assumed you'd helped yourself. It would be okay if you had." He was fully focused on Mabel now.

"Wait, do you not believe me?"

"Of course I believe you."

He looked up, then down again at the sweatshirt. Was he so offended by it? When it wasn't even his! Before he could say another word, I did a quick pirouette to reveal KERSHAW in large letters on the back.

"My dad's." I turned back in time to catch his nostrils flaring, his gaze fixed not on the jersey but my bare legs.

"Right. I just—never mind." He placed the bottle down on the counter and deftly switched Mabel to his shoulder.

"Hold on, you need this." I grabbed a burp cloth and placed it on his shoulder. "Unless you want to smell like regurgitated milk all day."

"My favorite." Once burped, he set her back in the highchair. The awkwardness of a moment ago appeared to have passed. "I know it's only been ten days, but I feel like she's grown an inch or two. Am I wrong?"

"Babies are like weeds and this one is happy and healthy and enjoying her food." We had taken her to see the pediatrician yesterday morning and she was meeting all the necessary milestones. "You're doing good, Lars."

He looked pleased at the compliment. "And how are you doing after last night?"

"Oh, fine. How about you?"

His lips twitched at my turning it on its head. I'd felt him, hard between my thighs. I'd heard him crying out my name at the peak of desire. Sure, he had told me it could never happen, and while it was hard not to take that personally, I also understood that there was *something* between us.

"Not great, but I'll live."

That made me smile. We both had our crosses to bear.

He cleared his throat, drawing a line under it. "I'm going to the gym, assuming you're okay with staying with her for a while."

"Of course. In fact, I was planning to take her to a class at the Chicago School of Folk Music."

"Music? Isn't she kind of young for that?"

"They're never too young for music. This is a JiggleJams

session, geared toward infants. Tilly used to love it. Now Mom takes her to one for older kids."

"I really appreciate this extra stuff you're doing. I didn't expect anything beyond feeding and changing her."

"Stimulating all the baby's senses is important. She's going to be a super well-adjusted baby. Don't worry."

His mouth scrunched up, like he had something more to say. "You should talk to your parents about what happened in Greece."

"Maybe ... when the season is done."

His brows V'ed together dramatically. I was starting to love that look, all scowly concern. "When it's done? That's six months away, eight if we go all the way."

"Now's not a good time, Lars. This year is so important to Dad, and anything that upsets him will only throw him off his game." And that included dalliances with teammates. What was I thinking?

"You think he can't handle hearing his daughter was hurt?"

"I think it would start to live rent-free in his head." Sighing, I headed to the coffee maker. "If something happened to Mabel, don't you think it would mess with *your* mind?"

"Sure, but I'd also want to know."

I tried another tack. "You might not remember this, but about thirteen years ago, the Rebels were in the Finals. It was Game 4 and they were 2-1 down in the series against LA. Suddenly my father was scratched from the game."

"Yeah, some personal issue." He shrugged. "So?"

"That morning, I had a fight with Rosie because she told me she liked my brother Hatch and she planned to marry him, which made me so upset that I screamed at her."

He squinted. "How old were you?"

"Ten. Rosie and Hatch were twelve. I thought if they

got married I would lose them both, so I ran away. I planned to go to my great-gran's cottage in Saugatuck and I thought I could take my bike there. I was missing for nine hours."

Bafflement gave way to awareness. "Your dad missed the game because he was worried about you."

"Yep. He flew home to Chicago, and when he landed, I had already been found, hiding in Erik Jorgenson's basement. It's where he keeps his very large Christmas collection." Erik was probably the most holiday-obsessed person I knew. "I got tired on my bike about ten minutes in, so I hung out with a weird Swedish elf and cried into Erik's Jul-themed cushions."

"Remind me how the game went."

"They lost that one and the next. Finals done. My dad was crushed, and it was my fault."

"Jesus, Adeline." He stepped forward and took me in his arms, and I let him because I needed the comfort. I needed the assurance that I was making the right call here. "I get it, sweet thing, I do."

Sweet thing? He'd called me that last night in bed (oh, how I wished that reference was as smutty as it sounded). He still held me, and it felt glorious.

Until the glorious feeling was replaced by a new, exciting enhancement against my belly.

He didn't take a step back which would've been the sensible thing to do. Maybe neither of us was feeling sensible. My hand lay on his chest, my fingertips absorbing the heat and vitality of him.

I looked up into those denim-blue eyes and saw something like hunger there. Again, the denial came fast, my mind racing to cover what instinct knew to be true.

He placed a hand over mine, trapping my palm against

his chest. "What I said before, about the jersey. Thinking it was mine."

I'd wanted to pursue it but chickened out. Now he was bringing it up and I was dying to know what was going on in his brain.

"What about it?"

"I saw you standing there in that jersey and I didn't like it."

A pit of disappointment hollowed out my chest, and I pulled my hand away.

"As I said, it wasn't yours. I wouldn't go through your stuff like that no matter how cold I was." The words emerged rusty, pained.

"I hope that's not true." His voice was even raspier than mine. "If you were cold, Adeline, I would hope you'd use anything of mine to keep warm."

Warm me with your body. "You sounded annoyed when you thought the jersey was yours."

His hand squeezed mine. "Because I liked the idea a little too much."

Surely, he could hear the thump of my heart. "Me wearing your jersey?"

"Yes."

Too stunned to respond, all I could do was remain frozen, my go-to in moments of shock or change. But then something in me reared up, a need to fight back and reassert control. I was tired of letting things happen to me.

"What am I supposed to do with that information, Lars?"

"Absolutely nothing, Adeline. I had a knee-jerk reaction of annoyance and pride and lust on seeing you in the jersey of my team. You look so damn good in it that all I can think of is how much better you would look out of it. It's wrong and I'm owning it. I had a hard time reining in my feelings there, and I didn't want you to think you'd done anything wrong. You haven't. You're just being you. But you being you is not doing good things for my dick."

My cheeks heated. "It's not?"

"Well, my dick is having a grand old time whenever I think of you, but my mental health is suffering. Hopefully a bout in the gym will help me work out the toxins."

I pushed at his chest. "I'm a toxin now?"

"The sweetest kind."

"It's not easy for me, either," I said, a touch indignant.

"No? Good." A slight smile curved his lips.

At least he could see the funny side of it. I was having a hard time getting on that page.

I pulled my hand away. "This isn't helping, Lars. You can't tell me I'm not doing good things for your dick and then push me away. That's not fair."

He looked like I'd struck him. "You're right. It's not."

We stared at each other for what felt like forever until finally he said, "I'm gonna head to the gym now."

With a brisk nod, I attended to Mabel—my job—instead of watching him leave the kitchen.

CHAPTER SEVENTEEN

Lars

GOING to the gym was the best idea I could have had.

Okay, unwrapping Adeline from her dad's jersey was the best idea, but as I didn't have that as an option, the gym was the next best thing.

I did everything I could to push thoughts of her away. Treadmill, elliptical, weights, all of it helped keep images of her sweet mouth on the down low for a few peaceful moments. Until Theo arrived and my efforts dissolved in the face of that all-too-familiar smile.

Was I forever doomed to this hell? One look at my captain and I think of his gorgeous daughter and all the wicked things I want to do to her? The sooner I could hire an official nanny, the better. Adeline would be gone, back to living with her parents. I would probably have to stop going to the Kershaws for dinner because there was no way I could avoid looking at her and keep my dirty thoughts to myself. Not after that kiss. Not after the feel of her in my arms.

Not after she put me in my place.

She had me dead to rights. I couldn't joke around with her, talking about my dick and her impact on it. Ownership of my shit was all well and good, but honesty wasn't always the best policy, not when I could never follow through.

I flexed my hands, trying to stretch and eliminate the muscle memory that had developed since holding her. Since touching myself with Adeline as the fuel to my fantasy. My cock twitched and I thanked the gods for my loose sweatpants.

"You okay?" Theo asked from the treadmill beside me.

"Yeah, why wouldn't I be?"

"Your life's upside down and you probably haven't been laid in a while because you're busy with a baby and worried about what'll happen the next time you ejaculate. Will it result in a baby brother or sister for little Mabel?" Theo shook his head, grinning like a total dick. "I get it. With Olympic swimmers like that, you start second-guessing yourself."

Kershaw wasn't far off the mark. I was cock shy, but that was the least of my problems.

Right now, the thought of sex with anyone other than Adeline repulsed me. I wanted her and for now, I was going to keep it in my pants, at least until she was out of my house, and my life took on more semblance of normal. If anything, her presence was a good way to prevent more mistakes of the conception variety.

"Sex is the last thing on my mind."

"Already putting your dick in cryofreeze, NyQuil?"

That delightful query came courtesy of Peyton Bell.

Before I could respond, Boden weighed in. "Cryofreeze

implies he's going to be ready for action at some unspecified time in the distant future."

"True. Once you have kids, your dick never gets *any* action again," Bell said with the authority of a guy who had experienced nothing in his short twenty-three years on this earth.

Jacobs put down one of the 5k hand weights and picked up an 8k. "Until your wife says she wants another kid, which I blame on Nyquist and his cute baby. Then suddenly she's all over you."

"So what I'm hearing is that my cute kid is actually responsible for you finally getting some. You're welcome."

Theo pointed at Jacobs. "You need to send him flowers, Jakey."

"Dear NyQuil, thanks for jumpstarting my sex life," Bell said, like he was writing in his tween journal. "Love, my Dick."

Everyone cracked up, even Jacobs.

"I think you're all forgetting something." I jerked a thumb at our captain. "This guy thought his child-rearing days were over and look what happened. Another surprise in his stocking." Theo and Elle had found out they were pregnant with Tilly around the time of a Rebels holiday party. "There's hope for us all."

Theo chuckled. "Yep. My sex life is stellar, even after five kids. So let's not give up on NyQuil just yet, even if he is a little worried about getting ambushed in the Empty Net with another of my niblings."

"The trainer is ready for you, Theo," someone called out from the gym entrance.

He turned off the machine. "Time to have them duct tape it altogether."

"You're going to outplay us all, old man."

I couldn't imagine playing at his age, but then I didn't have much to play for. Kershaw had his family, his son on the team, this entire world he'd built with him at the center of it. He could happily retire and enjoy the fruits of that, but he always had one more goal. One more reason to strive. As role models went, he was A-plus.

Would Mabel ever see me as a role model? Look at her genetics. I tried to go against the grain of mine, but I'd yet to be tested as a father. Would I be a dick when she started talking back? Would I lose my temper and take it out on her? Would I turn into Sven?

As much as I hated the idea of Vicki having custody, I still felt it would be better for Mabel. Growing up Nyquist was no picnic and no daughter of mine deserved the legacy of my family.

I was so consumed by all this negativity that I didn't notice Kershaw's replacement on the treadmill: MacFarlane.

"How's it going, Narquist?"

"What did you say?"

"Just a fun new nickname. Can't choose your own, y'know." He pressed a button on the treadmill. "Narquist."

Narquist. Narc. Got it.

My part in Sven's ban from the league wasn't a secret. Seventeen years ago, the draft was approaching, and I was about to be named, when I got a call from the Commissioner's office.

Are you betting on professional hockey games?

My world imploded. *No. Not me, sir. It must be some mistake.*

I knew what they were thinking: like father, like son.

Sven Nyquist had been suspended once, six years

before, when he was caught gambling. Another infraction and he'd be out of the league altogether.

I assumed it was an admin error or someone with a beef against my dad. He'd made a lot of enemies over the years and his lack of remorse around being caught for gambling had only made him more.

I immediately called him. "Dad, I just heard from the Commissioner's office."

Sven made a noise in his throat. "What does that asshole want?"

Close to forty, my dad was on his last legs in the NHL, holding on for dear life after a series of bad investments had threatened the security of his retirement. He drank too much and barely put in the effort anymore, but he had two years left on his contract with the Detroit Motors, and that team was in the second round of the playoffs. Sven had won the Cup once in his first year out and had flirted with a Finals run a couple times since. This was his last year. His final shot at going out in a blaze of glory.

"He says there's an investigation into me. For wagering."

My father remained silent, and that's when I knew.

"What did you do?"

Another cough preceded too long of a pause. "Me? Nothing."

"You did something. You—*Dad, what did you do?*"

"It's nothing. It'll blow over."

"I'm about to be drafted." It had been my dream from the first day I set foot on the ice. Every beating, every harsh word, every tortured moment as Sven Nyquist's son, I could forgive it all if I made it to the pros. Hockey was the scaffolding for the relationship with my father, the only thing we had in common. I'd been so ashamed when he was suspended before, but we got through it.

Now, this.

"Dad, did you place a bet on a game?"

He chuckled. "Well, *I* didn't."

Fuck. I hung up.

During the investigation, I wasn't allowed to take my spot in the draft. By then they'd figured out my father had placed bets in my name, and I was innocent, but the powers that be insisted the optics weren't good and I should wait until it all blew over. Sven was kicked out of the league one game before the Motors won the Eastern Conference. My father never made it to the Finals that year, or any year after. Banned for life.

The next year I signed a contract with Boston. But my father's stink followed me around for years.

He never forgave me for not taking the fall for him. He claimed that if I'd pretended those bets were mine, I would have gotten "a slap on the wrist." My career would recover. Instead, he had to suffer the ignominy of a ban in his twilight years, slinking off into the sunset in shame instead of full throttle in victory. Detroit won the Cup that year but he wasn't allowed to receive a championship ring.

I never spoke to him again. Seventeen years of silence. Not even when he got emphysema or cancer; he co-existed with one disease and was fighting the other when he snorted a line of coke, slapped pedal to the metal, and crashed into a tree.

These days, there was always some dick who thought it amusing to remind me of my roots. Of the fact I "sold" Sven out because I wouldn't take the rap for him. Sins of the father and all that shit.

Rowan MacFarlane had been gunning for my spot as Kershaw's partner since he arrived. He was hoping I'd blow up at him and give him an opening, but no way in hell was I surrendering my spot in Theo's last season. We were the dream team on defense, and I intended it to stay that way.

"You have something to say to me, MacFarlane, say it."

"Me? Nah, just messin' with ya. You're kind of prickly, so I'm guessing you're not getting much sleep. Your kid's a cutie, though. Saw her the other day when Adeline stopped by."

Since when was MacFarlane on a first-name basis with my nanny?

"Don't look at my ... kid."

"So touchy." MacFarlane grinned while I pushed the incline on the treadmill higher.

Adeline

THE CHICAGO SCHOOL OF FOLK MUSIC had recently opened a new branch in Evanston, much more convenient for one of their JiggleJams sessions, aimed at infants and toddlers past six months. Tilly had loved these as she was becoming more mobile. The combination of music, dancing—well, wiggling—and socializing was a great way to entertain while providing networking options for the parents.

I got the impression that most of the adults were parents and not paid caregivers. It would have been nice to have Lars here when I wasn't mad at him, but until then, I was determined to enjoy the sight of Mabel wriggling about on the large Turkish rug with several other kids her age.

A heavily pregnant Miss Emmy led the group in a

rousing rendition of *Row Row Row Your Boat* on a lovely Epiphone Masterbilt Texan guitar. The older kids joined in while the wigglers crawled, planked, and rolled their way through it.

"Now isn't she the cutest," the woman next to me said after the song had ended. "What's her name?"

"This tiny dancer is Mabel."

A crawling Mabel thrust out her hand at the mention of her name, which caused her to lose her balance and fall on the side of her face. Before I could intervene, she'd repositioned her palm on the rug for support and resumed her headbutting attack on a nearby child. A future hockey player, for sure.

"She's a clever girl," my neighbor observed. "Already knows the charmers."

I assumed she was referring to the Little Lord Fauntleroy lookalike, currently absorbing Mabel's assault with a solemn grace beyond his months. "Is he yours?"

The woman smiled proudly. "Yes, that's Tristan. Which preschool is yours signed up for?"

"Oh, none yet." Tilly had just started at Goddard in Riverbrook, and now that I thought of it, Mom and Dad had signed her up as soon as she was born. Another thing I should tell Lars, though it was hard to plan that far ahead when the mother's whereabouts were a mystery. "We're keeping our options open."

The woman regarded me with a suspicious smile before scooping up her little princeling. Best not to contaminate him with Mabel's sorry lack of ambition.

Miss Emmy launched into *The Wheels on the Bus*, while my mind strayed to that kiss and Lars's reaction.

He was right. Nothing could happen between us. But to have him tell me I was a sweet toxin that he needed to work out of his system through exercise, that I was bad for *his* mental health—I was all for honesty but sometimes there was *too* honest.

I took out my phone and sent a text.

If Lars was so determined to work me out of his system, then I needed to do the same.

IT WASN'T until I witnessed Lars at the Kershaw dinner table that I finally understood how embedded he'd become in my family's life. It could have been the glow attached to Mabel that had everyone in a good mood, but there was more to it. Aurora presented him with a martini before anyone else, the infamous Scandi Noir. My mom made sure he had a serving of chicken parm larger than Wisconsin, even bigger than the one she gave her husband. Meanwhile, Dad and Lars were deep in a discussion about some prank Peyton Bell had pulled on one of the other rookies (a jock strap took a starring role) and my dad had spent the entire time chuckling away at Lars's minimalist, dry commentary. Another uber-fan.

Even Tilly loved him. She insisted she sit on Duckman's lap after dinner, a vacant spot because Mabel was spending all her time being shuttled between Aurora, my mom, and my dad. (My father's comment that maybe he and Mom should give parenthood another shot, get it right this time, earned an apt glare from the woman herself.)

The only person who wasn't fully on board the Lars Fanclub Train was Hatch. My brother was friendly enough, but he also spent most of dinner watching me to see if I was watching Lars. After narrowing my eyes at him for the third time, he finally shrugged and gave up the surveillance.

Don't worry, bro. Lars Nyquist is no longer on my radar.

What a relief to be free of it. Seeing Lars so close to everyone, especially my dad, reminded me of the bullet I'd dodged. If something more than a kiss had happened between us, there would be hell to pay. My father might be the best man I know, but he would go ballistic if he knew I'd messed around with a teammate and friend.

The moment of madness had passed. Hooray for sanity!

After dinner, Tilly abandoned her new fave and found me.

"I want a song!"

"You do? Well, maybe H-man can sing for you."

Tilly shook her head in disgust. "Hatch is a terrrrrible singer!"

Hatch grinned. "She's got my number."

My guitar appeared courtesy of my father. It looked a little different. Shinier.

"You got it restrung for me?"

"Sure I did. Oiled, too. You've been so busy, stepping up and helping us all out." He meant Lars, and I didn't dare look in his direction. "This is the least I could do."

"Thanks, Dad. I really appreciate it."

Hatch scooped up a giggling Tilly and set her in his lap on the sofa beside me. "What song do you want, Tilly-Billy?" he asked.

Don't say it. "Duckman!"

Out of the corner of my eye, I saw Lars turn his head. The faint scent of linseed oil, used to condition the guitar, tickled my nostrils.

"I only have one verse for that one."

"You wrote a song about Lars?" Aurora asked, eying me over her martini glass. Hatch was staring, too, so I busied myself with finding a guitar pick in my pocket.

"Just a throwaway ditty. A couple of lines because Tilly is *so* obsessed." Unable to avoid him any longer, I made a face at Lars to make it clear the obsession was Tilly's and Tilly's alone.

His raspy chuckle poured water and sunlight on the withering roots of my crush.

"I want the Duckman song!"

"Okay, you got it." Tilly lay her head against Hatch's chest, waiting patiently for me to start. "Remember it's the *Twinkle Twinkle Little Star* tune."

I strummed a C chord, enjoying the resonant sound produced by the new strings.

"Duckman, Duckman, on the ice ... Skating faster than the ... mice." Everyone chuckled at that.

"With your silly beard so ..."

"Thick," Tilly chimed in.

"How you move about so ..."

My clever girl had no problem recalling the rhyme. "Quick!"

I didn't dare look at Lars, lest he think songs about his beard and speed might be further evidence of my why-won't-you-die-already crush.

"Duckmaaaan ..."

I strummed and waited until Tilly joined in, "Duckmaaaan!"

"On the ice," I continued. "Skating faster than the ..."

I sustained that final C chord, until Tilly and the rest of the room yelled, "Mice!"

We all exploded in laughter, but of course I was interested in only one person's reaction.

Which was why I avoided looking at him and instead launched into a song about Eggsbee's farts.

CHAPTER EIGHTEEN

Adeline

ONE LAST CHECK in the mirror, though I wasn't sure what good it would do. I looked tired, but that was the lot of the nanny.

A text came in from Rosie.

> You ready for some action?

ME

> No action. This is just a getting to know you kind of thing.

ROSIE

> You kidding? Rowan MacFarlane has the hots for you! When's the last time you got any?

Two days ago. Did not end well. Of course I couldn't tell Rosie. She'd let me have it for being a total fool.

ROSIE

Because I know when. It was that British
guy at the hostel in Bangkok. And
MacFarlane is hotter than him!

My recollection was that the Brit and his friend had practically duked it out over Rosie and I was left with the loser. He'd fallen asleep before anything memorable happened, leaving me relieved and with plenty of time to concoct a story for my friend. *All good, great orgasms!* Her concern for my sexual health was a tad intense.

ME

Just a date. Don't pressure me. And I'm
wearing my granny panties, so nothing can
happen.

ROSIE

Okay. Okay. I just want you to be happy.
And the sooner you get out there, the
quicker that'll happen.

This morning, we'd interviewed two more candidates for the nanny position. Neither came up to Lars's lofty standards—one was too nervous, the other too confident—which meant I was on the hook for this temp gig for even longer. If I was to continue working for Lars, I needed to start looking elsewhere for company of the male variety, hence my reaching out to Rowan. I was going into this date with high expectations of success. After all, I wasn't completely hideous. Lars Nyquist had used me as spank bank material once.

Armed with the confidence that knowledge gave me and ignoring the awkward aftermath, I headed downstairs. Outside the living room, I listened to Lars chatting with

Mabel. As usual he was having deep conversations with her about hockey, which made me smile.

"See that guy? That's Dan Fogerty, a semi-decent center but he's not getting by me next Tuesday."

Pause, while he weighed Mabel's response.

"You think he's better than me? Not sure where you're getting your information. Because I could totally take that guy."

Another pause.

"My stats are way better than his, sweetheart. Adeline told me so. You don't know what you're talking about."

Super. Cute.

But then I remembered I was supposed to be mad at him, or at the very least neutral, because he had the common sense to stop that kiss but still thought it was a good idea to tell me how frustrated I made him. We weren't *that* friendly.

I called out, "See you later!" When I pulled the front door open, it shut again without my input. A large hand spread flat against the oak.

I could scent him in my nostrils and that smell—cedar, citrus, what-the-fuck-Lars—made me weak at the knees. Annoyed with his effect on me, I turned.

Another smoldering gaze from him, this time dragging erotically against my skin, my breasts, my belly, which responded predictably and flipped like a dying fish.

"You're all dressed up." He took a step back and got a better look. "Going out with Rosie?"

"No. A date."

The words should have meant nothing to him. After all, he'd made his position clear.

This. Can't. Happen.

I knew where I stood, but right now my standing felt shaky, both metaphorically and literally.

"Who?" The word was a graveled utterance, more beast than man.

"It's just casual."

"Not what I asked."

This was none of his business. "I need to go."

I tried the door again, but didn't get far. Lars's many-muscled arm stretched over my head, keeping it shut and my body trapped.

"Who are you going on a date with?" His mouth was a slash. If I'd had my wits about me, I'd have said he was angry.

"You made it clear this wasn't your concern."

His eyes flashed. "That's different."

"Is it? You're not interested so I'm not going to wait around for you to become interested, Lars."

His voice was low, dangerous. "So your first response is to call up some guy and go on a date?"

"He already asked, and I figured why not? I haven't done anything fun since I got back from my travels." *Listening to you jerk off doesn't count.* "And I want to stop being such a ... coward."

He took a step back, hands on trim hips. "Because of what happened in Greece? Hell, you don't need to go on a date to prove your bravery, Adeline. You're here, living your life, saying fuck you to that Greek asshole. You were *never* a coward."

The words stopped me cold. Maybe he was right, but I still needed to test myself in the fires of real life. Mostly, I wanted out of here, away from that soulful stare and macho swagger. I almost asked, "Am I free to leave?" when the doorbell rang.

Shit.

I had told Rowan I'd meet him at the end of the driveway. Lars was already moving to the door, and I had no choice but to step aside. Nervously, I watched as his expression went from concerned to confusion.

"MacFarlane?"

"I'm here for Adeline."

"You're here for—" As Lars turned his head my way, I pulled the door open, so I didn't look like a complete weirdo, hiding away.

"Hi, Rowan."

"Hey, Adeline." Rowan smiled, then took a quick look over me. "You look gorgeous."

"Oh, thanks." I could feel my cheeks getting hot. "That's kind of you. Can you hold on a sec?"

Avoiding Lars seemed like the best option, which I managed by popping in to say goodbye to his daughter. Mabel was lying on her tummy in the octagon, doing dry laps. She had her arms outstretched, planking like a boss.

I leaned over and gave her a kiss on the top of her head. "Be good, Mabel. Look after your pop for me."

I turned to find Lars staring at me—or rather my ass. My bend over the bars of the playpen had exposed the backs of my thighs. The skirt of this dress was a little shorter than I was used to, but Rosie had claimed it made my tits look great.

Lars's lip curl indicated distinct disagreement. Apparently flesh offended him.

"I left a couple of bottles in the fridge. Just warm them to—"

"I know," he gutted out. "It's the one thing I *do* know how to do."

Rowan had stepped inside and was watching the dynamic between us with interest.

"Night in with the kid, Nyquist? Sounds like a blast." He smirked, and I had to fight my urge to say, "Watch your mouth, dick!"

Not a great way to start a date.

"Have a good night," I murmured as I walked past Lars.

"Adeline." I turned back to face him. "Call me if you need anything. And I mean *anything*."

"I won't." I said it with as much cheer as possible. The last thing I needed was Lars Nyquist's ghost on my date.

I LOOKED AROUND, a little surprised that Rowan had taken me to Viper, a famous nightclub in downtown Chicago. It was barely eight in the evening.

"They do really good sliders," he said.

Heading to a club for its cuisine was unexpected, but then so far it had been one awkward moment after another.

Once in Rowan's car, he took a selfie, or an "ussie" as Rosie called it, a term I despised because it was so stupid. He hadn't liked the first shot nor the second, but the third time was the charm. (*"You don't look like you've been taken hostage in that one."*)

"You're not going to post that, are you?" Asked because he then spent a few moments fixing the contrast and adding a filter. We hadn't even left Lars's driveway.

"You ashamed to be hanging with me?"

"No, not at all. But we've only just met." My social interactions with dates tended toward the old-fashioned. Didn't anyone want to start slow?

He smiled. "Sure, we can hold off on the PDA."

Not sure an ussie qualified as PDA, but I let it pass. As we headed to downtown Chicago, Rowan had plenty of questions about the setup with Lars.

"You live there?"

"It makes the most sense to keep things consistent for Mabel."

"The old man can't be dealing with this baby shit all that well."

My hackles spiked. *Old man? He's only thirteen years older than me.* Through gritted teeth, I said, "He's doing great. An absolute natural."

"The guy looked terrified when that chick dropped the kid in his lap. Wrap it before you tap it, that's what I say."

"Well, condoms have an 11 to 16% failure rate, so sometimes it can't be helped."

Rowan scoffed. "Yeah, but there are always ways to handle that after the fact. And this chick didn't even want the baby if she's dumping it on Nyquist."

It's really none of your business. I was about to open my mouth to say so, but we'd arrived at the club and Rowan was already handing his keys to the valet.

Once seated, a very attractive brunette wearing a backless halter top and a skirt that stopped just short of her vagina stopped by.

"Hi, I'm Candi. Want to hear about our slider de jour?" The smirk said double entendre, the arched eyebrow said there's more where that came from.

Rowan grinned while giving her the thrice over. It was as if he'd forgotten he was on a date. "Sure, tell me all about it."

She launched into a recitation of the slider de jour— lamb merguez with a slice of brie. It sounded pretty good, actually, but I was too nervous to eat.

"You want something, babe?" Rowan asked.

Babe. Shudder. "I'll just have a glass of Prosecco please."

Rowan put in four orders of sliders (*they're so small!*) and an Ardbeg single malt. Guess I was taking a taxi home.

"Your family must be thrilled to have you back."

"I think so. They're a busy lot so I haven't seen as much of them as I'd like."

"You close to Hatch?"

"Very." Though not as much as before. Hatch seemed moodier these days, not the fun-loving guy I remembered. Playing on the same team as Theo Kershaw had to be tough. "What about you guys?"

"Kershaw Junior? Sure, we're not rivals for the same lines, so we get along fine. Your dad's awesome, too. Not sure partnering with Nyquist is best for the team, though."

Alarm bells went off in my head. Yet another dig at Lars.

"But you're on the same team, right? Isn't it one for all and all for one?"

He looked at me like I didn't get it. Maybe I didn't. I wasn't a player.

Candi came back with the drinks and Rowan asked her if she'd take our photo. As she fiddled with the phone, he slid over to my side of the booth and put his arm around me.

"Let's make it a good one."

Unlike the others was the implication. I raised my glass because he raised his and I tried not to recoil at the way he pressed his body close to mine. He was attractive, supposedly interested in me, and most importantly, not my dad's closest friend. I should be enjoying myself.

We spent the next few minutes chatting about Chicago and favorite places to eat. All of his were clubs which, again, weird. I wasn't very good at keeping the conversation going but Rowan didn't seem to mind. He was a multitasker: drinking, eating, chatting, texting. I wasn't even all that annoyed at his phone etiquette. It just confirmed what I suspected: I wasn't interesting enough to date.

I excused myself to go to the bathroom and called Rosie.

"Oh, this can't be good."

She knew me so well. "Just checking in."

"Is it truly going terribly or are you trying to tank it?"

"I'm not sure we have any chemistry." Not like I had with a certain someone. "And he's asking tons of questions about my dad and Lars. It's weird." It reminded me of guys I dated in college who were only interested in me when they discovered my last name.

"He's asking you those things because that's what you have in common. Have you told him anything about yourself? That you like music? Art? Books? Hockey stats?"

"He hasn't asked."

Rosie sighed. "Take charge of the conversation. Offer things about yourself and see if he responds." She said something to someone in her orbit, then returned to me. "Go back out there and sparkle."

Sparkle. That was Rosie's approach to everything. It was easy to sparkle when you were as gifted and interesting as my friend. I didn't have the effervescence gene.

"Okay, I'll try."

I checked my reflection but unfortunately, I hadn't become more desirable in the last five minutes. My phone buzzed with a call from Lars. I answered immediately, worried about Mabel.

"Is everything okay?"

"That's what I'm calling to ask you."

I rolled my eyes. "It's fine. We're at some club." I added, "Having dinner."

"Dinner at the club. Sounds great."

I was allowed to think that, not him. "What would you know? When's the last time you went on a date? Oh, that's right, you just bang them in bar bathrooms. So romantic."

I sounded unbelievably jealous. There was a pause, then Lars spoke again. "I just wanted to be sure you were safe. That you ... *felt* safe."

Never mind safe, I now felt guilty. And stupid. Lars was just looking out for me, in a fatherly way.

"Yes. I'm—I'm fine. Go enjoy your night with Mabel." I hung up before he could speak again.

When I returned the booth was empty, but Rowan's phone was on the table and was blowing up with texts.

BODEN

Kershaw is gonna kill you, man. Messin' with his sister like that.

JONNO

She looks miserable with you, dawg. You need to treat her right.

MACKER

How far you gonna take this, dude?

Take what? Alarm streaked through me. What was going on here?

I looked up and there he was, leaning against the bar, flirting with the server. He spotted me, gave a bright smile, and headed back over.

"Hey, we good?"

"Yeah, great!" It sounded fake. "How about we get another round of drinks in?"

That surprised him. "Uh, yeah. Why not?"

CHAPTER NINETEEN

Lars

MABEL WAS IRRITABLE. I knew exactly how she felt.

Rowan MacFarlane showing up at my house to take Adeline on a date had to be the most outrageous example of trolling I'd ever seen. And I'd been a pro hockey player for sixteen years. Trolling was our currency.

But this asshole? It felt like he was trying to fuck with *me*, with his smirk and his hand on Adeline's back. And the way Adeline had looked at me as she left, like I was not worthy of an opinion here.

So what if she was right? I'd told her kissing her was a bad idea. I still believed that, but unfortunately this bad idea had felt so damn good I was getting hard just thinking about it. The way she'd felt in my arms, that supple strength and soft power. Her lips, her tits, the feel of her ass in my hands, the way my cock notched into the cradle of her body. All of it perfect.

And perfectly wrong.

I didn't need to count the ways, but I did it anyway because the reminders were the only things maintaining the thin veil of never between us.

Her youth.

Her father.

Her employment.

Her crush.

That was all before we factored in my unsuitability for a woman of that quality. Adeline was young and fresh and just starting her life. I was none of those things, not to mention I had a baby to consider. Leaning on Adeline, using her as a crutch right now was bad enough. Adding sex to the mix would not make the path any clearer.

I shouldn't have called. But I had to check in on her, make sure she was safe.

"Alright, Mabel, what are we going to do to entertain ourselves?"

There was a game tonight between Boston and Denver, but that was entertainment for me, not Mabel, so I switched over to the Disney channel and picked the first movie with a princess on the thumbnail.

Mabel was doing her crawling-but-going-nowhere thing, so I gave her a little boost, closer to the bars of her play-cage. The bright colors on the screen held her in thrall for all of ten seconds, then she flapped her arms like she was trying to fly. Back to the screen as the princess belted out something. Kind of catchy, to be honest.

I checked the score of the game and considered calling O'Malley or Jacobs, or even Theo to see if they wanted to hang. Only I wasn't good company. Neither did I want to explain to Theo why Adeline wasn't here.

Oh, haven't you heard? She's dating MacFarlane. Yeah, that MacFarlane.

Dinner at the club—what a joke. Where would I take Adeline on a date? A nice, romantic restaurant where we could be given privacy in a dark, candlelit corner. Where no one would know us. (*Because what you'd be doing was all wrong, asshole.*) I didn't know much about fancy food, but Adeline probably did. She'd traveled the world, and I bet she had a shit-ton more savvy than me who went nowhere and knew nothing.

Was she regaling MacFarlane with stories of her travels? I loved hearing the brief mentions, her excitement. I loved listening to her soft voice, especially when she sang to Tilly and Mabel. We hadn't discussed the fact she wrote a song about me to entertain her sister. She'd seemed embarrassed about it, so I let it slide. But now I was thinking, *she wrote a song about me! And my beard!*

I rubbed it now, thinking about abrading Adeline's thighs with my stubble-rough jaw, my beard soaked from her liquid pleasure. My chest felt itchy. I scratched but it was no good because this itch was under my skin. Inside my chest.

MacFarlane was always posting shit on Instagram. They'd left only an hour ago, so he probably hadn't had a chance to upload pics, or maybe he'd have some common sense and keep it on the down low. Did the guy really want to be messing about with his captain's daughter?

If I couldn't, then why should he?

There would be hell to pay if he hurt Adeline. I knew this how? Because I'd thought through every scenario involving this woman for myself and come up with the only conclusion that made sense: hurt her and die.

That was what Theo would think.

Except I needed to keep my paternal thinking for my own daughter, who right now was making noises that might be interpreted as singing along to Disney.

I resisted checking out my teammate's social media and focused on being in the moment with my daughter. She'd abandoned the movie and now she was rolling around on her back, waving her hands in the air. One of her booties had somehow landed on the other side of the pen, so I had no choice but to take possession of her baby foot and give it a squeeze.

Oh, she liked that! I tried to see Vicki in her smile, but all I saw was my mom. I hadn't thought about her in years. Sven had removed all trace of feeling I had for her, but Mabel's smile brought it rushing back.

She couldn't help dying and leaving me in Sven's care, but I sure wouldn't have wished a six-year-old kid on a gruff asshole like Sven Nyquist. Barely twenty when I was born, he hadn't matured much by the time he had to take me on full-time. Now here I was, in my father's shoes, forced to take on a kid I barely knew. But I could do better.

The muddle of emotions swirling around in my head hacked me off. My mom, Sven, Mabel, Adeline. I flicked a glance to my phone, resisted the impulse, and picked up the remote instead. Hockey would be the perfect distraction right now.

Boston was 2-zip up in the second period. I tried to get into it, but even a goal to narrow the deficit and the prospect of a Denver comeback couldn't elevate my mood. It wouldn't hurt to check my Instagram account, see if anyone was giving me shit about Mabel.

There was a new reel on there. Adeline must have added it after I'd given her access and told her to go crazy. A fun video of Kershaw and me, it showcased some of our best moves over the last couple of years, and even a few times we messed up but were laughing about it afterwards. The video was intercut with stats and details on our records. People loved it.

D'Legends!

Best defense in the game!

Superglutes and Superdad. (I laughed out loud at that one.)

I would never have expected a charm offensive like this to work, but Adeline really knew what she was doing. More interesting was that it was posted this afternoon after I had pissed her off. She didn't have to do this nice thing, yet she had because she was a good person.

In related news, I was a total dick, who still needed to know what MacFarlane was up to. Yep, he'd gone ahead and posted on Insta. The club, the drinks, the mini-burgers. One of Adeline with his arm around her. Her expression was deer in the headlights as she raised a flute to the camera. She didn't look happy, which I knew intimately because she had looked happy a couple of nights ago when I kissed her. She had looked abandoned and wanton and so damn needy that my entire body tensed with the pleasure of that memory. Then she'd looked scorned or maybe, scornful of my inability to take it any further. She had to know what a mistake it was.

But this thing with MacFarlane? That would be an even bigger one.

Adeline

"SO ROSIE just shoved him in the dumpster. It was absolutely priceless."

Rowan laughed his head off. "She seems like a cool chick."

"She is."

We were an hour in, and Rowan was close to hammered, getting his wrist rehab in with every raise of a glass. He'd given up any pretense of romantic or sexual interest in me, instead reserving his dubious charm for the servers who had started on the bottle service. We'd also acquired a few fans who loved that Rowan MacFarlane was here, drinking in their orbit.

"So what's the deal here?" I tapped his phone.

"What?" He looked a little worse for wear, but suddenly alert to my query.

"Boden just texted."

He looked down at his phone and Noah Boden's message: *Man, Kershaw is pissed. He called asking where you took his sister.*

"Why's my brother pissed?"

"He doesn't want you to date me. Of course it makes him mad."

"But you don't want to date me, either, do you, Rowan?"

His gaze sharpened. "I asked you out."

"Yeah, but not because you're interested in me. This is about Lars, right?"

He scowled at the mention of his teammate, then quickly adjusted. "Aw, Addy, don't be like that."

I had checked Rowan's profile on Instagram. He'd posted several pictures of us, cropping them to make us look close and personal. The hashtags were the usual junk: #clublife #hockey #chicagorebels but there was also one called #hockeyhos and another tagging #larsnyquist.

So, not a real date.

And all because no one saw me for me. I was Theo Kershaw's daughter, Hatch Kershaw's sister, Lars Nyquist's nanny. Even Rosie's friend.

"Tell the truth, Rowan. You have a beef with Lars, right? And this 'date' is some way to make him upset, so he'll what? Screw up and you get your shot on the ice?"

He made a face. "C'mon, Addy. So you have a crush on Nyquist. I heard you talking to Tara about it. This way we kill two birds—you make him jealous, and I make him mad. I saw how he was when I showed up."

"I don't want to—look, there's no point in talking to you about this. You clearly have an agenda. And I don't like playing games." I stood, fighting back tears. Rowan's actions might have been intended to make Lars mad, but they only served to earn my fury. Enough to pick up my glass of Prosecco and throw it in his face.

Which I did. "And you don't get to call me Addy."

THIRTY MINUTES LATER, I exited the Viper dance floor and ran into Candi again.

Her face lit up. "Another water or are you ready to hit the hard stuff?"

I grinned at her, feeling a touch breathless. "Still with the water." I'd already given her a twenty to keep me hydrated, but that was chicken feed for a server of her caliber, so I fished out another.

She shook her head as she passed the water glass over. "Nope. After the way you sorted out that slimeball, I can happily say your money is no good here."

Rowan appeared to have recovered from a glass of bubbly

to the face just fine. Right now, he was surrounded by an entourage more to his taste. Adoring women, braying men.

"Is it weird that I stayed?" I asked Candi.

"No. Though most women would be holed up in the bathroom sobbing instead of getting down solo on the dance floor—hello, what do we have here?"

I turned to where her avid gaze was drawn, then blinked to focus my own. But it didn't make a difference because the strangest image was still in my sightline.

Lars Nyquist in the club.

And he was heading this way.

As if that wasn't shocking enough, something else snagged my attention. In his hand, at knee level, he carried a large object. I could barely make it out, but then the crowd parted, and I understood.

The car seat—and it was occupied.

Lars had brought Mabel to a nightclub!

I slid a look to Candi, who *had* to have seen it all. Her mouth had fallen open. I was happy to provide this new experience for her.

He stopped a foot away. His eyes searched my face, followed by a quick glance over my body. To confirm I wasn't hurt? Or something else?

He came here for me.

"You okay?"

"Of course I am."

"You didn't look okay in those photos."

Lars had tracked me down through Rowan MacFarlane's social media?

Rather than respond to that, I moved my attention south. "You brought Mabel."

"Couldn't leave her on her own. At least not yet." He

grinned and my heart fluttered dangerously. "Besides, she should see what hockey players do in their spare time."

Mabel's eyes were dancing, the loud music and vibrant lighting keeping her interest.

"I think she likes it." I swiped at a tear.

"Hey now." He placed Mabel down on the floor between us, protecting her from the crowd. Protecting me. "What's going on?"

"I can't believe you're here." I added, "With Mabel," so it was clear *that* was the shocking part of it all, though it wasn't. I was having a miserable time, and Lars had come to fetch me home.

Somehow this man knew I needed him.

I turned to Candi and gave her my last twenty dollars. "Thank you for looking out for me."

"Sure, girl." She leaned in and whispered, "Is this your guy?"

"My boss." *Also my dad's teammate, closest friend, and the guy I'm falling hopelessly in love with.* "I'm Mabel's nanny."

Candi nodded slowly. "Right. Your boss. With the baby. At the club."

She was right. None of this made much sense.

"You ready?" Lars fixed me with another trademark intense stare, to which I could only nod. We threaded our way through the crowd and when we reached the exit, Lars handed a ticket to the valet.

"You want to tell me what happened?"

"Just mismatched expectations."

He faced me, his eyes fiery suns. "Meaning?"

"I thought it was a date, and he obviously didn't. He just wanted to use me to piss you off."

Lars didn't look surprised, which felt even worse. "He hurt you."

"Just my pride. I can patch that up no problem."

He stared so hard I had to look away in embarrassment. Here I was, being rescued from a fake/revenge date by the guy I was falling for and who had told me it would never happen, in this lifetime or the next.

The valet pulled the car around and I stood by helplessly while Lars affixed the car seat in place, expertly working the loops of the seat belt and securing it. Only two weeks ago he barely knew what a car seat was; now he was an adept handler of babies and distressed women alike.

He closed the back seat door and opened the passenger one. "Get in."

His hot palm on my elbow filled me with shame. Apparently I was now the kind of woman who needed to be rescued. First, Greece. Now Lars had uprooted his baby daughter from her crib to give me a ride. The burning humiliation was morphing into something closer to anger.

"I didn't ask you to come get me."

"No, you didn't. We should talk about that. Watch Mabel for me."

He closed the door and disappeared back inside the club. The valet glared at me, as if I was responsible for leaving the car in the no-load zone. A minute later, Lars was back.

Flexing his fist.

Had he—no, he couldn't have.

He clambered into the driver's seat and stared straight ahead.

"Did you—hit someone?" The only someone worth hitting here was Rowan and I couldn't condone that. Yet, a thrill skittered through my veins all the same. Was I suddenly one of those drama-llama *Real Housewives* types who enjoyed men fighting over her?

Calm down. No one is fighting over you.

Lars remained silent as he started the car and pulled out into traffic.

"Lars, tell me. Did you hit someone?"

"Hush now, the baby."

The baby? *Now* he was worried about the baby? I took a quick glance, and sure enough Mabel was sleeping, a damn conspiracy with this man to keep me from shouting at him.

I lowered my voice to a furious whisper. "Did. You. Hit. Someone?"

"Someone implies a human being. Not sure MacFarlane deserves that label."

My gaze dropped to his right hand, gripping the steering wheel. The knuckles were tinged red.

"Why would you do that?"

"You know why."

"Seriously, I don't." I thought on it for a second. "Because you don't get along with him?"

"Doesn't help."

But that wasn't it—or only it. "I don't understand you at all."

"Women are from Venus, right?"

"Don't know what that means."

He sighed. "It means men and women are from different planets. They don't always get each other."

"Sure, but I'm not an illogical person and this isn't logical behavior, Lars. You woke your baby up in the middle of the night—"

"She can sleep anywhere. And she likes the car motion."

"And drove thirty minutes to downtown Chicago to … rescue me. When I didn't need rescuing."

He snorted. "I saw the photos."

"What are you doing checking out Rowan's Insta? Is that what you usually do on your night off? See how the boys are spending it at the club?"

"He's always posting shit. And that seemed like the best way to see if you were having a good time with him. Because you weren't going to tell me."

"I threw a drink at him."

He caught my gaze in the mirror. "Good for you. What did he do to deserve that?"

"Oh, I just came across a few texts to his bros. Made it clear I wasn't his main target tonight." I held up a hand. "It's not a big deal. But you showing up—with Mabel!—and then hitting him makes it seem like a big deal. It's stupid, Lars, and does not make for good teamwork."

"But it felt good." He flexed his hand, and I couldn't help myself. I placed my palm over those pinked-up knuckles.

"Did it hurt?"

"Nah, sweet thing. Gloves off is what we do."

CHAPTER TWENTY

Lars

ADELINE WASN'T ALL that impressed with me right now.

I wasn't all that impressed with myself. So there was bad blood between me and MacFarlane, and tonight it came to a head. Knowing he hurt Adeline—maybe even used her to get at me—pissed me off in the extreme.

Or maybe I just didn't like knowing she'd gone on a date with that asshole. Or that I might have driven her into his arms because I was so afraid of these feelings I had for her. I was trying to separate them out from lust and gratitude. From jealousy and fear.

I was afraid of both hurting her and of losing her dad as my friend. Taking this to the next level, bedding Adeline, would have such dire consequences for my life. I'd found my place here with a good team, people I cared about, and now Mabel was in the mix, and I wanted to make that work.

I wanted her to grow up feeling safe and secure, which meant crafting a life that put those wants and needs at the center of it.

Fucking the nanny was not it.

But that didn't mean I'd made the wrong call tonight. I didn't regret strapping Mabel in and riding out to Adeline's rescue. And I certainly didn't regret curling my hand into a fist and introducing it to MacFarlane's stupid face. The expression on that same stupid face, priceless, as he realized what was happening, would fuel me to the end of my days.

"You still pissed at me?" I slid a look to a brooding Adeline in the passenger seat.

"I can't believe you stuck your dick in like that."

I blinked, surprised at her turn of phrase.

"I didn't like what I saw. And it turns out I was right, wasn't I?"

"That doesn't make it your business, Lars." More aggressive whispering, though Mabel was tuckered out. She wouldn't be waking anytime soon.

"You needed a ride, no matter what."

"That's what taxis are for. Or I could have called Rosie. A couple of minutes before you rode in on your white charger, I was having a fine time on the dance floor."

I was sorry to have missed that. Taking a deep breath, I banked my frustration. "Adeline, I didn't intend to embarrass you."

"That's not it, Lars. And you know it."

I did. She was mad because I was acting like a jealous cock-blocker when I had no right to interfere, not after I'd told her we could never happen.

"The other ni—"

"Can we not talk about it? I'd like to forget this entire night ever happened. Both of them."

I nodded dumbly, and we continued the drive in silence.

IF I HAD any doubt that Adeline wasn't an amazing person, it was immediately dispelled when we pulled into the driveway. Her first thought was to unstrap Mabel from the car seat and bring her inside.

"No diaper bag?" she asked over her shoulder.

"I was in a hurry."

"Oh, father of the year right here."

Disgusted, she went ahead into the house while I locked the car and took a breath. Remorse was creeping in, slowly doing a number on me. This was supposed to be her night off and I'd ruined it with my caveman antics. Not Rowan MacFarlane. Me.

All I could do was apologize.

I found her putting Mabel down in my room. Once done, she brushed by me, setting every nerve ending on fire.

Okay, enough. "Adeline."

She ignored me.

I called out again. She pivoted and made an urgent gesture at the room behind me. "*Hush now, the baby!*"

Sarcasm noted. "We need to talk."

"Do we?"

"In your room. Now."

Those moss-green eyes grew wide, and she backed up as I practically stalked her into her room and closed the door behind me.

"Get it all out, Adeline."

"You're the one who said we needed to talk."

"Yeah, but I have a feeling you have plenty to say. I

don't think you're used to that, are you? I think you're the quiet daughter in a rowdy family and you're used to keeping your feelings under wraps. You don't have to do that with me."

She shook her head. "You're unbelievable."

"Okay. I'm waiting."

Hands on hips, she started to pace. "You already made it clear how you feel and then you waltz into that club like-like-like you ... *own* me! You don't like MacFarlane, so you came to put a stop to it. But it's not about me. It's about him. And now you want me to talk, tell you what's in *my* head? What's the point? I tried that and look where it got me."

"Rejected," I whispered, feeling every ounce of her pain.

"Yeah. Rejected." She blew out a breath. "And I know why. Not all the reasons you said—my dad, my age, how complicated things are in your life—but *me*. I'm not the kind of girl who attracts a guy like you. You could have anyone."

She thought that? "Jesus, woman, did you not hear me jerking off to the fantasy of you?"

There was that pretty blush again, and instantly I was hard.

"That-that was just recency bias. I was the most recent woman you saw ergo I'm the one who enters your thoughts. It wasn't personal."

Give me strength. "It wasn't personal? I think imagining a woman's lips wrapped around my leaking cock is *pretty* personal."

Her slender throat bulged on a swallow, and my mouth watered, desperate to apply my lips, my tongue, my everything to that tender spot. I was supposed to be making her feel better, but instead I was making us both feel worse.

Frustrated. Horny. Desperate.

"This crush you said was done, Adeline—well, I can't stop thinking about it. Wondering if you still think of me like that. And now you're here all the time, it's magnified all those thoughts. All those fantasies."

"What fantasies?" Barely a whisper, but also a plea.

This was the moment to back away. Insist that we'd butted up against the line but that crossing it would be a mistake.

Only I'd already crossed it. In the shower. In the guest room. With that kiss.

Resistance was exhausting. I was wrecked between work, the baby, my dad, and the constant need to be better than him. No affairs, no gambling, no vices.

No fuckups.

The line was at my feet and God help me, I crossed it and stood inches from her.

"Very inappropriate ones."

Those green eyes flashed.

"Tell me." No longer a rasp, but stronger, pressing. Aware of the power she had over me.

I curled a hand around her jaw and rubbed a thumb over her pouty lower lip. "This mouth. I want to plunder and make it mine. With my lips, my tongue, my cock. I want to lay you down and explore every inch of you, figure out what'll make you pant and whimper and scream with pleasure."

That bottom lip trembled. "Lars."

The quiver undid me.

"When you said you were going on a date, I was annoyed but I realized I had no right to be. When I saw it was MacFarlane, I wanted to punch him there and then— and that's how I would have felt with anyone who spent a single moment with you, moments that by rights, belong to me. I know that's not fair but it's how I feel."

God, it was good to speak openly. Liberating.

"You really want to ... with me?"

"I shouldn't. I'm all wrong for you, Adeline. And it feels like a betrayal of your dad. I have to be honest about that."

She leaned into my touch. "I'm a grown woman. I'm not some child—"

"Except you're Theo Kershaw's daughter. And he would kill me if he knew I'd touched you."

She placed a hand on my chest. "Then we'll have to make sure he doesn't find out."

On tiptoes, she pressed her lips to mine.

CHAPTER TWENTY-ONE

Adeline

LARS DID nothing when I kissed him. No reaction, just his entire being held still. *Wrong again, Adeline. Another misjudged moment.*

But then the moment exploded in a barrage of fireworks. His mouth claimed mine, all tentativeness gone, replaced with a thrilling urgency, as if worried I might change my mind. Or that he might.

Was I taking advantage? I pulled back.

"Is this what you want?"

"More than anything."

"Because I feel like you're at the end of your tether, absolutely no place to go—"

"But in your pants?"

I tried for a humorous shade of gravity. "I'd hate to force you, Nyquist."

He put a finger on my throat then drew a line down to

the center of my cleavage. "I'm going to kiss you again and maybe grasp your lovely ass. If that's not something you're interested in, now would be the time to object."

I tightened my lips so there could be no doubt.

He grinned, then moved his lips over mine, still smiling. That mouth was perfect, his lips warm and giving. I luxuriated in the feel of being wanted with such purity.

His hand curled around one butt cheek, then the other, and I was pulled in, close, and left in no doubt that Lars Nyquist was interested in me. Carnally.

That made me hungry, hungrier than I'd ever been. I wasn't completely inexperienced, but neither was I an expert. Lars had years on me, several women in his rearview, proof of his virility sleeping next door.

Too many thoughts, too much doubt ... I pulled away.

"I have a crush on you."

His lips twitched behind his beard. "Right."

"A big one. Going back years. But that's all it is. Infatuation. Which is to say I'm not expecting anything more than tonight. I know your life is complicated."

If I insisted this was just a little crush, or even a big one, I could maybe steer my heart away from a rockier path. Not love. Not anything so stupid.

"Let's talk about the future later, unless it's important that I not promise you anything now?"

Said like that, it sounded weird. *Can you guarantee that you won't pursue me for a relationship after one smoking hot night? Sign here please.*

"Maybe no more talking," I murmured, my hands gripping the hem of his sweatshirt.

Ever helpful, he pulled it over his head and dropped it to the floor.

Wow. I'd seen him coming out of the shower—after

coming *in* the shower—so I should have been prepared. But that felt forbidden, a peek without permission. Tonight was different. I finally had leave to view this perfect man, all blocked abs and hard pecs with a light dusting of hair that made me itch to explore.

So I did. I ran my hands over his chest, mapping the topography of his body with a leisureliness I did not feel, committing to memory each bump and ridge, those copper penny nipples, that happy trail. If this was my one shot, I needed to make it my best one.

Placing my palm over his bulge, I squeezed through the denim and drew a grunt.

"Is this okay?"

"It's all okay because it's you."

I undid the button of his jeans, pulled the zipper down, and blinked at the sight.

"Commando."

"I was in a hurry to rescue the princess who didn't need rescuing."

I loved that he recognized his mistake, but I also adored that he'd shown up for me. Contradictory, I knew, but such was the lot of a modern woman. We wanted agency and wooing, often in the same moment.

Pulling his jeans down, I watched avidly as his cock sprang forward into my waiting hand, a magnet to my greedy grip. It felt like magic—hard, velvety magic.

"You'll tell me how you like it."

He nodded as I stroked, pulling on the skin, watching as the dark plum-colored head leaked at the tip.

"A touch harder, sweet thing. Don't be afraid to get a little rough."

His face was a mask of ecstasy, all because of what I was

doing. Dull-as-dishwater Adeline Kershaw was turning this man on.

Maybe I could take it further. I pushed his jeans down. "Off."

With an amused curl of his lips, he pushed off his shoes and jeans.

"Socks, too."

He sat on the bed and removed his socks, a little slowly like it was part of the seduction. But then everything he did was. Before he had a chance to stand again, I fell to my knees with my hands on his thick, glorious thighs. Pushing them apart, I ran my palms up them and wrapped one around his cock.

"You don't have to," he gutted out, almost breathless.

"I know."

And then I did. Because I didn't have to. Because this was my choice, and I wanted to take charge in a way I hadn't done before. Seduce the man of my dreams, exert some measure of control over a life that felt like a runaway train. Then I would decide what happened next.

Now wasn't the time to think about the single blowjob on my resume, from my first year in college, drunk and delirious and desperate to get this rite of passage done. I'd watched enough porn to have some semblance of how it should go, but Lars was bigger than any guy I'd encountered. I found it easier to lick along the underside and use my hands to stroke and squeeze.

He pulled back and lifted my chin. "If you keep that up, I'm gonna blow."

"Isn't that the idea?"

"I want to come inside you."

Oh. I wanted that, too. So much. I stood quickly and pulled at the tie for my dress.

"Adeline."

I kept going, trying to undo the knot.

"Enkelini."

"What does that mean?"

"It means 'Angel'. *My* angel. And I'd like you to slow down."

My hands shook. "Really?"

"Reveal yourself to me. Slowly."

My knees buckled, but I did my best to remain upright. My fingers felt stiff and uncooperative. He hooked a finger in the belt and used it to leverage me closer.

"Let me." Deftly, he loosened the knot. The dress parted, revealing my teal blue bra and ... non-matching navy granny panties.

He gave a breathy little groan, which created a hot throb between my legs.

"I-I wasn't expecting any action tonight. So, not my nicest underwear."

"Good."

With both hands on my hips, he inched me closer until his lips touched my belly. Inhaling deep, he moved his mouth over the border of the panties, then applied an open-mouthed kiss to my mound. I shivered at the sensation of warm lips against no-nonsense cotton.

"Lars."

His lips parted, his mouth pushed against the cleft of my pussy, wetness to match my own growing dampness. Pulling back, he hooked a finger to the edge of my panties and brought them down. Slowly, like they were the sexiest lingerie. Hot puffs of air dusted each newly revealed inch. I held my breath, waiting for him to touch me, taste me, anything. Everything.

"Please."

"Please what?" He licked his lips.

I squirmed. "I need you—"

He grasped my thighs and yanked me closer, using his thumbs to spread my sex. His tongue touched skin. I released a heartfelt moan.

He delved deeper, taking that slick instrument and burying it in my sensitive flesh. My knees went weak, but he held me upright as he plundered me with his tongue. Sucking, spearing, *ohGodohGod*. The tightness in my belly coiled until I could no longer stand it. Either I would explode or I would collapse, and I had no idea which would come first.

Explosion won the race. I gripped his shoulders, digging in hard enough to bruise as sensation crashed through me, leaving me whimpering with relief.

I felt my dress being slipped off my shoulders and my body being gently lowered to the bed, while I tried to catch my breath. Lars's hand splayed over my belly, and I didn't even care it was rounded and soft. That calloused hand made me feel safe.

I opened my eyes to find him staring at me, all intensity.

I tried to find the words. "That was—wow."

"That was only the beginning."

Lars

THE TASTE of this woman was the most intoxicating thing to ever cross my tongue. It could have been any combination of things: her sweetness, her strength, the taboo, but basically, it came down to the fact Adeline made me feel like no one ever had. Possessive, strong, a protector.

Now that I'd teased from her the first of what I hoped would be many orgasms, I took a moment to savor the sight of her lying on the bed. Tanned skin gilded by the moonlight filtering through the blinds, those curves I'd dreamed of for weeks, rosy-tipped nipples on teardrop breasts.

"You are gorgeous."

"The way you look at me ... I feel gorgeous."

I placed my palm on the flare of her hip, using this anchor point to explore. The round of her ass, the soft skin of her inner thigh, that thatch of dark curls with the musky scent of her arousal. Moving up, I mapped every inch, silently claiming this territory for my own. With a thumb over one peaked nipple, I gathered the other breast to my mouth. Sucked long and hard on the sweetest flesh. So much to cover.

"Open your legs."

Obediently she did as she was told and my fingers stroked between her thighs, then inside her wet pussy. She'd tasted so good earlier but now I used my fingers to prime her for my cock, stretching that tightly intimate space while my thumb sought her little clit. It seemed to bloom under my touch, and she squirmed, agitated to reach that peak again.

Soon, sweet thing. Soon.

Her fingers raked through my hair, her back arched off the bed. Hating to leave off my exploration, I paused, realizing the protection was in the other room.

"Back in a sec."

Mabel was sleeping peacefully, tired after her nightclub adventures. I grabbed the baby monitor and a condom from the nightstand, and tried not to think of the discordance of that. Of the choice I was about to make. Back in the guest room, I paused at the door, taking in the sight of a beautiful, naked woman. Sweet, sexy Adeline.

She leaned up on her elbows, studying me with those movie goddess eyes.

"You're thinking about the risks?"

I was. Not just the risk of a condom breakage or a surprise pregnancy, but also the threat to the life I was building. There were multiple borders here, points at which I could have said "enough." One more gate to smash through remained. I could stop here and insist to myself that I was still a good guy. That I hadn't yet betrayed my friend or taken advantage of the only family I'd ever known.

"It's a different world on the other side of this."

She nodded her understanding and let me sit with it for a moment. Then she spoke:

"If it helps, you're not the only one with something to lose."

But Theo would forgive her. He'd blame me and then eighty-six me out of his life, which I'd thoroughly deserve.

"Yet all I can think of is what I would win."

Her lips parted on a quickly drawn breath. Adeline was a prize, and any guy would be lucky to have her. I was the one she wanted, so why the hell should I second-guess this gift?

When I closed the gap, she took the monitor and placed it on the nightstand, then the condom and removed it from the packaging.

"I'm on birth control as well. We've got this covered, Lars."

I took the condom back from her, this exchange serving to reinforce both advice and consent. We were each taking responsibility for this decision.

I rolled the rubber on, then coasted my hand over her

ass, anchoring myself, getting a good grip. Nudging along her wet seam, I notched between her lips and gave a shallow thrust.

It was already amazing.

"Lars!"

That final invitation did it for me. With a deep, slow stroke, I filled her, loving how her muscles eased my way then tightened when I hit home. She arched into me and held me so close I groaned. That sound set us both off, a prelude to long, consuming thrusts that turned frenzied as the pleasure built, tight, taut, flushing to every extremity of my body, especially the one buried inside her. My groan became a roar, and milking my cock, she squeezed every last drop of pleasure from me.

No longer was she the nanny, my teammate's daughter, the innocent who was all wrong for me. With my release and claim, she was the woman who was right in every way.

She was the woman who would be my undoing.

CHAPTER TWENTY-TWO

Lars

LAST NIGHT I fell asleep wrapped up in a warm woman who had rocked my world.

This morning, I awoke from the slumber of the sated. As I reconciled myself to my surroundings, I did a mental check-in for regrets.

Adeline still slept beside me. Not a single regret remained in my head.

So this could go nowhere, but at least we'd satisfied the lust and hopefully dampened the spark. My phone said it was just after six, which meant Mabel was probably hungry.

I did my best to slip out of Adeline's arms without waking her and pulled my boxer briefs on quickly. I couldn't help taking a moment to appreciate her lying there, her dark hair fanned out on the pillow, her snoring soft and endearing.

This is it. The last time you'll see her in this well-fucked, pliable state.

Sighing, I headed into my room where Mabel was already awake. Though I had kept the monitor on the nightstand, last night was the first time she'd slept alone since she'd come to live with me. She had managed to pull herself up to a sitting position and was gripping the bar of the crib like an Alcatraz felon proclaiming her innocence.

"What's goin' on, Mabel? You trying to escape?"

I picked her up and inhaled her baby scent. A strange peace came over me. I might not be the best dad in the world, but Mabel didn't know that—at least not yet. I could figure this out. Adeline would help me.

Except her presence here was temporary. And while everything might feel better when she was around, I still had to take care of business.

I changed Mabel—I was a dab hand at it now—and after washing up, took her downstairs to eat. Formula and applesauce, her favorite combo. While I waited for the formula to heat, I checked my phone to see if my run-in with MacFarlane last night was on anyone's radar yet.

Bingo.

I had a text from Ryder asking me to call him ASAP. A voice mail from Natalie in PR. On the other hand, the Rebels text thread was unusually quiet, probably because MacFarlane was part of it, and no one wanted to appear to be taking sides without further information. There were also a couple of messages from Jacobs about inviting Mabel over to hang with his daughter and the Rebels toddler set.

Nothing from Theo yet. It wouldn't be long, and I needed to think about my strategy around him. For the first time, I would have to lie to my friend.

The bottle warmer beeped and I sat at the kitchen table,

feeding my daughter while I worked out how best to cover my tracks. It wasn't as if Theo would ask outright. I wouldn't have to lie to his face; I would just *not* tell him.

The classic fallback of liars and cheaters everywhere. Not so different from the old man.

When were you going to tell me you've been placing wagers in my name, Dad?

What you didn't know didn't hurt you.

Until it did. Until it almost destroyed my career before it started.

Mabel finished her bottle, gave me a gassy grin, and burped to her satisfaction. I puttered about the kitchen, noting the supplies I needed to order to make Mabel's food from scratch. Cooking was something I'd always enjoyed, a way to settle my brain when I wasn't playing hockey. Making baby food was probably not a good use of my time, but I liked the idea of my daughter eating something produced by my hands. I could buy her everything else.

I settled her back in her crib and watched for a few minutes as she punched the air and chatted away in that funny language of hers. I made sure she had Bear nearby, then I went back into the bedroom.

Adeline was still dead to the world—I'd worked that gorgeous body good, and just the sight of her constricted my heart. I hated the idea of giving her up, but the longer this went on, the riskier it became. I stepped into the shower, thinking I should head to the Rebels HQ gym and get some work in before facing the music in the front office.

A minute later, the shower door opened behind me and a soft hand touched my back. Looking over my shoulder, I found a naked Adeline. God, she was perfect.

"Did I wake you?" I placed my hands on her hips and pulled her close to the part of me that still ached for her.

"No. Maybe. I checked on Mabel. She looked like a happy, dry-bottomed, well-fed baby."

"Doesn't take much to satisfy her."

She smiled. "Don't underestimate your contribution here. You're better at this than you give yourself credit for."

"Couldn't do it without you." I inclined my head, nuzzled my nose against hers, and took her mouth with my own. Christ, the sweetness of her. Her taste, her pliancy, the support I felt with her near—it overwhelmed me with its purity.

"Last night," she murmured, her lips close to my chest. "Was amazing." Her eyes were round and tinged with a frankness that scared me.

"It was. You were."

"We both were." She ran a hand over my chest, coasted it down to by abs and wrapped it around my willing cock. "I know we didn't talk about what comes next—and if you want me to leave—"

"Said while she strokes me just the way I like it."

"Can't you stop anytime?"

I smirked. "Of course, but I get the impression you don't want me to. That you'd like … more." I flipped her so her back met the shower tile and gave her as good as she was giving me. My fingers between her thighs, rubbing and stroking through all that sensitive, supple flesh. I touched her clit, relishing how she arched her body, her breasts wet and slippery against my chest.

"This was my fantasy," I said. "The shower one."

Her eyes went wide. "That day I overheard you?"

"The day you eavesdropped."

"You were loud!" She squeezed harder, rubbed her thumb along the head of my rampant cock. "What was I doing? Something like this."

"That. And then you were on your knees, sucking me off."

She jackknifed to the tile and resumed jerking me, long, sinuous slides of her hand from balls to tip. I stepped back against the tiled wall, bringing her out of the shower spray.

"You don't have to, enkelini." *My angel.*

"But I want to." She licked the head, then applied the most delicious suction. I curled a hand around the back of her head and gently started fucking her mouth. Those ruby red lips, the sweet, velvet suction, had me in the hottest grip.

"That's it. That's my girl. So good. So fucking good."

My balls felt so damn heavy and the sizzle in my spine sparked hard. I pulled back an inch.

"Gonna come, sweet thing."

She sucked harder, and Jesus, that did it for me.

After, I tried to catch my breath. "You okay?"

With watery eyes, she looked up at me. "That was ... so hot."

"That's what you do to me."

I helped her to her feet and kissed her deeply.

She smiled. "Close to your fantasy?"

"A million times better. Now, let's take care of you." My fingers sought that sensitive flesh between her legs, stroking, owning, until finally, I made her come with the heel of my hand. For a few moments, we clung to each other, neither willing to end it. The world outside this steamy space was too cold and unforgiving for what we'd created.

Eventually, pruned skin and lukewarm water forced our hand. We stepped out of the shower, and I patted her dry. More kisses, more touches. I couldn't get enough of her.

The door to the ensuite was open, and the buzz of my phone carried through. Quickly I went into the bedroom and found three new messages blazing on the screen.

THEO

You up? Not a booty call, I promise!

I'm outside with the Halloween stuff for Mabel.

Okay, I'm getting worried now. Coming in!

That last message came through a minute ago. Cocking my ear, I listened for signs of life, a prelude to signs of death. My own.

I put my head around the door to the bathroom. "Your dad's downstairs."

GOD HELP ME, I used Mabel as cover.

Walking into the kitchen with my daughter in my arms, I found Theo helping himself to a coffee from the Keurig. A Safeway shopping bag sat on the kitchen table.

He turned on my entrance and raised a grave eyebrow. "You're in so much fucking trouble, NyQuil."

A chill gushed through my veins as I tried to parse the situation.

He knows. Somehow, he knows. And the only reason he's not punching me is because I'm using my child as a shield.

"You'll have to be more specific." I took a seat at the kitchen table, another ploy to avoid being thumped.

"It's all over the fucking Internet!"

"Could you watch your mouth?"

Theo grimaced before picking up where he left off. "You hit MacFarlane! And while the punch didn't make it onto ye olde videotape, there is footage of you leaving the club right after."

Relief flooded me.

"MacFarlane tattled, I suppose." I sounded so cool, an absolute sociopath.

"Probably. Or one of his entourage. Or someone at the club." Theo took a sip of his coffee. "Addy still asleep?"

"As far as I know." *Lie Number One.*

"Hatch told me MacFarlane was out with my daughter last night."

I picked my words carefully. "She wasn't having a good time."

"Did he hurt her?"

"Not physically. But he made her feel small and that's not right." The words sounded angry on my lips, and I soothed Mabel's back on the road to soothing myself.

"So ..." A frowning Theo was trying to connect the dots. "How did *you* end up there?"

"I called him, Dad." Adeline stood at the entrance to the kitchen in sweats and her dad's jersey, her lips still puffy from when she took my cock deep, all of ten minutes ago. She had never looked more beautiful, and I had never been more of a jerk.

She headed for the coffee maker. "I was feeling sorry for myself, and I needed a ride. I could have taken a cab, I suppose, but Lars had already offered to pick me up if I needed it."

Theo took a good look at his daughter. "You could've called me or your brother."

"Hmm, okay. Remember that time I got stuck in Ravinia when I missed the last train?"

Theo folded his arms. "Rosie's fault, if I recall. She was throwing up Mai Tais after the Doja Cat show."

"And everyone blamed *me* for not keeping an eye on her. Even though she's older."

"But you're the sensible one, Twinkle, always have

been. And I don't think we blamed you." He flicked a quick glance at me, seeking support.

I remained silent, not wanting to come between father and daughter any more than I already had.

Knowing he hadn't a leg to stand on, he sighed his surrender. "Thanks for picking her up, Lars. I appreciate it. And the rest. Though my sources say you waltzed into the party like you were walking onto a yacht. Except into the club and with a baby." He sipped his coffee and said to his daughter, "That's a Carly Simon reference."

She gave her father an indulgent look. "I know. Taylor sang with her in concert."

I spoke up in my defense. "Mabel slept all the way through it."

Theo went quiet, which was never a good sign. He knew something wasn't adding up, but his trusting brain refused to go there.

"I brought over Halloween costumes. I know you said you wanted to make your own"—he added finger quotes to "make"—"but when are you going to have time for that? Tilly's grown out of these, so one of them should work for May-belle." He shook his head. "I think Button might work better for her nickname, short for Belly Button? Still percolating on that. Or you can buy your costume at the Spirit store like everyone else, if there's anything left which there won't be because the party is tonight."

I didn't have it in me to be churlish. "Let's see what you've got."

Adeline unpacked the bag and produced bumble bee, pumpkin, and cow costumes. We cooed over each one, though I was pretty sure only the cow one would fit her without needing major alterations. It also gave Theo another nickname idea: Moo-Belle.

My phone buzzed with a text from Ryder. *My office. 8 a.m.*

Theo offered a knowing smirk. "Our illustrious leader?"

"Meeting in his office in an hour."

"That doesn't sound good," Adeline said, her voice threaded with worry.

"Probably a game suspension. Maybe two." Theo put his coffee mug in the sink. "You played right into MacFarlane's hands and now I'll have to work with him when I hate his guts. He's a good player but he's not Dream Defense material!"

"Sorry, Dad."

Theo kissed his daughter on the forehead. "This isn't your fault. If he hurt you ..."

"He didn't. Don't be an asshole to him. Be professional."

Her dad clutched his chest, wounded. "I am always professional! Okay, laters, kids."

And then he left as noisily as he'd arrived.

She raised an eyebrow. "Think he bought it?"

"Not entirely. But he'd rather not consider the alternative, that I showed up at that club because I was ragingly jealous." Mabel stuck her finger in my mouth, almost as if she knew I needed to shut the hell up now.

"You were?"

"Of course I was. I hated that you were going on a date. I hated that anything I'd said might have driven you to make that choice because I was too much of a coward to admit I wanted you."

She bit her lip, a very sexy move. As I didn't want to be thinking sexy things right now, I looked away. Or maybe I didn't want to be thinking honest things right now.

"Are you really going to be suspended?"

"Probably. But it was worth it."

She rolled her eyes. "And what about the aftermath? Was that worth it?"

Trust Adeline to refuse to dance around the issue. I'd once considered her shy, but now I saw someone different. A woman who called it how she saw it, who wasn't afraid to be direct with me. Last night, we went into this agreeing not to discuss what came next. But now the time had come to be straight with each other.

"Yes."

She held my gaze with those beautiful, shamrock-green eyes. I'd expected she would be nervous because her dad showed up and we were hiding something huge from him. She seemed different this morning. More assured.

"I know it can't go anywhere, Lars."

"That's supposed to be my line." Here she was, giving me an out, and I was arguing against it?

She smiled, rubbed at a scuff on the kitchen counter. "There are a lot of reasons not to do this—"

"And we've blown right past them and done it anyway."

"Have you had enough?"

Of her? Not a chance. But I couldn't say that. I couldn't make any promises.

"If we had any sense we'd call a halt." Her father had almost walked in on us. How long could we keep this between us in the company of other people, especially *her* people?

"Are you feeling sensible?"

I stood and approached her, Mabel still in my arms like the cutest of chaperones. Leaning in, I kissed Adeline, first a gentle press, then deeper, making clear my intent.

Sensible was not the word to describe this.

Adeline licked her lips, tasting me, savoring the sensual

promise in it. "My dad can't know. No one can know. This season is important for him. For you all."

"I know." Anything that interfered with the team's dynamic—and Theo finding out I was fucking his daughter was right up there—would tank our chances. My captain and I had built a partnership on the ice, and if I had any sense, I would kill this thing with Adeline before it could mess with that.

"Here, let me take her," she said. "You need to get ready for your meeting with Ryder."

I watched as she headed into the living room to put Mabel down in the play-prison. Following, I leaned against the door, my entire body itching to claim her. Instead I offered one more warning, one more grasp at common sense.

"I don't want to hurt you."

"I'm a big girl, Lars. Let me worry about my feelings."

The assumption being that mine were of little concern.

CHAPTER TWENTY-THREE

Chicago Rebels defenseman Lars Nyquist has been assessed a three-game suspension following reports of a physical altercation with teammate Rowan MacFarlane at Viper, a nightclub in downtown Chicago. Inside sources tell us that MacFarlane was on a date with Adeline Kershaw, daughter of Rebels captain Theo Kershaw and nanny to Nyquist's baby daughter, when Nyquist arrived to take her home. Witnesses say Nyquist had his daughter with him at the time, which has prompted observers to wonder if Child Protective Services should be involved. (And where is the child's mother?)

- Hot Goss

Lars

A COUPLE OF HOURS LATER, I walked into a scene straight out of a Western. In the Rebels saloon—sorry, gym —O'Malley and Hatch were restraining Theo, who was all up in MacFarlane's face. I immediately placed myself between them.

"Gentlemen, control yourselves."

"Like you did last night, Narc-*quist*?" MacFarlane poked a finger in my chest. The darkening bruise on his jaw gave me a shit-ton of satisfaction. "Heard from the league about your suspension yet?"

"Pretty sad about the lengths you'll go to get more ice time. Draw my fire so you can get me out of the way?" I tutted. "Like making enemies on your own team, do ya?"

"You might want to ask that of yourself." MacFarlane had that sly, know-it-all look I hated. "You're out at all hours rescuing the nanny. Do these guys here know you've got the hots for Adeline?"

This fucker. "I showed you my fist last night because you disrespected someone I care about. Talking smack about me isn't going to improve your shot at the D-line."

I turned my back on him and placed a hand on Theo's chest. Fury rolled off him, and it was kind of scary. The guy was so good-natured, rarely giving in to dark thoughts, not even on the ice.

This was my fault. I fucked around and now I was finding out.

Worse, this was going to be bad for the team. With my suspension, Theo would be forced to pair up with a guy he didn't like. MacFarlane was a good player, but that kind of dynamic never boded well.

"Let's cool off a bit. How about a smoothie, cap?"

Hatch squeezed his dad's shoulder. "Yeah, go to the lounge and take a breath."

Theo inhaled, and with one last glare at MacFarlane, exited and headed to the lounge. I followed.

He pulled at the fridge door and started laying out ingredients. "What did Ryder say?"

"That I'm an idiot for letting MacFarlane get to me."

"You were defending Adeline. I appreciate that, really, I do."

Shame washed over me. I'd broken his trust. He hadn't even warned me off her because it would never have occurred to him to do so. It never would have occurred to him to *need* to do so.

"She said it's happened before."

"What? MacFarlane?"

"Guys like MacFarlane. Guys who take an interest because of her family connections, or how they can turn it to their advantage."

Theo looked confused. "But ... she's beautiful. And the sweetest person in the world. I don't get how—shit, it sounds like she needs to date outside of hockey! Find some guy who doesn't even know the name Kershaw, except for Nik Kershaw, amazing eighties sensation."

I leaned on the counter. "She's feeling a bit fragile right now. And the last thing she needs is for you or me or Hatch getting into it with MacFarlane. She'll blame herself if what happened affects the team."

That I was a Grade-A hypocrite crossed my mind before I buried it deep.

"I could never blame her! Though why the hell she would want to date MacFarlane is a fucking mystery. Just the idea that anyone would take advantage of my girl, would do anything to hurt her, pisses me off big time."

"I get it." Hell's fire licked at my heels.

"Thanks again for picking her up last night and for

dealing with him. Just doesn't seem fair you get to play white knight while I'm supposed to set a good example. No one deserves a punch more than that guy."

I could think of someone much more deserving.

"I'll be your enforcer on and off the ice, Kershaw."

Theo shoved a few leaves of kale into the blender, added Greek yogurt, pineapple, ginger, and some protein mix.

"So I should just imagine feeding him to this blender instead?" He hit the button and we both watched as it created a pulpy mess. Once done, he added, "Not very satisfying."

I blew out a breath. "You have to work with him. The team needs stability and having the captain in a feud with one of his players is not the way to win games."

He nodded. "Right, but as soon as your suspension is done, I'll take care of Rowan MacFarlane."

With any luck, the storm would have blown over by then. However, I suspected that storm clouds of a different variety would be gathering force.

Adeline

I WIGGLED my toes though the toe-separator restricted my movement. The frosted blue sparkled, making me smile.

"Crazy Tart Red for me."

Choice made, Aurora nodded at the nail salon technician and picked up her martini glass, one of her "travel pair." The salon didn't have a liquor license, but they were fairly lenient in letting my great-grandmother drink from her hip flask. I stuck to Snapple in a martini glass since I was driving.

We clinked and giggled.

"So what's all this with MacFarlane and Lars?" Aurora took a sip of her French martini—with extra pineapple juice—and set the glass down. "Your father can't be too pleased about that."

He wasn't, but he seemed to be exercising superior levels of restraint. More concerning was Lars's suspension, which put pressure on the team to fill the gap he left.

"I probably should have thought it through a bit better."

"Dating one of your dad's teammates? The heart wants what the heart wants."

I scoffed. "Nothing even remotely close to my heart was engaged with Rowan MacFarlane."

Aurora eyed me beneath her silver bangs. "I wouldn't have thought so, either. So why did you go out with him?"

Reeling from rejection, I wanted to show Lars I was desirable. And it worked!

"He asked, and I thought it might be nice to do something outside my comfort zone for once."

Aurora nodded. "Instead you create an international incident! Lars rocking up to the club with baby Mabel and squirting MacFarlane in the face with formula! I would've loved to have seen that."

I'd read several versions of the story, which was only a story because (a) Lars brought a baby to a club and (b) he hit a fellow teammate. "People keep twisting the facts."

"Which are?" Shrewd eyes studied me over the rim of her glass.

"I needed a ride."

"She needed a ride!" Aurora cackled and almost spilled her drink. "Okay, honey. Whatever you say."

I rolled my eyes, determined to move on. "So how's the knee?"

"Fine! My tennis-playing days are over, but I can still move from the fridge to the wet bar. How's the Big Ponder going?"

"I've barely had time to think about it. Babies take up a lot of headspace." Hot hockey hunks, too.

"Well, I think you're a great person for doing it. Just don't get complacent. Not that being a nanny isn't a good job, I just don't think it's for you. You should be a photographer! Or a film director. Or a cam girl."

"A cam girl?" She couldn't possibly know what that was.

"Yes, one of those girls who strips on camera. For money!"

I stood corrected. "I admire your sex-positive attitude and confidence in my ability to make money like that, but it's not for me."

"Or a musician? You have such a sweet voice and Tilly loves your songs. Or how about a travel blogger? I loved watching your videos when you were away. I felt so close to you. But then you stopped a couple of months ago." She shifted her feet from the sudsy water to the towel-covered footrest. "Did you get bored with it?"

"Just so busy. Those videos take work."

Aurora assessed me, those all-seeing eyes piercing into my soul. "It was around the time you went incommunicado."

While my lip and cheek healed after the mugging. I could have covered the bruises with makeup, but no amount of Maybelline could have disguised my mood.

"I texted every day. I just didn't video call for one week, and that's all you remember."

"And no more fun videos of you and Rosie eating spicy soups and washing elephants!"

"We were in Europe by then. Elephants were thin on the ground." I sounded so defensive.

She nodded, her stare unflinching. "Your dad was worried about you, out in the world. I told him you've always been stronger than you seem."

"I'm not his little girl anymore."

"But he'll always see you that way. And how you respond might look like you're rebelling against his world-view." While I searched for a response, she added, "Like dating one of his teammates."

I chuckled nervously. "You think I went out with MacFarlane to show Dad I'm all grown up?"

"To show somebody."

Eighty-plus sure came with a lot of insight.

"I don't date people to stick it to Dad, Aurora. That would be childish."

She grinned. "But fun! My father once tried to lock me in my room to stop me from going out with the Masterson twins. Oh, they were trouble. But I climbed down the ivy trellis and met them in a little red Corvette at the top of the road."

"Twins?"

"One of them was a real charmer while the other one had muscles to die for. You really needed the combo to get the best experience." Her phone buzzed and she checked it. A shriek pierced the salon air. "Look at what your brother just sent me!"

Someone had created a video of Lars in his Rebels uniform with a baby strapped to his back like Yoda when

Luke was in Jedi training. Lars was surrounded by night-club strobe lights before he inevitably punched Rowan under a disco ball. AI finally being used for good.

"Conor says it has two hundred thousand views!" Another cackle. "Wish I had a young man fighting for my honor. Or an old one."

"He didn't do it for me. They have their own beef."

"Sure they do. But still, we need to be careful this doesn't send him off the deep end." She lowered her voice to a whisper. "He didn't do so well when his dad died. Full bottle of tequila, I heard. Couldn't play."

Of course his father's death would have affected him, especially given their estrangement. For all his bluster, that connection would be impossible to ignore. "He's talked about his dad a little, mostly about how he wants to raise Mabel differently."

"That Sven was a piece of work, by all accounts. And Lars is family, so you'll keep an eye on him, right? Our girl in Havana!"

"I'll do my best."

Aurora finished her martini and tapped into the photos on her phone. "Have you seen my costume for Halloween? Tell me if I'm showing too much leg!"

CHAPTER TWENTY-FOUR

Adeline

THE KERSHAW HALLOWEEN party was a must on the Rebels' social calendar. Most of the players, staff, and anyone vaguely associated with the org showed up, vying to outdo each other in the costume stakes. Tonight, all the toddlers and infants were gathered like a petting zoo of adorableness. We had a baby goat, two little pigs, a fox, and of course, our Mabel, now christened Moo-Belle, in her cow costume. My mom had put them in a playpen at the center of the living room and instructed the tweens to keep an eye on them, which gave their parents—and temporary nannies—a bit of a break.

I adjusted my antenna headband and took a seat beside Summer, who was wearing a Disney princess dress, a la Beauty and the Beast, though this one had weird detailing in the seams. Like brown and green rosettes.

"What did you come as?"

Summer patted her blonde wig and grinned. "Taco-Belle."

I looked closer. Those rosettes were minced beef and cilantro-colored pops of fabric.

"Awesome."

"And you're Zom-Bee? Love it!"

And I loved not having to explain my costume, a combo of a bee and the undead. Lars had spent an age on my zombie makeup, lovingly applying it with a care that told me he'd missed his calling. Enjoying the domestic comfort of creating costumes and getting ready together as a family were so enjoyable that I hated myself for even going there. But I was also determined to grasp these moments of joy and go with where the flow took me.

"And Lars looks so handsome as a Viking—uh, hockey player?"

"Fantasy Hockey League." A hockey jersey with a horned helmet and Thor wig was simple but effective. "He objected to every idea until I said he could wear his sweater."

"Well, it works." She leaned in close. "And how's the other thing?"

I played coy. "What's that?"

"I heard you went on a date with Rowan MacFarlane and Lars pulled a John Wick and punched him while he had the baby strapped to his chest like a weapons holster. I would have paid to see that."

The embellishments were getting fancier. "Not how it happened. He came to pick me up—with the baby—and I watched her in the car while he went back in to, uh, hit Rowan."

That sounded worse. I should probably apologize to the

poor guy, but he got his wish: a spot on the line with my dad for the next few games.

Summer's brow wrinkled. "You two are still boss/nanny? No funny business?"

"Yep!" Was that a slight twang I heard in her voice when she said "funny business"? I didn't know much about Summer's origins, and I itched to learn more. "So what did you do to my brother?"

Summer blinked, wide and slow, just like a Disney princess. "Hatch? Nothing."

"I've noticed that he's kind of off with you."

"I know!" She sounded amused rather than upset. "Anytime he comes into the front office, he's very 'just the facts, ma'am.' I think maybe I called him Hal the first couple of times I saw him? He's been snippy to me ever since."

I didn't buy it. My brother wasn't the grudge-holding type. I resolved to interrogate him later.

I let my eyes scan the room and rest longingly on Lars for a hot second. Enough to catch his eye, for both of us to recognize the danger, and reluctantly move on. To cover, I waved at Aurora, who had come as a 1920s flapper and was indeed showing decidedly too much leg.

Rosie in the guise of a lady pirate had been chatting with her brother Devon, a rubber chicken. She spotted my wandering gaze, so I jumped in with a question before she could. "How's the job hunt going?"

She rolled the eye not covered by a fetching patch. "I talked to Harper, but we both agreed the Rebels front office is not for me."

I'd thought as much.

"But! Jude got me an interview at the tattoo parlor where he gets his ink done." Jude Torres was a Chicago firefighter married to Hudson Grey, one of the retired Rebels players.

Summer smiled. "That sounds like it would suit you!"

"Just reception work, for now." She waved at someone who had just come in. "Hey, sis!"

Franky St. James was Rosie's stepsister and a lecturer at Lakeshore University. Pushing her glasses back up her nose, she grinned at my friend. "You never call, you never write."

Rosie hugged her, while doing her best not to crush the cardboard box around her waist. "That's what social media is for! We kept up with everyone there."

"Sure, and Vi would like a word."

Rosie stood back and looked her sister over. "What did you come as?"

From what I could tell, she was a cat, but the makeup on one side of her face was gray green. A cardboard box around her waist was covered in Sharpied question marks.

"Schrödinger's Cat."

At my baffled look, she explained, "I'm half alive and half dead to represent the cat's existence in a superposition of both states simultaneously." Adjusting her cardboard box, she took a seat beside me. "I heard Lars Nyquist is now a father. How did that happen?"

"The usual way," I said. "But he's figuring it out."

"With your help," Summer said to me. "Don't forget he couldn't do it without you."

"So did the condom break?" We all stared at Franky, who blinked owl-like behind her glasses. "I'm trying to ascertain if it was a faulty prophylactic, if he's particularly virile, or if he's merely careless."

Franky was known for some outlandishly direct thinking that tended to eschew social norms. I loved her to bits, but she did make an interesting first impression.

"No idea." Discussing Lars's prophylactic habits was not on my agenda.

Franky took out her phone and made a note.

"What's going on there?" It looked like a list of names, a few of which I recognized as Rebels team members. My uncle Jason's name was on there, too—he played for the Boston Cougars—but his had been struck through. Curious.

"Just some research I'm doing."

Rosie nudged Summer. "You're looking at the brains of the family. Franky studies slugs and teaches all about them at Lakeshore U."

"Gastropods, actually. With a side of mollusks." Franky pushed back her glasses again.

"Wow!" Summer looked suitably impressed, if a little skeeved out at the subject matter. "You're probably the smartest person here."

"She is." Rosie grinned proudly. "Her IQ is 151."

"152," Franky said. She was older than us, in her mid-thirties, and she never seemed completely comfortable at the Rebels parties. No doubt she found the jocks to be awfully tiresome.

"How's Kat doing?" I asked.

Kat was Franky's older sister and had recently had twins with her husband, an investment banker in New York. That prompted a review of photos, showcasing the little ones. A couple of minutes later I excused myself to go check on Mabel, and on my way, I ran into my uncle Jason dressed as a ... Rebel?

"Addy!" He hugged me hard.

"What are you doing here?" A defenseman with Boston, he should have been at home, getting ready for the Cougars-Chucks game. It was also a little freaky to see him because I had just spotted him on Franky's mysterious list.

"I'm on IR so I came home to visit my parents and you guys."

Jason Isner was my dad's brother and twelve years his junior. My dad hadn't known their father, Grandpa Nick, for most of his life, and their reconciliation had been bumpy, to say the least. We were all close now, and Jason and my dad were incredibly tight.

I studied his costume. Rebels' jersey, one fist strapped with a bloodied bandage, backpack with a creepy baby doll peeking out over his shoulder.

"Are you ... Lars?"

He grinned. "Lars at Da Club! Do you think he'll punch me?"

"We can only hope." My family were so weird.

He spotted my dad who was chatting with one of Rosie's dads, Cade Burnett, who was dressed as a "cereal killer"—a box of Cheerios wielding a plastic machete. "What's my brother come as?"

"French Kiss?" At his blank look, I tried to explain. "He says it's 'a concept piece' where he's a French mime but with the makeup style of some ancient band called Kiss?"

Jason shook his head. "Never simple, that guy."

I finally made my way to the menagerie where Mabel was the star attraction. On seeing me, she clutched the bars of the playpen and pulled herself into a sitting position.

"Hey, Moo-Belle, you having fun?"

She smiled, a big gummy grin that lifted my heart. Someone hunkered beside me, bringing with him his intoxicating scent.

"How's my girl?" He was looking at me when he said that, and feeling flustered, I passed over it.

"Moo-Belle's fine. And you look kind of ridiculous."

"I look amazing, and you know it." He leaned in and

scooped up Mabel. "And you're the sexiest Zom-bee here," he murmured to me on his way back upright.

"Lars."

"You gotta learn to control that blush, sweet thing."

"Stop. It."

"Uh, make me." Said with a sexy rumble I felt all the way to my toes. He seemed lighter in spirit, almost playful.

I changed the subject quickly, which I was becoming very adept at. "Did you see my uncle Jason's costume?"

"I've apparently achieved some sort of pop culture nirvana."

"People keep asking me why you showed up at the club. Of course the baby-in-tow aspect is making waves."

"Mabel and I had to pick up our third musketeer."

That made me feel warm. I had to get away because I was going to make a fool of myself. Before I could, I felt a tap on my shoulder.

My father stood behind me. From his expression I didn't think he had heard anything, but I was suddenly acutely aware of my reckless behavior.

"So, Twinkle, we were wondering if you'd play a few songs for the kids." He held up my guitar, his expression hopeful.

"I don't know, Dad. There are an awful lot of people here."

"It was Lars's idea. Tell her she'd be great, man."

Lars's idea? My boss cocked his head, his ear to Mabel's mouth. "Moo-Belle says you have the sweetest voice." His eyebrows drew together in concentration. "She wants to hear something about her people." A pause to get clarification. "The cows."

I should not have felt this giddy. "Mabel's pretty chatty for a seven-month-old."

"Seven and a half. And she's up for Mensa candidacy."

"You'll do it?" My dad grinned, clueless to the undertones between Lars and me.

"Sure, why not?" I shot a quick glance at Lars, whose lips curved.

Someone moved a chair near the playpen, and I took a seat with my guitar in my lap. My dad cut the Spotify, which of course drew attention to the live entertainment. God, this was nerve-wracking. I never sang for anyone other than my family, but I knew most everyone here. If only my fingers would stop shaking.

I sent a quick look to Lars, who stood off to the side with Mabel. He offered a smile of encouragement, and just the sight of him there in his silly Viking helmet, holding his little girl, gave me the confidence I needed.

As we had so many fun costumes, many of them animals, it made sense to go with Old MacDonald, though with a twist.

"Old Man Kershaw had a farm, E-I-E-I-O."

"Hey!" My dad whined, which made everyone laugh, and instantly relaxed me.

"And on that farm, he had a ... cow. E-I-E-I-O. With a moo-moo here ..."

To ensure each of the kids got a verse, I stood and started a circuit. It didn't matter that they weren't all dressed as animals; we managed to come up with fun, representative sounds together. Fairies wisped, princesses giggled, pirates arghed, and witches vroomed (on their brooms). By the time I had name-checked all the kids, the knocking of my heart against my rib cage was drowned out in the roar of approval from the crowd.

Lars was the first person to approach me right after with Mabel in his arms.

"Mabel says that was the best song she's ever heard."

Pulling on a felt udder on Mabel's costume, I whispered, "What about her dad?"

"He thinks it needed more references to Duckman's thick beard."

"Oh, shut it," I said with a giggle.

"We never did discuss you writing a song about me."

I rolled my eyes as my cheeks burned. "It was a special request for Tilly who has a big crush on you."

He didn't further embarrass me with a comment about her older sister having it just as bad. Instead, his eyes searched my face.

"Seriously, I loved it and so did everyone else. Maybe there's room for another bright star in the night sky."

I choked back the emotion in my throat. That night I talked about my envy of Rosie and fear of not taking chances seemed like a lifetime away, though it was only a week.

With a shaky hand, I set my guitar down beside the credenza in the living room. "I'm headed to the kitchen. You need anything?"

"Nah, we're okay. We'll miss you, though."

Swoon. Walking by, I couldn't help brushing my arm against his. Foolish, I knew, but I was falling hard here, and that kind of falling was characterized by idiotic behavior. I wiped the smile off my face, but obviously not fast enough.

Rosie intercepted me before I made it to the bar setup in the kitchen. "That was *so much fun.* How about we get some air?"

"Sure, but first I was going to—"

"Now, Adeline Aurora Kershaw."

We didn't make it to the back door. Rosie yanked me into the pantry and closed the door.

"I thought we were getting air."

"Are you kidding? It's cold enough to freeze my tits off. What's going on with you and the Hockey-nator?" Her lips twitched. "Work in progress."

Modeling good behavior for Mabel. Nothing to see here!

Instead of that perfect excuse, my next words came tumbling out in a run-on rush. *"Wesortofhadsex."*

Rosie's dark eyes sparked with glee. "Okay! Good thing the country isn't relying on you to keep its classified secrets."

"It just happened," I mumbled.

Rosie folded her arms. "Sure it did. When were you going to tell me?"

"Um ... never?" At her semi-outraged expression, I rushed on. "I knew you wouldn't approve because you'll think I don't know what I'm doing. And maybe I don't. But I'd rather experience *something* than feel like I'm ... hiding all the time. Like I'm this sad person who's too afraid to do anything exciting! Or go for what she wants. So it's been building for a while and then I went on that date with MacFarlane and Lars didn't like it. Not one bit."

"I assumed the animosity was team stuff. MacFarlane's always calling him names and stuff—"

"What names?"

"Narc-quist, Snitch-quist, the usual."

"Oh." Because of what happened with his father? Lars hadn't told me. He was so close-chested about his dad and the impact it had on him. Hatch must have said something to Rosie.

"But he came to that club—with a baby—and rescued you." Rosie wagged a finger. "And then you guys fell into bed. So sweet."

"And now we're going with the flow." I tried to sound grown-up, a woman of the world.

She took a curl of my hair and twisted. "You're not really a go with the flow kind of girl, are you? Casual isn't your thing, despite all my efforts to get you some on our travels."

"I knew you were going to be like this. It's why I kept quiet." But she was right. Casual sex wasn't my jam. Growing up the daughter of Theo and Elle Kershaw set near-impossible expectations in the arena of love and relationships. Now the worst had happened.

My crush had bloomed into something more serious. I'd fallen in love with Lars Nyquist.

While catching my breath, I tried to put this in context. The amazing lover, the hunky single dad, the man who was learning to connect with others through the process of connecting with his child—all were reasons to be attracted to someone. To even want to see where it could go.

But I knew it could go nowhere, and still I was the fool who had fallen for this man, all because he saw in me potential I couldn't yet see in myself.

Maybe there's room for another bright star in the night sky.

My family encouraged and loved me despite all my weird, but there was the usual judgment there. Our history was too embedded for it to be any other way. With Lars, I saw myself through fresh eyes.

Rosie's gaze softened. "Does he know about Greece?"

Preferring to talk about something concrete, I moved onto another of my least favorite topics. "Yes. I had a nightmare, and he was there to talk me down. He agrees with you and thinks I should tell the fam."

"At least he's getting one thing right. Is it possible you're acting out to try to exert some control over a situation where you feel helpless? And this is taking the form of seducing second generation Finnish hockey players with more issues than a magazine stand and the words 'No trespassing' stamped on their forehead?"

This crazy bitch and her razor-sharp insights.

"Of course it's possible! It's entirely possible!"

Rosie smiled. "Aw, Addy." And then she wrapped her arms around me. She gave such great hugs, and I really needed one, if only to confirm that she wasn't mad at me.

At least she wasn't accusing me of being in love with him. She would think I was too sensible for that nonsense.

"I'm pretending I know what I'm doing," I whispered, "but I really don't have a clue. If I keep saying I'm taking it one day at a time, then I don't have to think about what comes next. Don't judge me."

"Never." And then she hugged me tighter still.

CHAPTER TWENTY-FIVE

Lars

ADELINE WAS QUIETER than usual on the way home from the party. I suspected performing in front of people and all the attention that yielded had worn her out. She went to great lengths to hide her light, which was easy to do when you were the introverted one in a family of sun-seekers.

While I put Mabel down, Adeline went to her room to shower and clean off her Zom-bee makeup. I'd loved getting my girls ready for the party, loved being wrapped up in that domestic ease. It reminded me of the more stable years of my youth, in particular, my dad's short-lived marriage to Carla. She was the only woman in his life that I could recall doing normal family stuff—Halloween costumes, school lunches, cooking together. While the rest of Sven's girl-friends floated through in skimpy bikinis and clouds of perfume, Carla had acted like a mom and tempered some of Sven's worst traits.

I wanted that kind of stability for Mabel.

I wanted her to always know love and laughter and never a harsh word.

During the party, my agent had called and left a message. It was late but I phoned back, knowing he'd answer immediately.

"Any news?" It had been over two weeks and Vicki appeared to have gone off-world.

"We have her address in Cleveland but she's not on site. Neighbors say she and her husband have gone to visit his family in upstate New York. We could have the lawyer reach out and start proceedings to—well, that depends on what you want to happen here."

"If you'd asked me two weeks ago, I would have said she has to take her kid back, but now? She hasn't even tried to get in touch, Quinn. Is that the environment I want to send Mabel back to?"

Maybe I was reveling too much in the fantasy of a life that was going well. My cute little girl in her cow costume, the gorgeous nanny taking care of my kid *and* my sexual needs, the fact I was playing better than I ever had—or would be once my suspension was up.

How long could this dream state last? I hadn't lied outright to my friend, but every moment in his presence since had felt like a betrayal. I was placing Adeline in this untenable position, forcing her to keep secrets from the people she loved. And for what? A sad effort at a do-over for the life I'd missed as a kid?

"Get in touch with her. We need to start negotiations on Mabel's future."

"Will do."

We chatted a little more about my upcoming contract renewal and how we might want to play that, especially given the wrinkle of my suspension. We had hoped to use my partnership with Kershaw in his likely last year to leverage the negotiations, which required I actually play with the guy. When I clicked off, I looked up to find Adeline standing at my door.

In a Rebels jersey.

"Is that—?"

"Uh huh." She turned and there it was: 22 NYQUIST. The hem skimmed her ass. Her gorgeous thighs tapered to slim ankles. Just my jersey against her silky skin.

Blood rushed to my groin.

I grabbed the baby monitor, a condom, and her, in that order, hauling all that lush flesh against my chest, one hand supporting her perfect ass.

Bare. She was completely bare.

I crushed my mouth over hers. All those doubts weighing on my mind—Kershaw, Vicki, my spurious dad credentials—went poof in the pleasure of her lips. She tasted like toothpaste and perfection, and she met my kiss with such dirty sweetness I almost came on the spot.

I carried her to the guest room, one eye open so I didn't trip, and finally made it to sanctuary. Placing her on the bed, I watched approvingly as she scooted up a few inches with one knee raised, revealing that dark valley of pleasure between her gorgeous thighs. I stowed the monitor and the condom on the nightstand.

She sat up and curled her fingers around the jersey's hem.

"No. It stays on."

Those moss-green eyes flashed. "Like I'm one of your puck bunnies?"

Not where I would have gone, but I could tell this fantasy turned her on.

"Bunny Prime." Kneeling at the side of the bed, I pulled gently on her ankle and brought her closer to my greedy mouth. "Now let me see what this little bunny's got for me."

I pushed the jersey up past her hips and placed my hands between her thighs. Spread her wide and looked my fill.

"Aw, sweet thing. Is that for me?"

Her chest heaved, her breathing turned raspy. "If you want it."

"Oh, I want it. I want this sweet little pussy so bad."

She squirmed, rubbing her gorgeous bottom against the duvet. "Please, Lars. Touch me."

"You first."

Cheeks flushed, her lips parted. Adeline wasn't used to dirty talk, but she liked it. Her wetter-by-the-second pussy liked it.

I massaged her thighs, rubbing my thumbs close to the heart of her, but never touching. More squirming, now with added moaning.

"Larrrrs!"

"You heard me in the shower, baby, now it's my turn to hear you."

That connection flipped the switch. Feeding her hand between her legs, she started to stroke. My mouth watered, as I watched those fingers she'd used earlier to bring joy to so many play her own body like a musical instrument. A few seconds in, I couldn't stand not tasting her any longer.

Pushing her hand aside, I took over with my tongue. Instantly, she bucked against my mouth, forcing me to spear inside her. My hands got in on the act. My fingers slicked through her folds as the flat of my tongue rubbed her clit.

Her writhing became more fevered, so much so I had to use one hand to hold her still while I licked and sucked and fucked her with my tongue. One final suckle on that slick bundle of nerves, and she came against my mouth, my name on her lips.

Giving her a moment to recover, I reached over for the condom and rolled it on. She sat up, leaning on her elbows, her cheeks flushed, her tongue darting out to lick her lips.

"You ready for me?"

With a sly smile, she responded, "You ready for me?" and then she turned over on her hands and knees.

Jesus.

That perfect ass, her glistening pussy, my name on her jersey. I must have been good in a previous life because I certainly wasn't good in this one. I pushed that thinking away. Gripping her hip, I sank into the hot, wet clasp of her. Made my claim. This woman had me under her spell, and with that encouragement to take her from behind, she knew what she was doing.

Thank Christ one of us does.

I withdrew a torturous inch, stroked a tantalizing inch more, then found a rhythm that drew me deeper each time. Both hands on her hips now as she stretched her arms forward and flattened her body to heighten the angle, taking her pleasure and spurring mine to unrecognizable heights.

Reaching around, I rubbed between her thighs. She moaned, met my thrust until I felt her pussy tighten, and she gasped her release. Instantly, mine rocketed through me and blanked what was left of my brain.

Adeline

. . .

A FEW DAYS AFTER HALLOWEEN, I walked in on a scene that would have had stylist Tara in a tizzy: Lars was tying Mabel's hair in cute little bursts with rainbow clips.

He looked up at me with a grin. "I can't wait until it's long enough to French braid."

"French braid? Who is this person?"

"You look so cute, Mabel." He leaned over to nuzzle his nose against his daughter's before picking up his phone and tapping the screen. "Take a look at this video," he said to me. "Don't you think this would look perfect on her?"

It was an adorable video of a dad braiding his daughter's hair. But a kid had to have hair to braid.

"When it grows in."

"When do you think that'll be?" He sounded concerned. "I've checked and there's this Japanese baby that looks like a mini-Yeti and he's only five months old. I feel like Mabel should have more hair by now. When did Tilly start getting longer hair?"

"Six months? But we all have Kershaw hair genes. Dark and thick and wavy." I didn't know much about Vicki's hair quality, but Lars had great hair. "Any baldness in your family?"

Horror crossed his brow. "No! Don't you dare jinx it."

I ran a hand through his thick, lustrous locks, and because I couldn't resist, I parted it at the back. "Hmm, looking a bit bare here. Sure there's no baldness in the Nyquist family tree?"

"There is not!" I loved teasing him. Who would have thought Lars Nyquist would have this lighter side to him?

"Oh, and I bought this outfit for her today." He pulled a shopping bag from the side of the sofa, a bright blue onesie

that said, "I Try to be Good, But I Take After my Daddy."
"Cute, right?"

"You're doing things to my ovaries, Nyquist."

"Oh yeah? What kind of things?"

I put my hand on his chest. "Melting, exploding, the usual."

"Sounds serious."

"Oh, it is." Damn. "I didn't mean—"

"No, I know."

But I wanted to mean it. I knew it wasn't realistic, but I wanted him to know this relationship was important to me. Even if all that was left from the rubble was an awkward friendship and my broken heart.

I changed the subject. "So you went shopping with Mabel? Do anything else?"

"Went to the gym so I could stay limber during my suspension. Tara watched Mabel."

"I could have done that."

He shook his head. "You need time off. But I had an interesting chat with your brother."

"Hatch?"

"Basically grilled me about you."

That threw cold water over my domestic fantasy. "What did he say?"

"He just wanted to know why I'd come to your defense against MacFarlane. Sounded like my least favorite D-man's accusations about my wicked intentions had finally hit home. Guess he needed to think on it awhile."

"And what did you say?"

He sighed. "That looking out for you was a no-brainer. Listen, your brother is understandably protective of you."

"Understandably?"

"In the way any male family member is protective of a

female family member." He frowned at my sour expression. "What am I missing here?"

"I'm just tired of being considered fragile enough to need protection."

He took my hand. "You're a girl in a family of boys. From an evolutionary biology standpoint, that's hard to fight. But it sounds like there's more."

"Oh, there's always more!"

He settled back on the sofa and pulled me into his arms. "Then tell me. So I can learn and not be such a hard ass when it comes to protecting Mabel."

I rubbed a hand along his chest. "I doubt anything I say will change that."

He nuzzled his lips along my temple, giving me space to sort through my emotions.

"When I was a kid, I wasn't good at sports. Hatch was already there, the heir in waiting, but I think my dad wanted to raise a family of genetically enhanced superstars."

"His own hockey team, huh?"

"Right. But I was clearly the weak link. Clumsy, unco-ordinated, not champion material."

His hand rubbed my arm, soothing in all the right ways. He didn't jump in and invalidate my feelings, and I almost wished he had so I could put a mark in the Lars con column.

"Once the twins were born, I think Dad was relieved he didn't have to encourage me to be sporty. He could move on to the kids who would be successful." I sighed. "I've always felt a bit different from them. I like books and art and music. Conor used to joke I must be adopted."

"That had to hurt."

"A bit. You said your dad gave you a hard time when

you didn't measure up. My family didn't give me a hard time. Not entirely. I did it to myself, I suppose."

"We're our own worst enemies."

I smiled against his chest. "We are. My brothers didn't mean to, but they would inevitably treat me as different to them. Being a girl, not really into the same things, not as strong as them. And because I don't have a clear vision for my life, it adds fodder to the story of me. Aimless, weird, needs-to-be-cared-for Adeline."

"Well, that's bullshit."

I raised my head. "It is?"

"Do you believe that about yourself?"

"No. Well, sometimes." *Tell me something different.*

"The Adeline I know is kind of a dick."

Not the kind of pep talk I was expecting.

"Okay."

"In the sense that you are bossy as fuck. You're take charge when you need to be and all soft power when the moment calls for it. You've got this moral streak that keeps you and the people you care about on the right track. Plus you knew exactly what to do to steer me in the right direction. Not just with Mabel but standing up for myself and showing people that I'm not like Sven. I didn't want any PR soft soap, but you figured out a way to draw me in because you're—"

"Sneaky?"

"I was going to say persuasive, but sneaky works. A good type of sneaky. Manipulative in a way that I was already doing your bidding before I even realized what was happening. That takes a special kind of quiet strength."

That made me a bit giddy. "Or perhaps you were vulnerable to anyone who would tell you what needed to be done."

"Perhaps. Or you could take the compliment and recognize your strengths and how you could use them."

"I like babies, but I don't think it's a vocation."

"I'm not talking about being a nanny, though that's another amazing thing you've got going for you. Not only did you step up for me, but you stepped up for your parents. Taking time off from college to help with Tilly."

Only because I didn't like being away from home.

"And seeing you with Tilly and all those other kids at the party, playing music, showcased another of your talents."

My first instinct was to deny. "That's just for my sister."

"Yet every kid there loved it." He kissed my temple. "Adults, too."

"Not sure I can make a career out of that." Yet the idea gave me tingles. "Could I?"

"Who knows? But maybe it's worth exploring." He ran a finger over my jaw. "You don't have to decide it all now. You're still so young with so much potential."

His voice held a note of melancholy. Because I was young, full of potential, or something else?

Before I could ask, his brow lined. "We didn't get to discuss this last night—"

"Not much talking, if I recall."

"No." His lips twitched as we both indulged in a sexy memory. "Before you seduced me in my jersey, you vixen, I talked to my agent. They found Vicki."

"Oh, that's good. Right?"

He blew out a breath. "It is. We still have to get her to the negotiating table but it's a start. I have to be realistic here. I don't know what's going on with her, but we need to figure things out, for Mabel's sake. I can't rely on this patchwork of solutions or expect you to be here forever. You have a life to start, Adeline."

I swallowed my emotion. I could say I was happy to stay on as long as he needed me, but that would sound desperate. Like I was trying to insinuate myself into his life, taking that crush and magnifying it now that I had the leverage of his need for childcare. He was here, making suggestions for my career path, telling me that Mabel's mom might be back in the picture soon. Anyone with a brain could join those dots.

We had never discussed anything more than a day at a time. We had barely discussed it at all.

Take the hint, Adeline Kershaw. Take the hint.

CHAPTER TWENTY-SIX

Hockey Dads. Just like us!

Spotted in the wild! Three Chicago Rebels players visited Lincoln Park Zoo with their children yesterday. The second week of November saw the first frost of the year, which meant the Rebels kids were bundled up in the latest fashions. At almost two, Jane Jacobs, daughter of center Cody Jacobs, rocked a cuter-than-cute Burberry trench while her big-girl friend, Tilly Kershaw, radiated tomboy energy in jewel-embroidered Stella McCartney jeans and a varsity-style bomber jacket from Sadie Yates's kids' range. But the true star of the show was Lars's Nyquist's daughter Mabel, who shone in her pink shearling bodysuit from Zara, which still allowed enough range of motion for the curious little girl to touch the goats at the petting zoo. The usually stern Lars was seen laughing with his teammates, Theo Kershaw and Cody Jacobs, which we hope can only signals better relationships on the ice! Daddyhood suits you, Lars. Go Rebels!

- Hot Goss

Adeline

THE SCENTS of cooking wafted through the air, picking up strength as I entered the kitchen. Lars stood over the stove, stirring something.

"You cooked?"

"Yep. Come taste this."

I approached as he held up a wooden spoon coated with a red sauce. My tongue flicked out and tasted. A little spicy, absolutely perfect.

"I thought you wanted me to babysit." He'd texted to say he had a dinner date with his agent that he couldn't get out of.

"I lied." The corners of his eyes crinkled with a smile. "I wanted to make you dinner."

My heart flipped. A thank you dinner? A goodbye dinner?

In the last week, as Lars's suspension continued, we'd enjoyed each other's company, watching movies, cooking for Mabel, and playing songs, despite a faint ticking sound always in the back of my mind. Still no sign of Mabel's mom, but that last conversation about needing to start my life had stayed with me. The happy-family bubble had to prick soon. It was just a matter of who held the pin.

"I'll never say no to a man cooking for me. What can I do?"

"Open the wine? I've already fed our girl, given her a bath, and put her down." He nodded at the monitor.

"You're beginning to sound like an old pro at this, Lars Nyquist."

He shook his head. "Remember how terrified I was that first day? I didn't even know I needed to change her diaper."

"Your face when I told you." I smiled fondly. "You've come a long way."

He didn't deny it. "So you know how she says 'Yabby' a lot? Today, I'm pretty sure she said 'Yaddy'. Now before you say anything, I know that it's a little early in her development for speech, but she's such a smart girl, that it could be possible. I read today that some babies are speaking at ten months."

I wouldn't be the one to point out that Mabel was a few days shy of the eight-month mark.

He eyed me. "You think I'm crazy?"

"You're just a proud dad."

He grinned and passed me the corkscrew. "The wine, sweet thing."

Hiding my smile, I did as I was told. The table was already set with a bottle of red, real napkins, and candles. Between getting plates, silverware, and a block of parm, we criss-crossed the kitchen several times, a domestic dance that made me heady.

"Where did these flowers come from?" A gorgeous bouquet of roses, chrysanthemums, and eucalyptus was set in a pretty vase on the counter. Curious, I plucked out the card.

My dick sends his gratitude. –Jacobs

"Do I want to know?"

"Just Jakey thanking me for getting his wife in the mood to jump his bones." Chuckling, he filled me in on how Insta images of Baby Mabel had made Zara broody and kick-started the Jacobs' love life.

"Lars Nyquist, uterus whisperer," I said with a grin.

Ten minutes later, we were seated with spaghetti and meatballs.

"Not as fancy as burgers at the club," he murmured.

"Damn, those burgers were fine."

He leaned over and swiped at my chin, then sucked on his thumb. That little move, so comfortable, made me shiver.

We continued eating, chatting about Mabel, about last night's game, about my latest video on Peyton Bell's various cellies. It was easy, and I loved every minute.

I pushed the plate aside and rubbed my stomach. "That was so good. Did you really make that sauce from scratch?"

"Carla's recipe." At my curious expression, he added, "Dad's second wife. She taught me how to cook."

He hadn't talked about his childhood much beyond that initial panic about his suitability for fatherhood. But Sven's ghost hovered over everything, making Lars doubt. Was he good enough to be Mabel's dad? Could he offer her the best possible life?

"You liked her?" If she was teaching him recipes, then there had to be some affection there.

"I did. She lasted about eighteen months? Age ten until my twelfth birthday. Probably the most stable time of my childhood." He paused before adding, "Sven fucked it up as usual."

"How so?"

He rubbed a finger around the rim of the wine glass. "He hit her."

It shouldn't have shocked me. I knew he was a piece of work, between the gambling and substance abuse, but to hear he also abused a woman he supposedly loved took him from pitiful addict to total asshole.

"More than once?"

A slow nod. "They both drank a lot, so there were a lot of fights. They sometimes got physical, so I think Carla excused most slaps as a 'takes two to tango' kind of deal. But on that day—my birthday—he was pissed at me because I slept in. Typically, I'd be up at five for practice, Carla didn't wake me because …"

"It was your birthday."

"Right." He grimaced. "But Sven didn't care. He—" He broke off, the emotion of the memory obviously affecting him deeply.

"Hey." I jumped up, circled the table, and took a seat on his lap. "You don't have to tell me but I'm here for you if you want to share."

"No, it's okay." He rubbed a hand along my thigh, a move that seemed to soothe him. I'd noticed him rubbing Mabel's back when he was upset. "He dragged me out of bed and beat the living shit out of me. Carla tried to intervene, and he hit her so hard it knocked a tooth out. That's when she decided she'd had enough."

My heart dropped. "And she left you? With him?"

He frowned. "She had her own stuff to deal with. Her own healing to complete. And I got a decent spaghetti sauce recipe out of it."

She abandoned a child to an abuser. This reminded me of Lars's concern for Vicki, that she might be in a tough spot with her husband. He understood about a woman's need for self-preservation after his experience with his stepmom. "Did he continue to hit you?"

"I told him I'd quit hockey if he got physical with me again. It was the only leverage I had so I used it, though the idea of giving up hockey killed me. It was my way out. I called his bluff, and he caved. The odd slap here and there but nothing that left bruises. I could handle that."

My eyes welled. "Lars, that was so unfair."

"Hard to say if it was or not. It shaped me, gave me grit, built character." He swiped at my tears. "Don't be sad for me, enkelini. I'm okay."

But was he? I'd grown up with so much and it wasn't right that Lars didn't have the same. Mabel was truly a gift. With her he could finally appreciate the miracle of a close-knit family.

I was still pissed at a dead man, though. "Then he almost got you kicked out of the league before you'd even started."

His lips twitched, probably amused at my defensiveness. "I was furious at how he tried to throw me under the bus. It definitely left a bad taste. I'd always felt like I was of use to him for one thing—to make him look good—but once he tried to blame me for his mistakes, I knew we could never be a real family. Luckily hockey has no shortage of mentors."

Like my dad. They were closer than I had imagined, becoming even tighter in recent months. It made what we were doing so much more reckless.

"Aurora says you need someone to love, something to give you focus other than hockey. She seemed to think Mabel would be the making of you."

"Did she now?" He considered that for a moment. "Your family have been good to me, this last year especially. I wasn't in a great place when my dad died. Everything was unresolved. Your dad pulled me back from the brink, your mom welcomed me at her table, and your great-gran makes the best martinis on the planet."

"The Scandi Noir! I can't believe she named a cocktail after you."

He shrugged. "What can I say? She's always had a thing for me and my beard."

Not the only one. "We Kershaws tend to go all in on people."

He paused a moment, like he was gathering his thoughts. "I know I've said I'm grateful, Adeline, but it's more than that. It's not just the practical help, shopping, appointments, and all that. It's the assurance you give me that I'm not like Sven. I can be a good dad to Mabel, no matter what happens with Vicki."

"What'll you do if she shows up?"

"Can you believe I'm almost hoping she doesn't? I know that sounds strange—"

"It doesn't."

"If she does, we'll come to some sort of arrangement. Now I've had a taste of fatherhood I'm not going to just hand Mabel over."

This man was in love with his little girl, and it was so beautiful to see.

"What are you smiling at?"

"I love seeing a happy ending. You and Mabel are so great together." Only there was no room for me in this happily-ever-after.

"I love our chats," he said, before dropping a light kiss on my lips. "I love our time together."

My eyes stung, and I tried my best to hold it together. "So do I."

The unspoken lay between us. *I'll miss this when it's gone.*

We both knew we were on borrowed time. This new life with Mabel, how in-sync he'd become with his team and especially with my father. I couldn't compete with that.

He moved in to kiss me. He tasted of wine and need, and I couldn't get enough of him. Of this. Of us.

But there was no us. This was a precarious time for Lars. This conversation today had only confirmed what I suspected: he needed the support network of my family. If he lost that—if he lost my dad's friendship—then he might fall apart. We had Mabel to think of. The Rebels. The success of my dad's final year in the pros.

Everyone but us.

Lars

WE CLEARED UP THE DISHES, working side by side in the kitchen like the team we were solidifying each day. It was strange to think it. Teamwork up until this point in my life had meant hockey, and nothing else. I had no other family that qualified.

Now I had the Kershaws. I had the Rebels. I had Mabel. And I had Adeline.

People said it took a village to raise a child. For me, it had taken paid employees and abused women, not exactly the most heartwarming of combinations. Talking about my father and his bad behavior made me wonder about Vicki. Was she safe wherever she was with this husband who made her choose him over her child?

Then there was Adeline. I had no idea how this was going to play out. I just knew that I wanted more with this woman, and that was going to cause problems with my hockey partner and closest friend on the Rebels.

The dishes squared away, I poured the last of the wine into her glass and rinsed the bottle. We stood at the kitchen counter, staring at each other.

"You trying to get me drunk, Lars Nyquist?"

"You're already intoxicated by me."

She giggled. "Oh, really?"

"C'mere, sweet thing. Let me take care of you."

She fell into my arms and damn, the feel of her was powerful. Not just the physical molding of her curves to my body, but the way it pulled my heart and stretched it like taffy, like I could do anything because this was the endgame. Adeline and Mabel, the family I would fight to protect. My beautiful girls.

We kissed, the connection between us suddenly deeper and more compelling than ever. I'd unburdened myself tonight, shared the hurts inflicted on me, the doubts I had about my potential to be a good dad. She had listened, defended, supported. She had stood in my corner, cheering me on. No one had ever given this to me.

"Thank you," I whispered as I applied another lingering kiss. "Thank you."

"You don't need to thank me. I'll always be here for Mabel."

I drew back. "Not thanking you for Mabel—well, I am, always—but for being you. For being my rock, but also for being my angel. For lifting me up. For offering your strength, your body, your wit. Everything about you is so damn perfect."

Her eyes welled. I thought she might say something, but words appeared to fail her. She kissed me instead.

Breathless, we separated, again gazing upon each other

like we were seeing for the first time. I didn't want to impute too much significance to this, but it felt big. Real. Terrifying.

She clasped my hand and led me upstairs. I loved seeing her take the lead; I was a slave to her and would happily follow her anywhere.

In the bedroom, we stripped each other slowly, taking our time. Recognizing that this thing between us had entered a new phase.

I kissed down her body, spending a few heady seconds on those perfect breasts, the flare of her hip, the curve of her ass. Those soft inner thighs were perfect against my lips, and when I tasted her, the tang of her arousal sent blood rushing to my cock.

After the slow strip, I tried to keep what followed on the same speed setting. But I wasn't getting any younger and waiting had never been my strong point. Suited up, I entered her in a single thrust. She bracketed my body with her thighs, pulled me deeper, whispered sweet words of desire and need in my ear. Rocking into her, I let myself fall into pleasure and push away the trouble rearing its head.

And when she cried out, I captured that pleasure with my mouth, holding it, dragging it inside me, until I could no longer keep it behind the gates. Mindless, I let go with a final stroke inside her, loving how she held me tight. Loving her.

Knowing this was likely the end of one important relationship, but recognizing in my heart that it was the start of another.

A family of my own.

CHAPTER TWENTY-SEVEN

Rebel sources tell us Theo Kershaw has been placed on IR with a lower body injury ahead of tonight's game against Tampa. Given the Rebels' poor results after Nyquist's unfortunate suspension, Coach Graham will be hard-pressed to adequately stock the lines on a team with such a shallow defensive bench. Will he put the terrible twosome, MacFarlane and Nyquist, on the same line? Maybe these two can work out their differences in a more productive manner on the ice. Then again there's that saying about pigs and their ability to transcend the usual laws of physics.

- @RebelsInsider

Lars

I HAD TO TELL KERSHAW.

Last night with Adeline, I'd felt so close to her. Like I was finally where I belonged, with the right person in the right moment. I couldn't imagine my life without her, which meant I had to take action to make it happen. It would be rough for a while. Theo would probably pummel me to a pulp, Hatch would join in, and Elle would stop speaking to me. (I suspected I might have Aurora and Tilly on my side.) Most of all, the team dynamics would suffer. But it was early in the season—we might recover.

Ahead of the home game against Tampa, the press was loving this new angle of me forced to play with my sworn enemy, almost daring me to lash out at Coach or make some crack about how much I hated MacFarlane. Stuck on IR, Theo was watching up in the box and God help us, Dex O'Malley had been given the captain's band.

Me and MacFarlane as partners? O'Malley in charge on the ice? The end times had arrived, it seemed.

It didn't start well. Your own teammates weren't supposed to be chirping away but this dick had decided getting under my skin would somehow contribute to our on-ice partnership.

"Aw, you miss your bestie?"

"Screw you."

He grinned behind his mouthguard and skated off.

Ten seconds later: "So sad."

"Get fucked."

Boden called out from goal: "Aren't you guys on the same team?"

Tell that to my so-called partner on the defensive line.

At the end of the first period, as I accepted the skate guards from the assistant, MacFarlane bumped shoulders with me. We were one goal down, owing to some miscommunication between me and my new buddy.

He offered a parting shot. "Maybe pay attention the next time I call for it."

"Eat shit, asshole."

Real mature. We were losing this game for sure.

I headed down the tunnel. Theo was waiting for me outside the locker room in his game day suit, his face grim. *Fuck, he's found out.*

But he wasn't coming toward me, ready to fight. This was something else.

My heart crashed, instant awareness hitting me. "Is Mabel okay?"

"She's at the hospital with a fever. Elle just called." He pushed me into the locker room. "Get changed and I'll drive you."

I SLAMMED through the ER doors and barreled up to the nurses' station.

"My daughter is here. I need—"

"Lars."

My gaze snapped to the source of the voice. Elle and Adeline were seated in a cluster of chairs near a vending machine. Rushing over, I tried to get the words out.

"Is she okay? Tell me she's okay."

Elle squeezed my arm. "She threw up at the house before the puck dropped. And then she threw up again about ten minutes later."

"Lars, the doctor's assessing her now." Adeline's expression and soft voice beseeched me to be calm, but how could I be? "She went in about thirty minutes ago and they're running some tests."

"I need to speak to someone in charge." I looked over

my shoulder. Theo was chatting with the nurse behind the desk.

Elle guided me to a seat. "All my kids had bouts of this. It's usually a viral infection, like gastroenteritis. It looks more serious than it is because a baby vomiting tends to be dramatic."

I placed my head in my hands and leaned my elbows on my knees. I wanted to bow to Elle's experience here but what if she was wrong?

I looked up at Adeline. "What happened?" Right now, she was the one person I could trust not to sugarcoat it.

"She seemed a bit fussy before I took her over to Mom and Dad's. A little high in color, too. But she ate well, and I thought she'd be fine. Then she threw up. We didn't want to risk it—" She broke off and shot a glance at her mom, then back at me.

"You did the right thing. I'm just—just worried."

Ten minutes later, a doctor appeared disguised as a pimply kid. "Mrs. Kershaw?"

Elle rose to greet him. "That's me. This is Mabel's dad, Lars."

The doc's eyes went wide. "Lars Nyquist? Wow."

"How's my daughter?"

"She's doing okay. Basically, it's a bad stomach bug. We're hydrating her and keeping her under observation."

Theo clapped me on the back. "See? Usual kid stuff."

"Can I see her?"

"Sure. Come on through."

I took a couple of steps, then turned back to Adeline. "Come with me? I think she'd be more at ease with a face she knows." Suddenly I felt like I knew nothing about parenting. If I'd been there, what would I have done? What if it happened at night while I was asleep or ... having sex? I could have slept or fucked my way through her choking to death.

Adeline closed the gap. "Of course."

We headed into the bowels of the ER, past curtained cubbies with people moaning and monitors beeping. They must have placed Mabel at the end because this walk seemed to be taking forever. She was in the last cubicle, half-sitting, red-faced, a baby-sized drip attached to her arm. A nurse stood at the end of the bed with a clipboard.

I could've sworn my baby's eyes lit up at seeing me.

"Mabel, sweetheart." I leaned over her and kissed her on the top of her head.

"Mr. Nyquist, Mrs. Nyquist. Mabel's doing fine. Just a touch of stomach flu, nothing she can't handle."

"Why is she hooked up like this?"

"Just keeping her hydrated. It's easier than hoping she'd hold it down. Once the bug is out of her system, she can go back to ingesting fluids the usual way."

"Can I sit with her?"

"Of course." She nodded at the seats, then left to attend to another patient.

I took one and looked up at Adeline. She was wearing one of those Theo's Tarts jackets that all the Kershaw women sported for the games. "Will you stay?"

"Are you sure you want me here?" She looked teary-eyed. "I was so scared for her."

Pulling on her hand, I brought her down to the seat beside me. "Of course I do. No one I'd want here more."

"She looks better than before. Not so flushed and hot."

I clasped Adeline's hand to mine. "You took good care of her."

"Thankfully Mom was there. She knew exactly what to do. If I'd been on my own—"

"You would've known too. You have all the right instincts. If it had been me or happened when I was asleep or occupied, I don't know if it would have turned out so well."

"Lars." She cupped my jaw and brought my face close. "You would have handled it like a pro because you're her dad. And this dad knows how to look after his daughter."

"Sometimes I don't know. Sometimes I think I shouldn't be doing this at all."

She held my chin tightly. "So your dad was a dick. He hurt you. You thought you could hold that inside, but you don't have to." She placed a hand on my chest, above my heart.

I didn't push her away or deny what she said. I listened, as if every word she spoke had the potential to heal. Give me the answers I sought.

"The scars he left don't make you a failure. They mean you overcame obstacles that no one should have had to face. They've given you a perspective, a way of seeing things like no one else can."

"Doesn't mean I'm going to be a good dad. Or a person."

"Doesn't automatically disqualify you, either."

I searched her face, looking for evidence she was blowing smoke up my ass. She was so damn sincere it scared me.

"You're the best person I know, Adeline."

And I love you. So fucking much.

Her eyes welled and I kissed her, taking some of her sweetness for myself. It mixed with my sharpness, my doubts, creating a brand-new flavor that was only us. Surely Theo could see what I did. Could recognize how amazing we were together.

The curtain behind us swished, and with it came a

sound like a tiny gasp. I looked over my shoulder at the swaying fabric.

"I think someone just came in."

She blinked. "A nurse?"

"Not sure."

The tension was broken when my little girl went "Yab-by!" I reached for her and squeezed her little finger, the one on the hand with the IV. I hated seeing her in such discomfort.

Adeline stood. "I'll go check on my parents, let them know Mabel's looking better." She leaned over and gave my girl a kiss on the forehead. "Be good, Mabel. I'll see you soon."

I took a second to try to process my feelings. Mabel's health scare was surely playing havoc with my emotions, but I knew this much. Tonight I was prepared to tell Theo that I wanted Adeline. That I was in love with her.

This woman was my rock, the one person I could trust to have my and Mabel's back. I loved having her around. I loved her smell and her curves and how she didn't let me get away with anything. I loved how she felt in my arms and wrapped around my body. I loved being inside her and I loved sitting on the sofa with her in quiet moments where neither of us had to say a word.

To be honest, it would be better if I wasn't in love because I was the worst person for her. I'd eventually hurt her, no doubt about it. And that was before I factored in the atomic bomb that would explode when Kershaw found out.

But for now, Mabel was on the mend, and I had finally stopped fighting my feelings for this wonderful woman. Everything else could wait until tomorrow.

Adeline

YOU'RE *the best person I know.*

It was a lovely thing to say, but it also sounded final. A kiss-off. My mind was whirling as I headed out to the waiting room. I was in love with Lars but did he feel even a tenth of what I did? I desperately wanted to think so, but I also understood he was in a weird place right now. Nothing like a sick baby to send your head spinning.

On reaching the waiting room, I found that several of the team had arrived. My dad bounded over. "How's Button?"

"She's okay. They're hydrating her and keeping her for observation. I'll probably stick around for a while if that's okay."

"Of course! Lars needs you right now." He thumbed over his shoulder. "The team wanted to help."

"They're good guys." I flicked a glance at my mom and that's when I knew.

She had seen me with Lars.

She was trying her best, but her face said it all. My dad headed off to give the team an update.

My mom took his place and rubbed my arm. "You okay? I know you got a fright there."

"I did. I'm just crazy about her."

She nodded. "I know. I think I've always known. Not sure it was a good idea to push you into this."

"It was my decision, Mom. I made the call."

"Right, but it's certainly ... complicated."

We were talking about something else. Someone else.

"You don't need to worry about me, Mom. I know what I'm doing."

Tiny tears appeared at the corners of her eyes.

"Oh, Mom." I pulled her in for a hug, then steered her to a quieter corner near the snack machine. I checked the offerings, looking for a Twix but resolved to settle for a KitKat. "It'll be okay."

"Is it serious?"

If my mom thought I was in love with Lars, she would insist I come clean to Dad. The fallout would be catastrophic. I needed more time. More space to think it through.

"Lars needed someone to be his support at this time—"

"And you were there to give it?" Fury sparked in her eyes. "I can't *believe* he took advantage."

"He didn't. I seduced him."

She looked supremely skeptical. *Thanks, Mom.*

"Honestly. He wouldn't have made a move if I hadn't gone there first. I've always had a crush on him."

"Well, I knew that." Oh. Who else did? Not my father. He would never have encouraged me to become Mabel's nanny if he had an inkling. "I just can't believe he'd go there."

"I'm not a kid who can be taken advantage of, Mom. I'm a grown woman." Was it any wonder I couldn't tell my parents about Greece? They still saw me as the naïve innocent who had things happen to her instead of the other way around.

"I don't want to see you hurt, sweetie."

I looked over her shoulder to my dad, who gave me a big smile. Guilt shuddered through me.

"Don't tell Dad. It was just a short-term thing, and he'd just worry."

She raised an eyebrow. "That's not really how my marriage works. I kept a lot of secrets from your father when we first started out. It almost broke us."

She was talking about her sketchy family's history. Her con-artist parents had long retired from their schemes to Costa Rica. We rarely saw them, but I understood my mom's concern. Secrets and lies tended to break the murky surface eventually.

"I don't want you to lie, but if it's not serious, how would it help?" I lowered my voice even further. "Dad would blow up with Lars. Their partnership on the team would be destroyed."

It wouldn't matter that I was crazy about Lars. My father would never forgive him, and a part of him would always blame me for coming between them. For destroying the team in this important year.

I couldn't be responsible for that. Yet I couldn't give Lars up, not yet. There had to be a way.

"Your father won't be pleased, whichever route we take here. But ..." She looked over at him, watching as he corralled his teammates into a huddle and led with the purpose he'd always shown. "Knowing you and Lars were ... it wouldn't go down well. If you two were committed, then it might be worth it. It would still be rough, but we'd get through it."

We'd get through it. That was the problem: my relationship with Lars wasn't just our business. It was everyone's.

CHAPTER TWENTY-EIGHT

Lars

I WOKE up with a stiff neck and a heavy pit in my stomach. Straightening in the bedside chair, I checked in with Mabel. She was awake and looked so much better. Color, and not the fire-engine-red kind, bloomed on her cheeks. Her eyes sparkled with pleasure, and I could tell she was happy to see me.

I grasped her little finger. "You okay, Mabel?"

"Yabby!"

"Yeah, yabby to you, too. You gave me quite the scare, ya little monster."

She chattered on with her usual baby talk and I listened, thanking my stars she was in a better mood. Last night when we were moved to a private room in Pediatrics, I sent Adeline home. There was no reason why both of us should get no sleep.

I regarded the empty chair on the other side of the

room, wishing she was here, that I could have woken up to both my girls. When she left, she'd been in a subdued mood, which I put down to her worry about Mabel.

Numerous texts had come in overnight from the team and org staff, checking in on Mabel. Even one from MacFarlane, telling me she was in his thoughts, which meant pigs might actually have transcended the laws of physics after all.

The only person who mattered was Adeline. I needed to be up front with her about what I wanted. Not just a nanny for Mabel. Not just a village to raise my child.

I wanted this woman with every part of me.

The door opened, and I looked up expecting a nurse, or better yet the woman I loved. It was Elle, toting two cups of coffee.

"Hi," she whispered. "How is she?"

"Good. She's awake." I stood, took the cup she offered, and kissed her cheek. "She's been talking up a storm, which usually means she's in a good mood."

"Oh, thank God. I thought you could do with a break."

I didn't like the idea of leaving her, but Elle was as experienced as anyone. I trusted her, the heart and soul of this family who meant the world to me.

"I probably stink."

"No, you're fine. But I'm here if you want to nip home and get a shower or some rest." It might have been my imagination, but she seemed on edge.

I sipped my coffee, let its magical properties lift me. "Is everything okay?"

A small sigh, nothing dramatic, but I sensed what was coming. "Last night, I saw you and Adeline together." She didn't need to elaborate. We both knew what she meant.

"Okay." I put the coffee cup down. "I can see that

would be upsetting for you." I had to assume Theo didn't know because my balls were still intact.

"She says you didn't take advantage, Lars, but I find that hard to believe. You're the more experienced person here."

I snapped my gaze to hers. "You and Adeline discussed this?"

"Once I knew, I couldn't exactly ignore it."

Adeline hadn't said a word. Maybe she worried about piling on, given Mabel's condition.

"She's too young, Lars."

I swallowed. "Yeah, she is."

"And she has very little experience with relationships. She's always set my and Theo's relationship on a pedestal. She wants what we have."

My heart cheered. *Yes, that's what I want, too.*

"So it surprised me when she said what you two had was merely a short-term thing."

My jubilant heart pricked like a spent balloon.

"That it just happened because of the living situation and ..." She gestured at me. "Her crush."

Her crush. Right.

While I tried to process that, Elle went on. "The thing is. She's lying."

"She is?"

"Lars, my daughter's in love with you."

Snap, I'm in love with her, too. I should have been over-joyed to hear this. But Elle's expression wasn't giving "welcome to the fam" vibes. As kind as she had been to me over the years with the invites, the fond words, the pitching in with Mabel, it all meant squat because now I was a threat to her daughter's happiness.

"She didn't say that, though," I said.

"No, but I know my daughter. She's had a thing for you

for years. A teen crush, rather harmless, I thought. It seemed to have vanished while she was away, and once she started looking after Mabel, I had hoped she would see it for what it was. The reality of it."

I struggled with the words. "The reality?"

"Lars, you have so much going on right now with Mabel and working out custody with her mother. The more embedded my daughter becomes in your family, the less likely she'll figure out her own path. Adeline's a sensitive girl, and she's always been the caregiver in our family, the one who puts everyone else before herself. She might confuse her feelings for you with obligation. Set aside her own needs."

Everything she said resonated. I had been using Adeline, weaponizing her selflessness to make my life easier. I knew she had a crush, and while I wasn't convinced there was more to it despite Elle's claims to the contrary, I recognized a mother's concern.

You're not good enough for my daughter.

"I took advantage, Elle. Of your hospitality, of your support, of your kindness."

A flicker of something in her eyes—disappointment, perhaps—tugged at me before her gaze hardened.

"I'm not sure where to go from here," she said.

"You mean, with Theo?"

She nodded. "I'm not in the habit of keeping secrets from my husband."

Need advice? I'm a freakin' expert.

I was betraying this man every day, and I had thought I could tell him about Adeline? About how my feelings for her had developed. About how it had gone from lust to love in an instant.

That would not be happening. I had taken the trust of a

friend, his family, his daughter, and abused it. Not so different from the old man after all.

"I wouldn't ask you to do that."

"Really? My daughter did. She doesn't want to upset the team's strongest partnership. But if she's serious about you—and I think she is—that will have to happen. I don't want my daughter or my husband to be hurt, Lars."

That said it all. I was all set to rip that partnership to shreds last night, but the collateral damage would be monumental.

Mabel made a sound, looking for attention. The sight of her should have warmed me, but all I could think of was her short life's volatility. Her mother missing, her father a traitor to his legacy and his friends, not to mention what I was doing to Adeline. Clinging to her for dear life because she and Mabel were the only good things in it.

"What happened with Adeline was a mistake. I'll take care of it."

Elle studied me. "She'll be hurt."

"She'll get over it. First major crush and all that." She looked like she wanted to say more, but this conversation had to end. "You don't need to stay, Elle."

She looked taken aback. She had to realize that this knowledge between us changed everything. What I had done to her daughter and her family had expended all my goodwill. I could no longer use the Kershaws as a crutch.

"It's okay," I assured her. "Thanks for the coffee. Thanks for everything."

Adeline

. . .

DRAGGING a heart-shaped balloon and with a tartan teddy under my arm, I rounded the corner of the hospital corridor just as a nurse was leaving Mabel's room.

"Is everything okay?"

"Yes, Mabel's with her dad. We've just discharged her, so she'll be heading home."

Relieved, I headed inside. Lars was pulling her tiny pink jacket on, but Mabel was resisting.

"Hey, team!"

He looked up at me, his brows drawn together in a V. "Hello."

"The nurse told me she's coming home." I rushed in to help with her sleeve. "There ya go, Mabel." She fisted my hair and gave it a good tug. "You must be so pleased," I said to Lars.

"I am. Thanks for looking after her."

"Of course. I would say it's my job, but it's more than that. It's Mabel. I'm crazy about her."

A curious range of emotions danced across his face. "I'd better get her home."

Something about the way he said it pulled me up short. *I*, not *we*.

He was still fussing with Mabel's jacket, not looking at me directly. "I called the childcare agency this morning. Janet's still available and she can start on Monday."

My heart plummeted. That was mere days away. "I didn't realize you were ready to hire someone. You don't feel like you're settling?"

"I'm learning that compromise is the essence of parenthood. You said she was the best candidate we interviewed."

I had, weeks ago, but I expected more discussion, that these decisions would be made as a team. As a family. I chuckled nervously. "Lars, are you firing me?"

Finally, he looked at me squarely. "This had to end sometime, Adeline."

I resisted going to where my sorry heart was leaning. Surely, we were just talking about the nanny gig. My pulse was hammering a million miles an hour.

"I didn't think you'd want to make such a drastic change. Mabel needs stability."

"Then the sooner she starts with an official nanny, the better. And the sooner you can get on with your life."

Enough of this dancing around the issue. "Lars, are you ending *us*?"

"We knew it had an expiration date."

As far as I was concerned, that had never been discussed. I had suspected we were on borrowed time yet a part of me hoped we'd figure something out. Suddenly, I saw what I wanted so badly slipping away—and I was no where near ready.

"Is this because of Mabel getting sick while in my care? I know I don't have the same experience as an officially-certified nanny, but my mom was there and—"

He cut me off. "That's not it. You've been amazing with Mabel, an absolute godsend. But it's time to part ways. It's best for everyone."

"Is it?"

"Adeline, don't you see how much I'm hurting you?"

Right now? Yes, you dick. I shook my head, feeling like it might roll off my body at any moment.

He went on. "You're too caught up in this, your first grand affair. You don't see the damage this thing we got going on is doing to your relationship with your dad. Your family. You're lying to them. I'm lying to them. I'm dragging you down because I wanted you. I wanted your sweetness and goodness and everything in between. I used you to make myself feel better."

My debate skills were no match for this multi-pronged attack. "I wanted to be here. I *want* to be here."

"In the gutter with me?"

I had no idea why he was doing this. "Lars, what's going on?"

"I'm not the good guy here, Adeline." He allowed Mabel to curl her cute hand around his little finger. Sure, real villain stuff.

"You are to me."

"You sure about that? The guy who knocked up a married woman in a bar bathroom, who barely resisted when faced with the temptation of his friend's daughter, who continues to lie to that friend every day. Such strength of character." His tone was more than disgust. It was self-loathing.

"There's such a thing as context. None of those things exist in a vacuum."

That didn't impress him much. "Is that what you told your mom?"

"My mom?"

He rubbed his beard. "She stopped by this morning to see Mabel. She mentioned that she'd seen us together last night. You and me."

"Lars ..."

"Don't worry. I told her it was just a one-off. And I'd appreciate it if she kept it from your dad."

"You told her it was a one-off?" My voice sounded like I was trying to talk through razor blades.

"Better that than mentioning the gritty details."

I had told my mom it was a fling, and she must have shared that with Lars. In my own fucked up way, I had told him that our future wasn't important enough to override the fear. Was this why he sounded so blasé about us? Had I hurt his feelings? Or was he truly relieved that I'd given him an out, a means for him to bury his guilt and maintain a relationship with my father?

"What I said to my mom—it was a moment of panic. That's not how I feel. I don't think of this as a short-term thing. I just wanted more time to think through a solution, one that would work for everyone."

I was the people pleaser, the peacemaker. Surely he could see that changing that pattern couldn't happen overnight.

With each word out of my mouth, his eyes appeared to harden until they achieved peak ice. Pure, dark discs of indifference. But I could warm them up again with three little words.

"I love you."

A muscle twitched in his jaw. "You don't."

Pain stabbed me in the heart. "Are you seriously telling me I don't know my own mind?"

"Adeline, you once told me you wanted a great love story, something epic like your mom and dad. Now you're saying you'd settle for *this*?" He waved a hand between us, as if this was meaningless. "You have your entire life ahead of you. Why would you want to waste it on me?"

"It-it wouldn't be a waste," I said faintly. "It would be my choice."

"Then you need to choose better."

Apparently, I did. My throat felt thick with tears, my heart a ball of lead. I needed out of here, but I couldn't just run. That would confirm to him that I was a stupid school-girl, crushed by my crush.

That was no longer me. I had become a different person, partly owing to him. More confident, more open. Yet he was prepared to teach me so much then throw me away?

Anger flared, hot and swift. "I never expected you to choose me over my dad. But I thought that if it came out, like it has, you wouldn't be a chicken about it."

That shocked the hell out of him. Cowardly Adeline Kershaw suddenly had claws.

"Hold on a sec—"

I offered an imperious hand. "My mother confronts you with what she knows, and your first instinct is to tell her it was a one-off?"

Never mind that this was my initial reaction as well. My response came from a need to protect him, to protect his relationship with my father and the fortunes of the team. But deep down, I had hoped that he would claim me for his own, like he had that night he came to the nightclub.

"You've given me so much, Lars. Shone your sun on me and shown this wallflower how to bloom. Soothed my fears and stopped the nightmares. But I guess I haven't helped you in the same way. All this time you were worried about Sven's blueprint for shitty fatherhood imprinting on you, along with his history as a rotten partner and an abuser. You're nothing like him, Lars, but as long as you think you've inherited his bad traits, then you'll *never* be ready for something real. You'll never be ready for me."

Shock rendered him speechless, which gave me time to kiss the top of Mabel's head and mutter a goodbye. I loved her and would miss her so much.

"Be good, little one. Take care of your daddy for me."

He finally found his voice. "Adeline."

But it was too little, too late. With my heart broken, I turned and left, one tired foot in front of the other.

CHAPTER TWENTY-NINE

Lars

CRACKKK!

The sound of Kershaw's stick striking a bench reverberated through the Edmonton visitors' locker room. In the five years I'd played with him, I had never seen him so pissed.

Our third straight loss.

Theo and I were back on the first line together, though I had to wonder if something had broken, the Dream Defense turned nightmare. My suspension was over, his injury was healed, and MacFarlane was keeping his distance, but we were abruptly out of sync.

"Listen, guys, it didn't go our way." O'Malley had seen that Kershaw wasn't in the mood for a post-game debrief, so he was stepping up to the plate. "Sometimes the other team has a better night."

"Yeah, we'll get 'em next time." Cody patted my

shoulder clumsily, making it clear where the blame lay, but being nice about it as was his way.

We had a plane back to Chicago to catch, so everyone made quick work of the clean-up. A subdued Kershaw sat beside me on the bus to the airport while I texted Janet to check in on Mabel. She sent me a picture of her sleeping and a thumbs up.

"Button okay?" Theo asked.

"Yeah, she's fine."

"And the new nanny?"

"No complaints."

Janet had moved in a week ago, and we were finding our way with each other. She treated Mabel as a job, not that there was anything wrong with that, but I was used to getting more updates about Mabel's welfare. What she had eaten, how she had enjoyed her bath, how cute she looked in her fifty-fifth Rebels onesie. The discussions with my new nanny were purely baby logistics and travel schedules.

No songs filled the air.

Last week, while I was at practice, Adeline collected her stuff from my place and left her key on the kitchen counter. Janet had already moved into a different room, further down the hall, so Adeline's room remained empty, a void I tried my best to pass without remembering.

"Adeline's in a funk."

Swallowing hard, I turned to Theo. "What's wrong with her?"

"I think she misses Mabel." He frowned. "It was a good gig for her."

"For me, too. But I needed to get Mabel settled, given that there's still no sign of Vicki. Adeline can come see her any time."

He nodded abstractly. "I'll let her know."

I moved on to another tricky topic. "About tonight ... Sorry I wasn't on my game."

He gave me a long, hard look. Didn't deny it. His next words offered me an out. "You worried about Mabel with this new girl?"

"A little."

Still lying to my friend. But once I started this thing with his daughter, there was no going back to the honesty of before. I wanted to say this shift in my relationship with Theo was twisting me up, making me lose my edge, fucking up my game. But that wasn't it.

I missed Adeline.

Not the woman who cared for my child, but the woman who made my life a million times better. She had told me she loved me, then told me I was a coward. She was right. Once Elle knew, I had a chance to come clean. To proclaim from the rooftops that I loved her daughter and to hell with the Rebels.

To hell with Theo.

But my feelings of self-loathing at what I'd done to this man, my identification with Sven, would always win out. Adeline loved me, but my love wasn't pure enough for her. It was tainted with my betrayal.

I had never resisted touching someone as much as I had the moment the words of love left her lips. Instead, I balled my fists and denied that love. Told her how she felt because it was easier than admitting how *I* felt. I was a dick and every word out of my mouth that day only confirmed it.

Adeline was better off without me.

***

Adeline

. . .

ZARA JACOBS LED HER TWO-YEAR-OLD, Jane, to the big rug in their living room and set her down in the front row. The birthday girl wore a neon-green tutu, a bubblegum-pink cardigan, and silver Wicked-themed slippers that matched her sparkly tiara.

Her mom grinned at me. "Sorry, she needed to potty."

"Not a problem." The delay gave me time to run through my set list for the zillionth time. As if this audience cared about whether I sang *Itsy Bitsy Spider* before the *Hokey Pokey* (though *Hokey Pokey's* dance moves made that number a good closer). Gazing out at the crowd, ranging from infants to four-year-olds, I caught my mom's eye. Tilly, elder stateswoman among her peers, waved regally. I waved back.

"Hey, guys! Are we ready for a song?"

None of these kids had become jaded yet, so only toothy grins and dancing eyes shone back at me. As long as I kept their interest, we should be good.

I stroked the strings and launched into *If you're happy and you know it.*

Zara had seen my performance on Halloween and asked me to entertain the kids for Jane's party (*I'll pay you, of course!*). As I had recently been fired from my nanny job and had no career prospects, I immediately agreed, then whined to Rosie about what a huge mistake I'd made.

But it wasn't a mistake. I'd loved planning the set, practicing with Tilly as my test audience, and learning from Aurora that the classic, *Alouette,* was a touch too gruesome for inclusion at a children's party (it might be sung in French, but I drew the line at lyrics about plucking out a lark's feathers and eyes). Focusing on this new phase also kept my mind off what I'd lost.

Fifteen minutes later, we had covered the classics and were in the exercise portion of the session. The more coordinated kids were sticking their left leg in, the less coordinated were opting for both legs. That's when I spotted him.

He was at the back of the room with his daughter, his hands under her arms, holding her upright. Mabel, nightclub aficionado and music lover, danced with her daddy's help. I had to blink away, or I would have strummed a bum note.

Once the song finished, everyone headed to the other room to light the birthday candles. Songs and dancing before cake and ice cream ensured less likelihood of the party turning into a pukefest.

"Amazing, Addy, so much fun!" Zara gushed. "I've Venmoed your payment. Don't forget to grab a slice of cake!" Off she went to manage the Happy Birthday chorus and a crowd of dessert-ravenous ankle biters.

I placed my guitar in its case and tried to hold onto the good vibes of happy children and the joy I'd just created. My heart had never felt emptier.

"Hey, Adeline."

Lars stood before me, his arms full of his daughter, who looked delightful in a green jumpsuit with a tartan belt.

"Hi, there."

"Mabel insisted on congratulating you herself. She loved the set."

I smiled and rubbed her tummy. God, I missed her like she was my own. "I saw you dancing out there, Mabel. You have amazing moves."

"She does, but then she's been to the club." He smiled at me. "Lars thought you were great as well."

"Lars has started talking about himself in third person, huh?"

His brows drew together. "He finds it helps him achieve distance, so he doesn't have to examine himself too closely."

Amusing but not enough to make me feel better. So he knew he was a dick. Good for him.

"This is a good move for you," he said after the silence had gone on too long. "You're where you're meant to be."

He made it sound like I wouldn't have made it this far if I had stuck around in his life.

"You think you did me this big favor?"

"Not what I meant."

"You're probably right."

He got that wrinkle between his brows, coupled with a note of suspicion in those navy-blue eyes. "I am?"

"I was getting kind of settled as Mabel's nanny. I needed a push to get me thinking about what came next."

As long as we talked about this in terms of my career plans, then we could avoid the rest. The hole in my chest where my heart should be. I had offered him that heart and he turned it down.

His brow furrowed. "I was too abrupt. I could have been … kinder."

"Lars, it's okay."

It wasn't, but I could hardly argue the point at a children's birthday party. Lars had his chance to claim me. I'd made my own mistakes, for sure, but once it was out there, I had hoped he might choose me.

That he didn't broke me in half.

A small hand clasped mine. I looked down at my little sister. "Hey, Tilly-Billy, where did you spring from?"

"A tadpole pond. I'm going to be a frog when I grow up."

"Cool! I have a song about tadpoles."

Tilly grinned. Her mouth was rimmed with pink and white icing. "Sing it!"

"How about when we get home?"

She tugged on my hand, my cue to leave. *Thanks, sis.* I smiled at Lars and Mabel. "See you guys."

Lars nodded and stepped aside to let me through.

"Bye, Duckman! Bye, Mabel!"

"Bye, Tilly," Lars said.

I closed the gap between us and my mom.

"We're gonna sing about tadpoles, Mommy!"

My mom smiled at Tilly. "That's exciting."

She met my gaze, her own filled with concern. She knew I'd lied about it being merely a fling, but she had never pressed or talked about her conversation with Lars that day in the hospital. And I hadn't asked.

"Are you okay, sweetie?"

"I will be."

CHAPTER THIRTY

Adeline

MY MOM DID a silent count of the various sides. "Addy, could you bring the sweet potatoes in?"

"Maybe Conor could stop sexting and help out."

My brother looked up from beneath his too-long hair. "You're so obsessed with my sex life."

Mom grimaced. "La la la, my son does not have a sex life."

Conor chuckled. "Yes, Mom. I'm still a virgin."

I made a face at him. He stuck his tongue out at me. Parity restored.

As much as I loved Thanksgiving and especially loved that the entire Kershaw brood was under one roof for the first time in two years, I was still out of sorts. This morning, my mother had asked if I'd be okay with Lars's presence at the table and I'd acted like this would be my favorite thing in the world.

Of course! I miss Mabel so much! I can handle passing the onion and sage stuffing to the guy I've fallen hopelessly in love with. Bring it on!

My mom had given me a sad smile. She knew the wounds still festered, but I needed to be a big girl about it. The new nanny was visiting her family in Michigan, Lars and Mabel were at a loose end, so of course they were welcome for Thanksgiving dinner. I wasn't a complete monster.

Bringing the sweet potatoes out to the table, I tried not to cast my gaze through the French doors to the living room where Aurora was happily bouncing Mabel on her knee and Lars, my dad, and brothers—except Conor who was too busy texting whichever girl he'd charmed this week—were all watching the Bears suffer against Green Bay.

I fussed about with the table settings and moved the place cards so Lars was down at the other end of the table. Moments later, I heard the door squeak open. I didn't dare turn.

"Anything I can do to help?"

"No, we're fine." Hauling a breath in deep, I pivoted and got a good look at him. He appeared drawn and tired. That should have cheered me, but I was concerned that Mabel might not be getting a caregiver in tip-top condition.

"How's Mabel doing?"

"Aurora is spoiling her with Aurora kisses, which she claims are the best kind."

A distant second to yours.

"She loves babies." I moved a fork. "How are things with Janet?"

"I don't see her much. It's weird having a stranger in the house."

"She hasn't tried to jump you then?" I forced a chuckle,

but it died on my lips at the look on his face. "Sorry, too soon?"

"Much too soon." He shuffled a step forward. "Sorry about invading your holiday. I hate to make it awkward."

"It's not. Well, it is, but this is your family, too."

He nodded, his blue eyes troubled and searching my face. Keeping our secret meant he got to keep the Kershaws, but at what cost? I was supposed to be happy for him, but I'd never felt more miserable.

"Any more musical gigs?"

"I'm filling in for Miss Emmy's JiggleJams class at the Chicago School of Folk Music. She's on maternity leave."

"That's amazing news. Congratulations."

"Thanks. I even get to play a few original compositions."

He rubbed his beard, a move I loved. But then I loved all his moves.

He seemed to gravitate closer to me. I couldn't help it; I did the same. We didn't touch. We didn't need to. I felt a strange comfort in his presence, a lovely salve to the ache in my chest. He was both the disease and the cure.

"Is Duckman going to finally get a couple more verses?"

"Wouldn't you like to know?"

"Duckman, Duckman, on the ice ..." he started, low and a little tuneless.

"Skating faster than the ..." I raised an eyebrow, feeling a weird giggle coming on.

"Mice?" He chuckled. "How did mice come into it?"

"We songstresses think long and hard about the perfect lyric."

"First rhyme that popped into your head, right?"

I laughed. Moved closer. "Careful now. It could have been lice."

"Aren't I lucky?" he murmured, his breath a hot puff of air on my lips.

"So we have three kinds of cranberry ..."

We jumped apart.

"...sauce." My father stood at the entrance to the dining room, his expression confused. Several seconds ticked by, then several more. The temperature in the room dropped ten degrees. He knew what he'd seen but his mind was stuck, playing catch up.

"What's going on?" The good guy, who thought the best of everyone, needed someone to tell him his brain wasn't getting the right inputs.

Lars spoke first. "Theo, I'm completely to blame."

Shit. Quickly, I stood between him and my dad. "Don't get mad."

"Don't get mad? Are you kidding me?"

"Theo," Lars repeated, but my dad cut him off with a look.

"Don't. I trusted you. Invited you into my home. Included you in my family, and this is how you repay me? By making moves on my daughter?"

"Dad, please."

Lars placed a hand on my hip and moved me aside. "It's okay, Adeline. Your father and I need to talk. It's been a long time coming."

Dad's gaze focused on Lars's hand, which had touched my hip with such easy familiarity. Fury blazed in his eyes.

"You think talking will save you. No fucking way."

The raised voices brought in spectators, starting with my mom carrying Mabel. The rest of the family crowded in behind her.

"What's going on?" Mom looked at me, then her

husband as no one spoke. "Will someone tell me what's happening?"

"Nyquist has been messing around with Addy." My father could barely get the words out. "He took advantage—"

"No one took advantage. I'm a grown woman—"

"You're barely twenty-one!"

"I'm twenty-three, Dad."

"And he's what? Forty?"

I rolled my eyes. "He's thirty-six. And I'm not a child. Yes, I'm *your* child, but you were going to hate anyone I date anyway."

Out of the corner of my eye, I caught Hatch's wince.

My father threw up his hands. "Nope, not good enough. I'd like to see you with someone age-fucking-appropriate. Not this guy. A user, like his old man."

"That's not fair."

"No, Adeline, it's okay." Lars placed a hand on my back. "Your dad's not wrong. I'm not what any man would choose for his daughter. And if I'd thought this was right, I would have been up front about it."

"What's happening?" Aurora came barging in, plowing her way through her gawping great-grandchildren. "I was in the bathroom. What's the fuss?"

"Lars has been hooking up with Adeline," Landon said.

"Lars? Well, of course he's with Adeline. She's perfect for him."

"Bopping the nanny, though?" Conor side-eyed Landon, then Aurora. "Kind of a cliché."

"Could you both be quiet?" My mom handed off the baby to Aurora. "In fact, everyone into the other room now. I'd like to talk with the principal players here."

"Apparently we're only supporting cast in this tragedy,"

Landon sniffed and left the dining room with the rest of them.

My mom closed the French door and stood with her back to the windows, protecting us somewhat from prying eyes. "I thought you two were no longer together."

Dad cut to Mom, his eyes wide with shock. "You knew?"

"I was under the impression it was finished."

"It is," I said. "We were just talking."

"Well, you have your official nanny now," Dad growled. "So you can quit sniffing around my daughter."

Lars gutted out, "That's not how it was, Theo."

"Not how it was?" My father lunged, and again, I stood between them.

I turned to Lars. "It might be better if you go."

"What? No. I'm not leaving you to face this."

"He needs to settle down."

"Stop talking about me like I'm not here."

"Then stop acting like a caveman, Dad."

My father looked so betrayed. We never argued. Sharp words between us were a novelty neither of us knew how to handle.

A wail went up from the other room. Mabel. Lars looked defeated—and torn. "I need to look after her." He flicked a glance toward my father who had not suddenly softened on hearing the baby's cry, then back to me. "I don't like leaving you here to manage the fallout."

"It's really for the best." I felt awful, sending him away on a day that was supposed to be about family and goodwill. But Thanksgiving was already ruined, and I didn't see my father and Lars reconciling over pumpkin pie.

Lars squeezed my hip, which yielded a growl from my father. I searched Lars's face and tried to tell him it would be okay. Of course, we were no longer a couple—if we ever had been—but I cared about him too much to inflict my father's wrath on him.

He left the dining room, and a tense minute later I heard the front door open and close. During that time, my father paced, barely looking at me.

"Okay, give it to me." I wanted it over with as soon as possible.

My father stopped wearing out the hardwood and turned to face me. "I'm not mad at you, Twinkle. He took advantage and broke my trust. Of course you're not to blame! I can't believe he was in my house, eating my food, wearing my kids' clothes—well, you know what I mean! And this is how he shows his gratitude. Helping himself to my daughter."

Enough. "This isn't a case of big evil Lars seducing some innocent. I made a play for him."

He stared at me, completely baffled. "Don't make excuses for him. He's older, a *former* friend of mine, and he should've known better."

"And I have no agency here? You think I'm some wide-eyed virgin who can't say no?"

Dad sent a beseeching glance my mom's way. "Help me out here, Ellie."

"You're doing fine all by yourself."

"Oh, right. You're in on this, the big conspiracy."

My mother looked uncomfortable, and I felt awful about that. Keeping my confidence had damaged the trust with her husband, one that was usually rock solid.

I grasped my father's arm. "Dad, that's my fault. Mom found out the night Mabel got sick,. I told her it wasn't serious, and that it would be better all-around if you didn't know. We were trying to protect you."

My father fisted his hands on his hips. "Protect me? I'm a big boy, Adeline. I can handle the truth."

"Sure about that?"

He glared at me.

"Lars and I are consenting adults. We had a fling"—I actually felt his wince that time—"and now it's over."

"It's over? Didn't look like it. Did he hurt you? I mean, your feelings?" Hearing him phrase it that way gave me hope. He knew that Lars was a good man and would never hurt me any other way.

"No, Dad," I lied. "We both went into it knowing it was just a casual thing. Not a big deal at all."

My father clearly couldn't decide which was worse: that his friend and teammate saw me as a sex-only proposition or that Lars might want more.

"And it's definitely done?"

My heart broke all over again. "Completely."

* * *

Lars

I HATED LEAVING ADELINE BEHIND. That she could handle her father better than I could was a given, but she shouldn't have to face that alone. She was right, though. Theo would stay mad as long as I was in his sightline.

Once home, I changed Mabel and placed her in her playpen. I sent a text to Adeline: *let me know you're okay.*

Nothing.

I knew Theo would blame me completely, which was fine because I was supposedly the should-know-better adult here. I should have resisted every impulse to fall for her but fall for her I had. Then I pushed her away. Not because she was the daughter of my friend, or completely too young for me. But because I wasn't suitable as a mate. I was barely making it as Mabel's dad.

But she had told me she loved me. Brave, beautiful Adeline had spoken those words even when I made it clear it would never work. Still she forged ahead, speaking her truth. She stood between me and her father, ready to absorb his anger. I'd wanted to give her space to fly, but now I wanted nothing more than to claim her for myself.

I checked my phone. Why wasn't she answering?

The doorbell sounded. Thank God. She'd managed to slip away and now I could tell her the truth.

"Hold up, Mabel. Back in a tick."

I bounded to the door, feeling weirdly happy despite the fuckery of before. Kershaw knew, we didn't have to hide anymore. So I was still the asshole screw-up who told Adeline I was no better than Sven. That might not have changed, but knowing my sins were public gave me hope I could now work on fixing it.

I pulled open the door, ready to tell Adeline I loved her.

"Hi, Lars. Happy Thanksgiving."

Vicki had finally decided to show her face.

CHAPTER THIRTY-ONE

Lars

I DIDN'T THINK the day could get any worse, but this dumb jock clearly lacked imagination.

"Oh, someone doesn't look happy to see me!" She giggled nervously.

"What are you doing here?" I should have been asking if she was okay but after the events of the last couple of weeks, I'd run out of fucks to give.

"Now, Lars." She stepped forward and I blocked her. "No need to be a dick about it."

"Are you fucking kidding me?"

Her brows angled down in confusion. "I took a break and now I'm here."

"My lawyer has been trying to contact you. They even sent notices to your in-laws in New York."

"We were on a cruise. Marriage rehab, you know how it is." She made a face. "Didn't work."

As if I cared about her damn marriage. "And you think you can just waltz back into your daughter's life after dumping her without a care?"

She had the audacity to look surprised. No one could be this obtuse. "I know it was a shock for you, Lars, but surely you can see it as a blessing in disguise. Aren't you crazy about her?"

Not just about Mabel. All I wanted was to get rid of my daughter's absentee mother and run to the woman I adored.

"Vicki, you abandoned your daughter in a bar with a complete stranger."

"I told you. I needed the break. I needed a chance to save my marriage." A sour look crossed her face. "For all the good that did. But I've realized that maybe he wasn't the one for me. I did everything he asked, and he still made me beg—on my knees, mind you—and it made no difference. He just wanted to humiliate me."

This made sense now. She'd tried and failed with her husband, and now she was here for Plan B. I pinched the spot between my eyes, trying to stave off an incoming headache. This was exhausting. Vicki was exhausting.

"Vicki, why are you here?"

"To see my girl. And you." She moved back to her car, a Range Rover, and opened the trunk, which was filled with shopping bags. "I brought her some gifts. The cutest onesie you ever did see. Picked it up in Aruba during one of our port excursions." She tilted her head. "Now where's my daughter?"

Adeline

· · ·

I SAT in Aurora's kitchen, letting the French country chic calm me while she poured hot water into two cups of Earl Grey.

"Hob nobs, honey?"

"Is my name Adeline Kershaw?"

She smiled at my nervous joke, put them on a plate, and set it before me. At just after six in the morning, I shouldn't have been eating chocolate cookies, but I needed some bite-sized comfort.

Taking a seat, she grasped my hand. "That was one of the livelier Thanksgiving dinners in memory."

After Lars and Mabel left, we'd tried to pretend everything was normal. Thankfully my brothers, Aurora, and my uncle Jason, who had joined us for his second meal of the day, managed to Band-Aid the silences and keep the dinner chugging along. Occasionally I'd catch my dad looking at me, like he couldn't believe what I'd done. Then he'd avert his gaze and study his turkey.

I was a stranger to him.

After dinner, I'd put together a care package of turkey, sides, and two slices of pumpkin pie, and drove to Lars's house. He wasn't alone. A Range Rover was parked behind his SUV, the vanity plates announcing its owner.

VICKI 3.

The wandering momma had returned.

A bolt of jealousy slammed through me, though I truly didn't think Lars was going to fall for Vicki's charms. He'd come a long way since that night in the Empty Net bathroom, just not far enough for me.

I considered turning back, not leaving the food. Instead I crept up the drive, tiptoed to the door, and left the meal outside, a different brand of cowardice. Once back in my car, I texted to let him know Thanksgiving had come to him.

He sent me a text thanking me an hour later. Nothing since.

"Dad's disappointed in me."

"Pfft! Like he's never done anything risky."

But had he? Sure, we joked about the one-night stand that resulted in Dino Boy, the start of the Great Love Story, Trademark. But my father had always lived his life with zero regrets. All his choices came from a heartfelt and decent place, while mine were selfish and immature.

"I really hurt him." I stood to finish the tea, adding a drop of milk to both, and a spoonful of sugar to Aurora's. "Do you think he'll ever forgive me?"

"Nothing to forgive, Twinkle."

My father stood at the doorway, looking like he had barely slept. I hated to see it, not only because it meant he was upset, but because he had a game tonight. The Cross-Town Classic against the Hawks played annually the Friday after Thanksgiving, and he needed to be in top form. He carried a Boba tea in one hand—my favorite—and a coffee cup in the other.

"I see you already have a Jean Luc Picard." Earl Grey, hot. He lingered at the entrance to the coach house, as if unsure of his welcome.

"I never say no to Boba."

Aurora stood and picked up her teacup. "I'm going to take a shower and leave you two to talk." She kissed me on the forehead. "Go easy on him."

Go easy on *him*? I nodded all the same, my throat heavy with emotion. Dad took the seat Aurora had vacated and pushed the Boba tea my way.

"Thanks," I muttered.

"You get any sleep?"

"Not much. You?"

"I can nap later before the game." After a fortifying sip of coffee, he asked, "Where do you want to start?"

"A schoolgirl crush." At his arched eyebrow, I continued. "I didn't want that nanny job. I did tell you."

He frowned at my disjointed thinking. "So this is my fault?"

"Can we say it is and move on?"

He snorted. "So you had a crush on Lars."

"He overheard me talking about it with Rosie last year before I went away."

"And?"

I sipped my Earl Grey. "He was embarrassed about it. But kind."

My father nodded, approving. "And then I threw you together under the same roof. Gosh, if only I'd known that someone had a crush on someone else."

"Okay, point taken. I wanted to help, be a team player, contribute to the Kershaw enterprise. I don't always feel like I do that in the way the boys do. And I ... I wanted to spend more time with him. I can admit that now. The more time I spent with him, the more I started to like him beyond the silly infatuation. Seeing him grow and learn as he became easier with Mabel, as they fell in love with each other. It was beautiful to witness. And then we became closer." I broke off there, so it was clear what exactly I meant by "closer."

Dad grimace. "Okay, I don't need to know the details. From my viewpoint, and not just as the father who wants to wrap you up in cotton wool and never let you date, he took advantage—"

"Dad."

"No, hold up. He knew you had this crush. He knew anything between you would have to be a secret. He's older, more experienced, and *supposed* to be my friend. He took advantage, Twinkle, that's all there is to it."

There was no reasoning with him when he was like this. Still, I tried.

"I made the first move on him." No need to mention overhearing him jerk off with my name on his lips when he came. My cheeks flushed at the memory. "And he tried to tell me how wrong it was. I agreed—at first. But after a while it became too hard to resist what was happening between us. Our chemistry. He came to the club because he knew I wasn't having a good time with Rowan, and the only reason I went out with him was to make Lars see me properly."

I swiped at a tear.

"Twinkle." He put his arm around me and pulled me close.

"So, please don't blame him. We both went into it with our eyes open."

"Okay." Said with a reluctance bordering on fury.

"There's more, Dad." At his tightening grip, I met his concerned gaze. "Not about Lars. There's a reason we came home from our travels early. I-I was mugged in Greece."

"Addy ... you were hurt?" He sounded positively woebegone.

"I healed quickly. Physically, anyway. I didn't want to tell you and Mom because you're so protective of me and this year is such a big deal for you and your career. Nothing should get in the way of that."

"Nothing should get in the way of *that*? You mean, my daughter's well-being shouldn't get in the way of *that*?"

He rubbed his forehead, like that could wipe away

everything he'd been through in the last twenty-four hours. Adeline Kershaw, the ultimate trial.

"I didn't want to rock the boat."

"Then I guess you shouldn't have started sleeping with my teammate!" He pushed off the stool and paced for a few seconds, hands on hips.

"And this is why I didn't tell you."

"Are you saying I'm overreacting?"

"No, this is completely within the range of Theo Kershaw's standard responses to stimuli."

His eyes narrowed to slits at my smart-assery. "This is because of the Finals thirteen years ago, isn't it? That's why you didn't tell me ... *anything!*"

"Dad, if I can't contribute to this family positively, the least I can do is keep my actions carbon neutral."

Emotion gripped him. "You actually think you don't contribute to this family positively? Twinkle, have you any idea how much joy you give me? How you complete us? You took time off college to help when Tilly was born. That was epic. I don't think I could have kept playing if you weren't here during that first year."

"What are you talking about?"

"I was *this* close to retiring but knowing you were keeping the home fires burning and the support this family needed gave me the confidence to keep at it. You're the reason I'm a legend!"

No one had ever told me this. "Really?"

"The Kershaws would be *nothing* without you. I would be nothing without you. So I missed a game thirteen years ago. Big deal."

I sniffed. "An important game."

"But my family is more important. My daughter is more precious to me than any championship ring. If you're hurting, I need to know. Don't hide that from me. Ever."

I swiped at another tear. He gave me a moment to get over myself before resuming the interrogation, dad-style.

"What happened in Greece?"

I told him an abridged version.

"Did you tell Lars about it?"

"Yeah. He advised me to be up front with you."

He scoffed. "So he does know right from wrong!"

"He's not the villain here."

I could see him recalibrating, retooling his attack, looking for another way in. Defense turned to offense. "Are you in love with him?"

Well played, old man. Yesterday, I'd insisted it was a fling, but I'd already lied enough. Besides, my mother would have told him her suspicions.

"Yes."

"And who broke it off?"

"Why does it matter?"

I'd had time to think it through. I was under no illusion that Lars loved me, but I did think he cared. His upbringing with Sven had done a number on him. He didn't think he was good enough. For fatherhood. For friendship.

For me.

Telling him that Lars considered himself a failure because of Sven felt like a betrayal. Better to keep the blame centered on me.

It didn't work. My dad remained silent, which was always a bad sign, but he did gather me in his arms again and held me close.

"I'm sorry I lied to you, Dad, about everything."

"You have nothing to be sorry for."

The "you" in that sentence said it all. Lars wasn't off the hook just yet.

CHAPTER THIRTY-TWO

Lars

I BARELY GOT a wink of sleep. Vicki finally left at just after midnight, after several hints that a baby needs both parents, and she wasn't just talking about co-parenting. She had to know I wasn't interested in her, no matter our connection in Mabel.

Adeline had texted last night.

Dinner outside. Talk soon.

My sweet thing was still looking after me. To show how mature I was being, I even allowed Vicki to share. A family meal. Feeling even more magnanimous, I didn't get overly possessive with Mabel. I was too interested in watching how Vicki acted around her. I could tell she'd missed her daughter, though the fact she chose her fuckface husband over our little precious still got me all riled up. But then I wouldn't have had her all to myself and I wouldn't have needed Adeline to take care of her and—*fuck.*

Vicki's selfishness had gifted me Adeline. And look what I did with that. I was glad when she left, when it was just me and Mabel.

But our third musketeer was in the wind. I missed Adeline like crazy, but before I could fix things with her, I had to sort out my relationship with Theo.

Janet was taking the holiday weekend off, so I was in a bind for childcare during the Thanksgiving Friday game. I'd burned my bridges with the Kershaws, so I moved down the phone tree to Tara, who had heard about the drama and was still thrilled to babysit.

Then I headed to the locker room.

Word of my transgression had obviously reached the team. Of course they would all be on their captain's side. I expected nothing less. I got a few curt nods before the air chilled with Theo's arrival.

He headed right to his cubby without looking my way. I wasn't going to avoid this, or him, and we needed to reconcile before the game. I was thankful Hatch was on IR, spending it in the press box, because I really did not want to have to tackle them both.

I walked over and leaned against the neighboring cubby. "Is Adeline okay?"

He looked straight ahead. "I don't want to hear my daughter's name out of your mouth."

"I just need to know she's okay."

"She's *my* daughter and I love her. Of course she's okay." He snapped his gaze to mine. "Or maybe you think she's upset because she knows how much you used her?"

I could easily think that, but I couldn't imagine Adeline sharing that opinion with her dad. "Where's that coming from?"

"God, you're something else." And then he shoved me.

"Guys!" Boden yelled, his voice high-pitched with panic.

"I get that you're pissed at me, T."

"Oh, you do, do ya? You've been jerking my girl around for weeks, maybe months, I dunno! And if that wasn't bad enough, as soon as you get a shot, you're back with your baby mama."

Shock coursed through me. "What? Where'd you hear that?"

"From the woman herself. She's all over social media with pics of you holding your kid. And it was the same onesie Button was wearing yesterday—I recognize it because I bought it for her, *you dick.* So the minute you bail on my daughter, you head back to this other chick."

Another shove. Last night, Vicki had taken photos of Mabel, some of them with me in the frame. Planting her flag now that her marriage had failed. I was too tired to police it.

"I'm not going to fight you."

"No?" He pushed again, hard, forcing me to choose between standing my ground and stepping back. I chose retreat.

Dash Carter slid between us, as smooth as a figure skater.

"In case you ladies haven't realized, the puck drops in less than forty minutes."

Theo shook himself back to reality, the one where the captain had to be the bigger person. I hated that for him—I truly deserved to be smacked hard—but I also wanted to get our frustrations out on the opposing team instead of each other.

Usually, Theo would give a pre-game pep talk, but tonight, nada. For the first time ever, I wished Coach would put me on the same line as MacFarlane because I wasn't sure Theo and I had what it took to overcome this hump. I prayed his professionalism would outweigh his need to avenge his daughter's honor.

For most of the first period, we ignored our problem and worked our asses off. Every time Coach put us in, we hopped that wall, assumed the positions, and let muscle memory take over. Skating as partners for almost five years, our innate fluidity did a lot of heavy lifting. When I was out of position, Theo was there. When he got pinned back, I took over. One crucial difference, though: each time we returned to the bench, someone sat between us. The guys were taking turns to chaperone us.

Still scoreless, we had three minutes to go in the first period, and Coach was about to send the D-Man Dream Team back in.

"What's going on with you two?"

Theo merely scowled, so I spoke for us both. "Nothing, Coach."

Coach divided a glance between us, then landed on Cody Jacobs who was the current designated driver in the babysitting rotation. "Care to comment?"

"Wouldn't dream of it, Coach."

Coach shook his head in disgust. "Right, get in there. Let's make something happen."

This time when I cleared the wall, Theo shoulder-checked me. If that was his worst, I was getting off easy.

It was not his worst.

Thirty seconds into the shift, he was slashed by Ranally, the Hawks center, and I did what I always did when an opposing player high-sticked or slashed my partner and I was within range. I checked that fucker and slammed him against the boards.

"Don't need your help." Theo bumped me on the way back to his position.

"Don't care, you got it."

He skated back over. "I said—"

"Heard what you said, but we're still a team here, so you're getting my help whether you want it or not."

My best friend in all the world came right at me. "Adeline said it wasn't a big deal—only a fling, she said. But I know my girl. You hurt her. You broke her heart."

"I need to talk to her—"

"Over my dead body." At which point all hell broke loose and the gloves came off.

The first blow landed clean because I removed my lid to let him at me. I took that punch. And the next. I had hurt Adeline, and I deserved everything coming my way.

No one was stepping in. Hell, not even me. Let him whale on me and enjoy his vengeance. Flabbergasted by this turn of events, the crowd lapsed into silence. Even the zebras were stunned.

One of the most revered partnerships in hockey was breaking down right before their eyes.

The next punch broke my nose. *Crunch.* Seeing first blood, the crowd came to life and my teammates decided it was time to step in just as Theo got off another haymaker. Jacobs and Bell pulled him off me. I needed to speak before blood filled my throat and words were no longer possible.

"*Ith-wanneth-a-flinth!*"

Still restrained, Theo yelled back at me. "What the fuck did you say?"

I held the bridge of my nose—damn, that hurt—and snorted out a spurt of blood that made the crowd go, "Ooooh!"

"I said 'It wasn't a fling!'"

"You liar. You fucking liar." And then more curious than pissed, "What does that even mean?"

"For Christ's sake, Kershaw, I love her!"

Gasps all around. Ladies and gentlemen, welcome to the latest episode of *Real Housewives on Ice.*

The ref finally rolled up. Veteran Johnny "Gally" Gallagher had officiated all manner of rumbles, including that one game twenty-five years ago when Cajun legend Remy DuPre beat the shit out of the asshole who had once struck his future wife, our CEO and Rebel queen, Harper Chase-DuPre.

Gally pointed at me. "Off! You need a medic. And Theo, you're out."

"Yeah, I'm headed to the sin bin now," he muttered as he defiantly shrugged off his teammates' grip.

Gally looked uncomfortable. "No, you're out of the game."

Theo threw up his blood-covered hands. "You're ejecting me?"

Fuck. This could not get worse.

CHAPTER THIRTY-THREE

Adeline

FOR THE ENTIRETY of the first period, the only friction I'd had to deal with was a bickering Conor and Rosie. First, it was the Ice Girls, and whether they took dance lessons. Then the beer concessions got the treatment. Seedless grapes were next (*if you can make them seedless why are some of the varieties available with seeds? Who's the market for that?* I kind of agreed with Conor on that one.) It was so odd because they rarely saw each other, and Rosie got along with everyone else in my family. She and Conor just rubbed each other the wrong way.

Landon nudged me before the game started. "You okay?"

"I don't know. Not sure I should be here tonight, it's just kind of stressful."

I'd happily played with fire and was now regretting my singed fingertips.

"It's going to work out," he said. "Sure, Dad's pissed at him, but the game is too important for them to let *your* drama get in the way. Don't be so conceited."

I watched the game with my heart in my throat from the tenth row behind the players' bench. The body language on that stretch of pine was more frigid than the rink. My father and Lars were not speaking to each other, that much was clear. Yet on the ice, they appeared to have everything under control.

Until what was likely their final shift before the break, when a scuffle graduated into my worst nightmare. My father dropped his gloves, yelled at Lars, then started to pound him into the ice.

"Oh my God!" Rosie stood, along with everyone else in our section. I didn't feel the need as the entire spectacle was playing in glorious Technicolor on the 'tron.

Conor yelled, "Take him, Dad!"

An outraged Rosie pointed at him. "Stop being a jerk!"

"What, I'm *not* supposed to support my own father against the asshole who deflowered my sister?"

"He did not deflower me!"

Landon sat beside me and offered a bag. "Chocolate-covered gummy bear?"

I covered my eyes, only peeking through the cage of my fingers when the crowd went "Ooh!" After what seemed like forever, a couple of players—Cody and Peyton—separated them.

"That's a lot of blood but it probably looks worse than it is. Broken noses bleed a lot." Rosie reached over and squeezed my arm. "This is good, Addy."

"How's that now?"

"They need to get this out in the open—no way!" She jumped up again. "They're throwing him out!"

Now everyone was on their feet, booing the ref's decision to eject my father. Both players skated to the gate, and it might have been my imagination, but I thought my father made a gesture, offering first dibs through the gate to Lars. Was Rosie right? Had this helped?

"I have to get down there."

Ejected players returned to the dressing room while injured players were brought to an exam room. Back of the house was where I needed to be.

The game restarted quickly while the crowd was still buzzing. Twenty seconds later, the Hawks scored a goal, with a minute to go in the period.

Oh, well done! Your love life is already ruining the Rebels' game.

I stood, only to have Rosie grasp my arm and yank me down to my seat.

"You've got to let this play out. Give it time."

"They could be killing each other down there!"

Landon grimaced. "Let them figure it out—and to the victor the spoils."

"Am I the spoils in this scenario?"

"If the jock strap fits."

I looked at Conor. "Is Rosie right?"

"Rosie is never right. But Landon has a point." He blew out a breath as the Hawks made another shot on goal, which Noah Boden saved by the skin of his teeth. The Rebels were trying their best to regroup without their usually rock-solid defense.

I was trying the same.

Lars

DR. SYKES ADJUSTED the bridge of my nose. "Does that hurt?"

"Yes, it fucking hurts!"

An evil chuckle sounded from some point to my left.

"Definitely broken," the doc confirmed. "You did this?" That question was for the other person in the exam room.

"Some of my best work."

The doc raised one straggly eyebrow. "Hold this ice pack on it. I'll be back in fifteen minutes to assess once the swelling's gone down."

I did as I was told while the doctor left the room.

"You still here?" I couldn't be mad at Theo over what happened. He had every right to go there. I just wished he wasn't sticking around to keep an eye on me, like his captain instincts trumped his paternal ones.

"Where else am I gonna go?" We looked up at the monitor. The Rebels were a goal down and we were a few minutes into the break. No one other than the doc had come to see us, and I wasn't sure how to interpret that.

"How about to the locker room to inspire the troops?"

"O'Malley will have to do it."

"Can't believe that guy's gonna wear the band when you're gone."

We both chuckled at the familiar absurdity, knowing we were merely biding time until we could revisit our grievance. Adjusting the ice pack, I winced and waded in.

"I'm sorry."

"For?"

"Lying to you."

He stuck his tongue in his cheek and assessed me. "But you're not sorry for starting this thing with my Adeline, are you?"

I shook my head. Slowly, because my head hurt along with most every other part of my body. In the immortal words of Danny Glover in *Lethal Weapon*, I was too old for this shit.

"What you said out there, did you mean it? Or were you just trying to stop the beatdown of the century?"

"'The century'? Maybe the decade." He offered a grim smile, which lifted my spirits a tad. "I'd have let you continue even though you just broke my nose and I'm fairly certain a couple of teeth might be loose. Theo, you could break every bone in my body, but it wouldn't change how I feel. I love your daughter."

He stared at me for a good ten seconds, which was an eternity in Theo-time.

"You saw your baby's mother?"

"She showed up when I left your place yesterday. A surprise drop-in."

"What did she have to say for herself?"

I blew out a breath. "She's been on a cruise trying to save her marriage, which apparently didn't work. She brought gifts for Mabel."

Theo looked horrified. "And she just expects you to forgive her?"

"We're going to work out a custody arrangement but to be honest, I don't want to switch off with her in a city five hours away. She's talking about moving to Chicago."

I suspected that would set him off. It might even have been why I mentioned it.

"She doesn't deserve a second of Button's time! And now she expects you to upend your entire life to suit her? And maybe slither back to you? I hope you told her where to go." He pointed at me. "Right, you didn't. You just took some happy family photos and let her post them online."

"T, I let her have some time with her kid, who she obviously missed. We're not playing at happy families. We're just trying to adapt to a shitty situation." But I hated that Adeline might have seen that, right after she showed at my place with Vicki's car parked out front. "I won't be spending any time with Vicki beyond what's necessary to create a loving environment for my kid. Mabel's my primary focus here and I'm going to fight like hell to keep her in my life. My little girl means everything to me."

Theo sat with that for a moment. "Okay, that was the undercard. Time for the main event, killer. Why did you break my daughter's heart?"

It felt like he'd whacked me in the chest with a stick.

"Because I'm not a good guy."

"Fuck that. Tell me the real reason."

Another adjustment of the ice pack, this time to make it hurt a little more. Focus my thinking.

My life was imploding. Adeline was everywhere, haunting my senses and spring-loading my dick. She had a crush on me and who's gonna say no to that? Once I had my fill, it was time to end it.

Except I couldn't say any of that. Not because it was about this man's precious daughter, but because it wasn't remotely true.

"All the stuff you said about taking advantage of her, how I should have been the adult, the guy with all the experience, burrowed inside my head. That was all true. At least,

I felt it to be. Once Elle confronted me, I got to thinking about the mistakes I've made. The poor decisions. The reckless choices. Vicki. MacFarlane. Adeline." Especially Adeline. "Here I was, getting in between the two of you, dragging her down to my level. A sneak. A liar. And for what? Because I'm selfish, like Sven. I saw her. I wanted her. I made her mine." For a short while, and how glorious was that? But it was time to pay the piper. "I knew it would hurt her now, but she'd be free," I finished.

"You think you're like your dad?"

"It's crossed my mind."

Theo's brow crimped into furious lines. "You know I've had issues with my dad. Sure, we get along—now—but I hope to God no one ever thinks I take after him. Do you really think I would give you the time of day if I thought you were an asshole like your father?" Obviously rhetorical, because he plowed on. "Look, I said you were a user like your dad. That was a low blow and I'm sorry. Here's the thing: I welcomed you into my home, my family, my life. I don't do that for just anyone, y'know. You had this great thing going as a bit player in my blessed existence, and then you go and sabotage it by seducing my daughter!"

"Maybe I just wanted Adeline more."

It wasn't as if I could have both. And now I had neither.

His mouth twitched. He liked that.

"You were willing to fuck it all up to be with her?"

"Crazy, right? There was something so strong between us, a spark so real that it couldn't be denied. And I know you think that as the older, supposedly wiser person here, I should have known better, but you're not giving your daughter enough credit. She knows her own mind. I might be more experienced, but I'm a complete novice when it comes to the heart. Adeline knows how to give it her all.

How to be open and generous and loving. She gets that from you. From how you raised her."

A flicker of pride lit up his expression. "Suck up."

"Is it working?"

"Not in the slightest." He inhaled a deep breath. "I just want her to have what Ellie and I have. Can you give her that?"

The Great Love Story? Damn right I could. "Why is everything a fucking competition with you?"

"You're the one who seems to think you're not good enough for her."

"Doesn't every guy think that at some point?" Maybe every guy but Theo Kershaw. "I might not be now, but I'd like to spend the rest of my life working on it. She owns me, Theo. My heart, my soul, every cell in my body. She's the strongest person I know. She thinks she's the weak link in your family when really, she's the lynchpin. The soft power. Does that make sense?"

He nodded. "I keep trying to tell her, but she won't listen to her dear old dad. Maybe you can do a better job of it."

"Excuse me?"

"I give you my blessing to try and fix things with my daughter."

"Don't need it."

He nodded sagely. "You have it anyway."

I growled.

"You're welcome, NyQuil."

This *asshole*. I was so damn lucky to have him as a friend. "There's something else I need to tell you."

His good humor vanished in an instant. "If you're about to say you've knocked her up with your super sperm—"

"Christ, no!" I blew out a breath. "Some fucker mugged her in Greece."

"Yeah, I know. She told me this morning around the same time she fessed up to being in love with you." Theo stood and headed for the door. "Thanks for being there for her. Now quit worrying about your beautiful face and tell her how you feel."

CHAPTER THIRTY-FOUR

Adeline

A NEW SECURITY guy we hadn't met was giving us a hard time.

Conor puffed up his chest. "Man, I hate to say 'do you know who I am' but seriously, do you know who I am?"

"No access pass, sir, no entry."

"Good job, Conor," Rosie murmured. "Now you just made him mad."

"Hey, kids, need an assist?"

Over my shoulder, I spotted Hatch approaching in his game day suit. He must have just arrived from the press box where the players on IR often watched the games.

"We need to see Dad," Landon said.

"And Adeline needs to see Lars." Rosie looked at me and shrugged. "Well, you do."

Hatch nodded at Security. "Damon, these idiots are with me. Can we let them through this once?"

"Sure, Mr. Kershaw."

Conor snickered, "Mr. Kershaw," and led the rest of us into the arena's inner bowels. "Dad'll be in the dressing room."

He walked on with Landon while Hatch pulled at my elbow. "Could I have a word?"

I slowed my roll, then stopped altogether. Rosie threw a quick glance of support over her shoulder and kept on walking.

Hatch and I had barely spoken at dinner last night. I had assumed he was mad at me along with Dad.

"Hatch, I'm so sorry about the game. I know it's my fault—"

He shook his head. "No, it's not. Look, I had a talk with Dad this morning. He told me you've been feeling like you don't contribute to the family. And if I've ever given you that impression, I'm sorry."

Hatch had blamed me when Dad lost the Finals all those years ago, but he was a kid at the time, only twelve. I'd agreed with him, but maybe I'd done something else. Internalized my difference so much that it kept me at a distance from the people I loved more than anything.

"I'm not the same as the rest of you. And sometimes that bothers me."

"Like we need more of whatever it is *we* offer." He meant the boys and their masculine energy. "Addy, you're my sister, completely unique, and one of the most amazing people I know."

"Even though I've just ruined one of the best defensive partnerships in professional hockey?"

"They'll get over it. The question is, will you? Do you want to?"

"I need to see Lars."

He grinned. "Not Dad? He did just get ejected from the game."

"He's not the one with a broken nose."

"Which he thoroughly deserved." Dad stood at the corner of one of the myriad corridors in the arena's backstage maze.

"I can't believe you hit him." I closed the gap and grabbed his jersey. Not gently, either. "Is he okay?"

"No idea. I'm mad at him, remember?" But he didn't sound angry. Quite the opposite, in fact.

"This isn't funny!"

"I'll say. Your reckless disregard for my feelings has screwed with this team's dynamic and put my swan song season in jeopardy. What do you have to say for yourself?"

I rolled my lips in to hide my smile. "I choose him, Dad. And I still love you."

"Exam room's that way." He thumbed over his shoulder, then pulled me into his arms. A big hug, no words, absolutely perfect.

With one last look at Hatch, I headed toward the exam room and its open door. Lars was seated on a table, holding an ice pack to his face.

"Hi."

He lowered the pack. I winced at the damage.

"Hi." He sounded understandably nasally.

"Is this a bad time?"

"It's never a bad time when you're here."

I stepped inside. "Just ran into my dad. I can't believe he did that."

"Can't you?" Okay, he had a point. "Thanks for the meal last night."

"Did Vicki enjoy it?" I tried not to sound sour.

"She did. Sends her love."

That made me smile.

"She's looking for an angle into my life, but all she's got is Mabel. I'm not interested in Vicki."

I breathed a sigh of relief. Hated myself for it. Onto the next mess.

"I ruined the game."

"Nah, your father and I did that all by ourselves. We had a good talk after. An important talk."

I suspected as much, given my dad's attitude, but it was gratifying to hear it confirmed. "So, the Dream Defense will be back in action for the next game."

"Sure, but that's not the partnership I want to discuss this minute."

His nose was broken, his eye sockets bruised, his cheek raw and red. He was beautiful, my big-hearted warrior coming home from battle. Not that he thought so.

"I screwed up, Adeline. I didn't fight for you when I had the chance."

I took a seat beside him. "Want to tell me why you panicked?"

He took a moment. "If I could hold a grudge like that against my father, one that lasted long past his death, if I could betray your dad, my closest friend, if I could lie to all these people who had accepted me, given me the family I'd always craved, then what kind of man was I? How could I be worthy of someone as good and kind as you?"

I snorted. "I'm not that good. Or kind. I wanted you and I was prepared to sacrifice my relationship with my dad and my family and destroy a billion-dollar hockey franchise's season into the bargain, all to get my way."

"Yeah, you were."

I thumped his arm. "You don't have to agree!"

His chuckle turned into a wince. My poor guy.

"What I'm trying to say is that it might have been self-ish, but you went for it, Adeline. For me. You saw something you wanted, something worth putting your heart and a lot more on the line for."

"And you saw it, too. I don't think even my feminine wiles are powerful enough to get you to risk everything that means so much to you." I bit my lip. "Are we actually justi-fying all our selfishness in the name of—"

"Love," he finished. "Yeah, we are. I love you, Adeline. And I'm sorry I told your dad before I told you."

"You did?"

"Out there on the ice. After the fourth, or maybe fifth punch."

"Looking for an escape route from the beatdown?"

He snorted. Another wince. "That's what he said. But no, I needed him to know the truth. I needed him to know I wouldn't have crossed this line, created this chaos, and risked my partnership with him if the prize wasn't worth it. My sweet, lovely Adeline."

I considered his words. "But, when I told you how I felt —how I truly felt—you rejected me." That had hurt and I needed him to know it. "I thought once my mom told you she knew, it would start this snowball of reveals and you'd ... pick me."

He closed his eyes, opened them again, and the pain I saw there told me how much he regretted it.

"I made a mess of it. Never think that in that moment I was choosing Theo over you. Or the team over this amazing love I'd found. I truly thought I was giving you an out, a chance to start your life without the baggage of me. I thought I was choosing the best path for you."

I sniffed. "The best path is the one I choose for myself. And I choose you."

He touched his forehead to mine. "I should have known better than to second guess you. You've taught me so much, not just how to look after Mabel, or fight for what I want, but how to open my heart. Because you opened yours and showed me purity and love. And I've a feeling you have so much more to show me."

He curled a hand around my jaw. "When Mabel arrived and I was in panic mode for that first hour, day, week, I thought my life was about to become smaller. Constricted and bound by my mistake. I was so wrong. Little did I know it was the start of my life becoming bigger, richer, brighter. Not just because of Mabel but because you came into it and showed me a new world. A love I couldn't live without."

Tears flowed freely down my cheeks now, and he caught them with his thumb.

"I'm not saying I deserve you, but I *want* to be the kind of man you deserve. The kind of dad Mabel deserves. The kind of friend your dad deserves. Mostly, I want to stop expecting everyone to let me down. To be like Sven. That's not the blueprint I should set for my kid. For my life. For you and me."

My lungs tightened. "I won't let you down. I'm not going anywhere."

"About that." He rubbed a thumb along my bottom lip as I swiped at my wet cheeks. "I'll wait for you."

"Where am I going?"

"On another adventure. Maybe travel, school, a job somewhere. It could be here or there. What I'm trying to say is that you have the world at your feet. I've got maybe a couple more years in me at this game because there's no way in hell I'll be working as long as your dad. I'm hoping those years will be here, so Mabel can grow up singing silly songs with people who love her in the Rebels village, the best place I can imagine for her. I'm going to fight Vicki for full custody because that's what's best for my daughter. But I don't want you to feel you have to be on hand, supporting us. You already did that for your mom and your family. This is your time. Spread your wings, fly into your future."

I'd known I loved this man for weeks now, maybe years. But with those words of support, I knew I would love him for the weeks and years ahead.

"I love you so much, Lars. It might have started as a schoolgirl infatuation, but I've peeled back a lot of gruff man layers—"

"And you're still here?"

"I'm still here. I see you, Lars Nyquist." I touched his chest with my fingertips, then spread my hand over his heart. "I see the heart and soul of you. The good dad, the great friend, the amazing lover, the better man. I've traveled the world, seen a few cool things, but I can't think of any better adventure, any place I'd rather be, than right here with you and Mabel, my family and my music."

He sucked in a breath and in his deep blue eyes, emotion shone back at me.

"How did I get so lucky?"

"You worked hard to be this lucky, Lars. You deserve good things."

He leaned in. "Or maybe I deserve sweet things. Adeline, the sweetest thing of all."

His lips brushed mine, and I fisted the front of his jersey and took what *I* deserved.

My Great Love Story.

Trademark.

EPILOGUE

Lars

IN THE PARKING lot of St. Martin's Episcopal Church, I scooped up Mabel like she was a puck on my blade and quickened my step.

"No!"

"Yes, sweetheart. I know you want to walk but we're in a hurry."

My daughter growled, a habit she'd picked up since the arrival of our new dog, a Yorkshire terrier called Biscuit. At close to fifteen months old, walking was Mabel's favorite pastime, closely followed by "singing" the Duckman song, now with more verses—though we kept the X-rated ones for after Mabel's bedtime—and saying "No" to everything.

Want your dinner? No! (Even though she did.)

Shall we go to the park? No! (But Adeline had no problem persuading her.)

Who's your favorite Rebel? No! (Which Rebels goalie Noah Boden had insisted meant him.)

As well as "no," her vocabulary had broadened to a host of new words such as "Dada," "Adda," and "Tea" for Tilly, who was her best friend, mostly because Tilly loved dressing Mabel up in her old clothes while fondly reminiscing about each item. For a four-and-a-half-year-old—and she insisted on that extra half—she had remarkable recall.

At the entrance to the church, the groom, Dash Carter, was huddled with Bell and a few guys I didn't recognize. I wasn't part of his wedding party, but like the rest of the Rebels, I'd been invited to the ceremony.

Dash nodded at me. "Hey man, you're cutting it fine."

"Yeah, had to run back home to get Adeline's lucky pick." I held up the plastic shard. With it, she'd written one of her best tunes—The Banana Peel Song, a huge hit with the under-five set at JiggleJams—and wanted to have it on hand today. Summer had asked her to sing "Something" by the Beatles during the ceremony.

Bell asked, "You seen Kershaw?"

"The cap's not here yet?"

"I meant Kershaw Junior."

I shook my head. Hatch was one of the ushers, which had surprised me because he and Carter didn't seem all that close.

Mabel was getting antsy, and I needed to finish my errand. "Good luck today, Carter."

"Thanks, man. Don't think I'll need it, but I appreciate it."

Fair enough. Inside the church, I walked up the aisle

lined with white roses, baby's breath, and greenery until I found Elle and Theo.

Elle's mouth dropped open on seeing Mabel. "There's my girl!"

"Mommy ..." Tilly tugged at her mom's hand. "I'm your girl."

"Oh, I know, honey. But Mabel's cool, too. And look at her pretty dress!" True, Mabel looked even more adorable than usual today in a seafoam green number with a skirt made of what I called gauze, but what I'd been told by people in the know was tulle.

"Adeline's looking for you," Theo said. "I tried calming her down, but I guess that's your job now."

"On my way. Do you mind ...?" But Elle was already relieving me of a very heavy Mabel and settling her in on the pew beside Tilly. "Sweetheart, can you be good for Auntie Ellie?"

I braced myself for the inevitable "no," so I was surprised to earn a big grin. My kid loved the Kershaws, but then didn't we all?

"Tea!" my daughter said, swiping at her friend's curls.

"Hi, Mabel," Tilly said with a world-weary indulgence as she fingered a silver-gilded rosette on Mabel's chest.

Theo leaned over and booped my daughter's nose. "Hey, Button."

A giggling Mabel grasped his tie. "No!"

He winked at me and gestured for me to get going. As he was still my captain, I did as I was told.

Two weeks ago, we lost the Finals in the seventh against the LA Quake, throwing a vat of water on Theo's exit in a blaze of glory. Then the guy surprised us all by *not* announcing his retirement. The Rebels had offered him a one-year extension and he was thinking it over. After all,

Theo Kershaw was good business: for the team, for the city, for hockey. If he had one more push left in him, and his body still cooperated, then who could argue with that?

With time to reflect, I'd wondered if the craziness of the early part of the season had contributed to us not getting over that final hump. But every day I was reminded that Theo and I were tight, that we'd had an amazing year, and our bond was as strong as ever. Maybe stronger now that we had so much connecting us, on and off the ice.

I found Adeline wearing out the carpet in the corridor outside the church's anteroom, where the bride and her wedding party prepared for the ceremony. With her phone to her ear, she hadn't seen me yet, so I took a moment to drink her in. Her inky dark hair was piled high with one little wisp crafting an escape as it curled against her slender neck. Her strapless sheath bridesmaid's dress in a dark pink emphasized the delicate roundness of her shoulders and dipped in a sweetheart cut over her chest. She rarely wore heels, but when she did, her legs went on for miles. Like today.

My phone rang and Adeline turned. On spotting me, those moss-green eyes fired, and she moved toward me with purpose.

"You're here!"

I placed my hands on her waist and pulled her close. "Now where else would I be, sweet thing?"

"I just called you."

"I was too busy watching."

A pale pink bloom appeared on her cheeks at my turn of phrase. Last night, I had been *very* busy watching as Adeline explored her body, while I did my best to follow her instructions to keep my "hands off." That lasted all of three minutes.

Where Adeline was concerned, I've never been all that good about following the rules.

"Did you find it?"

"Uh huh." I passed over the pick. "How are things in the War Room?"

"Tense. Dash's sister and his mom are scary society types, and Summer's gone very, very quiet."

"I'm sure she's just nervous." I kissed her nose. "How about you?"

"Nervous, too. Think I'd prefer an audience of five-year-olds."

"You're going to be fine. Hearing you sing is one of my favorite things, so I don't see why it shouldn't be everybody else's, too."

Her gaze softened. "I couldn't have crushed on a better man."

"Or ..." I suggested.

"Or?"

"We could just ditch the lot of them and go back to our place." While Adeline had moved in with Rosie six months ago, she spent more time at mine. To be honest, it only felt like home when she was in it. I had hired a new nanny, who didn't live in, but stayed over while I was away, a necessary arrangement now that I had full custody of Mabel. Vicki was making another run at her ex, and had decided our daughter didn't fit with those plans.

I continued, "We've already got sitters out there for Mabel, and you won't have to worry about strumming a bum note or forgetting the words."

"Tempting, but I couldn't do that to Summer. However, I've no doubt Mabel will get fussy around the time of the first dance—"

"Because she'll want in on the action."

She chuckled. "She's got the moves. So we let her get her John Travolta on, then I'm forecasting an early night ... for all of us."

"Love that idea."

To make sure she was primed for later, I gave her lovely ass a gentle squeeze while I kissed her deep and true. Every day I counted my blessings, one kiss, one ass squeeze at a time. My plan to ask her to be mine forever would have to wait until later because not even a jerk like me would upstage another couple on their wedding day.

"Sorry to break this up, folks." A slightly pitchy voice cut in. "We've got a problem."

I unlocked my lips from Adeline's and turned to a frowning Rosie.

"What's wrong?" Adeline asked. "Is Mrs. Carter still trying to put makeup on Summer's tattoo?"

Rosie grimaced. "She probably would be ... if we could find Summer."

"What?" Adeline blinked and looked at me, then back at Rosie. "You can't find the bride?"

"She went into the bathroom, the one connected to the anteroom. The only way out of there is a window and now there's no sign of her." Rosie shook her head. "Guys, I think she's gone AWOL."

Up next in the Chicago Players series: *Rebel Bride.*

Duckman, Duckman, on the ice
Skating faster than the mice

With your silly beard so thick
How you move about so quick
Duckman, Duckman, on the ice
Skating faster than the mice

Duckman, Duckman, on the ice
Skating faster than the mice
With eyes so blue they can't compare
And copper highlights in your hair
Duckman, Duckman, on the ice
Skating faster than the mice

Duckman, Duckman, on the ice
Skating faster than the mice
When you lose, we're sad and gray
When you win, we all go "yay!"
Duckman, Duckman, on the ice
Skating faster than the mice

(*Adult only version*)
Duckman, Duckman, on the ice
Skating faster than the mice
You're not so quick beneath the sheets
You slow right down to eat your treats
Duckman, Duckman, on the ice
Last night I came not once but twice

BONUS EPILOGUE

Four years later

Adeline

COURTHOUSES WERE NOT the most soothing of places, but unfortunately coming here was a necessary evil. I gazed down on Mabel's head of red-gold, an autumnal fall over her shoulders, and marveled at how lucky I was to be here.

Not just lucky, but nervous. More nervous than my appearance on *Sesame Street*, more nervous than when I lost a Grammy for Best Children's Music Album, *The Duckman Chronicles*, more nervous than on my wedding day.

My husband reached over and placed a calming hand

on my neck. I looked over Mabel's head, gave a wobbly smile, and wiped a tear.

"You okay?"

No. What if there was a paperwork problem? What if someone rose to their feet and objected? What if the judge had found something in my background, such as the fact Lars once punched a fellow player in a nightclub because *I made him do it?*

I nodded anyway. This day was just as important to Lars, to Mabel, to my whole family, all sitting behind me, ready to erupt.

The judge appeared, we all rose, and the questions began. I answered the best I could, affirming I knew what I was doing and that I understood the consequences.

Up until this point, Mabel had been quiet, but now she felt a need to be heard.

"Daddy, is it over?"

A few chuckles sounded behind us, and the judge looked out over her glasses.

"Miss Mabel, I'm guessing you just want this to be done, huh?"

"We're having a party. I'm worried the ice-cream will be melted. And my little brother needs his diaper changed. He poops *a lot.*"

More laughter, even from the judge. I looked over my shoulder at my mom who held Mabel's brother in her arms. Little Niko, our eight-month-old son, pumped a fist toward me. I gave him a wave.

"Well, we're almost finished here, Miss Mabel," the judge said.

Ignoring her, Mabel turned to me with those gorgeous blue eyes, the color of her dad's. "You're my mommy now."

I swallowed. "Not until the judge says so, Moo-Belle."

She shook her head. "No, now."

She was right. Over the last few years, Vicki's visits had become less and less frequent until finally they stopped altogether. Mabel barely remembered her. I was the one who soothed my little girl when she had a bad dream, who cleaned up her scraped knees, who sang her to sleep. She knew how to play a few chords, though she preferred her baby keyboard. Music was our connecting bond, and Mabel was mine, as much as Lars and Niko. Not only that, she was a Kershaw through and through.

I placed an arm around her shoulders and gathered her close. For a moment, the courtroom fell away and it was just the two of us.

"And you're my precious little cowgirl. No one can take that away from us." I locked eyes with the judge and dared her to say differently.

Her lips twitched. "Well, it looks like Mabel has made her decision. Along with Mabel, this court also believes that it's in her best interest to be adopted by Adeline Kershaw-Nyquist. You are now officially Mabel's parent under the law with all the rights and duties of the parent-child relationship. But most importantly, all of the joys. And Mabel, this is now your mommy."

"I know!" Don't try telling my daughter something she already knew.

The courtroom exploded in applause and hoots so loud that the tap of the gavel was a faint echo. But Mabel heard it, and soon we were behind the judge's bench, where all the Kershaw kids got a chance to bring down the hammer. (Even the older ones like my dad, who went back in for seconds.)

"Granddad!" Mabel ran into my dad's arms. After Lars, Tilly, and me, he was her favorite person, though she had a soft spot for her Uncle Conor as well because he was "goofy."

About a year ago, as the adoption proceedings started in earnest, Mabel had switched to "granddad" from "uncle" for my dad. We hadn't even told her about our plans just in case Vicki changed her mind, but our best girl knew in her heart that the Kershaws would soon be her forever family, for real.

"Hey, Button," my dad said as he lifted her into his arms. "You ready for your big party?"

She gazed at him, wide-eyed with adoration. "Yes! With ice-cream!"

"Hmm. Not sure we were able to get any after all ..."

"Granddad!"

"Just kidding, button. We've got ice-cream and cake and gummy bears and those cookies you like—"

"Macarons!"

Eventually we had to vacate the courtroom to give someone else a chance to be so happy. In the courthouse corridor, Lars had retaken custody of Niko and was now seated on a bench, filling his son in on who was who for the millionth time.

"And that's your uncle Jason—"

"Great-uncle," Jason said as he walked by with his youngest baby daughter, sleeping in his arms. "In all the meanings of the phrase."

"And this is your aunt Tilly, who is the best aunt in the world."

"Hi, Niko." Tilly leaned over, and her dark mass of curls brushed my son's cheek. "You're much quieter than Mabel was at your age."

"You can't possibly remember that," I said. Also, Mabel was a pretty well-behaved baby.

My supremely wise eight-year-old sister sniffed. "I remember everything."

Lars and I shared a smile. Since his retirement just before Niko was born, he had thrown himself wholeheartedly into being a stay-at-home dad. We had built a studio at the house, and while I worked on my music, recording, and teaching, Lars kept the engine of our little family ticking over smoothly. No more nannies, just us.

My mom called out for Tilly. "We're heading back home for the party, Til. You ready?"

"Okay. See you later, Niko! Bye, Duckman!"

"No bye for me, then," I murmured as I watched my sister skip off.

"What can I say? The Kershaw women adore me." Lars smiled after her, then turned to me. "How's it going over there, sweet thing?"

"We did it, Lars."

"We sure did." His eyes turned glossy. "And none of it could have happened without you."

I thought back to those early days with Mabel, how the panic and fear was soon evicted by excitement and love. Niko made a little snuffly sound and sighed, half-way to the land of nod. Mabel was chatting excitedly with Rosie as she explored her new tattoo. She looked over and waved at me.

My daughter.

"Without us. The other dream team." And then I kissed my husband, tapping the gavel on my promise to love and cherish, and marveled at how days like this only made our blessed life better.

ACKNOWLEDGMENTS

Thank you to my editor, Kristi Yanta. Our fourteenth book together! You are amazing. Thanks also to proofreader Julia Griffis for your perfect attention to detail.

To the team at Qamber Designs, my gratitude knows no bounds for the beautiful illustrated covers you've created for this series.

All my thanks goes to Miranda for helping me stay on top of communication with my readers.

Thanks also to my Rebels fans, especially my reader group, Kate's Kittens, and all of you who have been with me for so long. I know I said the Rebels were done, but it seems I was wrong there!

And thank you, Jimmie, for all your support these last few years as we adjusted to a nomadic life. Onward to the next adventure!

ABOUT THE AUTHOR

Originally from Ireland, *USA Today* bestselling author Kate Meader cut her romance reader teeth on Maeve Binchy and Jilly Cooper novels, with some Harlequins thrown in for variety. Give her tales about brooding mill owners, over-sexed equestrians, and men who can rock an apron, a fire hose, or a hockey stick, and she's there. Now traveling the world with her soulmate, she writes sexy contemporary, sports, and LGBTQ+ romance featuring strong heroes and amazing women and men who can match their guys quip for quip.

WRAPPED UP IN YOU

Hot in Chicago Rookies
COMING IN HOT
UP IN SMOKE
DOWN IN FLAMES
HOT TO THE TOUCH

Hot in Chicago
REKINDLE THE FLAME
FLIRTING WITH FIRE
MELTING POINT
PLAYING WITH FIRE
SPARKING THE FIRE
FOREVER IN FIRE

Laws of Attraction
DOWN WITH LOVE
ILLEGALLY YOURS
THEN CAME YOU

Hot in the Kitchen
FEEL THE HEAT
ALL FIRED UP
HOT AND BOTHERED

For updates, giveaways, and new release information,
sign up for Kate's newsletter at katemeader.com.